THE COVID KID

Another Marshall Morris Adventure

Robert John DeLuca

THE COVID KID
Another Marshall Morris Adventure

ISBN: 978-1-7320596-5-8 *(paperback)*
ISBN: 978-1-7320596-4-1 *(ebook)*

Published by Stanley Kramer Books
Bulk orders of this book may be obtained by contacting Robert John DeLuca at www.bdlauthor.com

CONTENTS

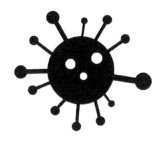

CHAPTER 1

A Ha! Apartment 4B. The right place. Up the stairs on the second floor. He had learned over the past few months delivering pizzas you had to hustle if you wanted to make any money. The pies came out of the oven and were given to whoever was ready to grab them. You could carry six a night or twenty-six. It was up to you. Marshall Morris was a high-motor guy. No sitting around for him. Get in, get out, get another delivery. You also had to be careful. Most people felt their adorable pooches could do no wrong. The tattered bottoms of his jeans showed otherwise.

He carried the pizzas in an insulated sack, which had to be held parallel to the ground or risk ruining them—something he learned early on by tipping them up like a lunchbox. He shot up the stairs and held the sack with one hand as he searched for the doorbell. Of course, there it was, on his lower left under the pizza bag. Having encountered this situation many times, he merely turned around with his back to the door and jabbed the button with the back of his free hand. After a few seconds, when there was no click from inside of the door being unlocked, he was about to ring again when he heard a woman's voice.

"Our buzzer is broken. The door is open. Just bring the pizza in, please?"

Sure enough, not only was the door unlocked, it was ajar. He hesitated, but only for a moment. These days, most folks couldn't be too careful and were reluctant to let anyone in, no less a complete stranger. There were so many weirdoes out there, and that flu epidemic didn't sound good. Marshall was in a hurry, though, and a little extra effort usually resulted in a good tip.

He pushed the door open and entered a typical two- or three-bedroom place with white walls, a small square of floor tile near the entry, and standard-grade beige carpet. The blinds were closed, and the room was lit only by a small table lamp and a large flat-screen TV hung on a wall, blasting away on what had to be TikTok music videos. The room had no other furniture. The distinct smell of cannabis wafted in the air. Marshall didn't partake in pot smoking but tried not to be judgmental about those who did. He recognized how widespread it was, especially among younger folks.

"Hey. Hi there." The same voice said, "Thanks for coming in. Would you mind setting it over there on our dining table?"

Marshall looked over and saw a young woman sitting on the couch with her legs tucked up under her. She had stringy blonde hair and was wearing a bathrobe. He noticed a slipper on one of her feet, dangling on a big toe. A cigarette or joint was smoldering in an ashtray on the coffee table in front of her. In the poorly lit haze, he couldn't tell her age, which might have been anywhere between twenty and forty. He spotted the dining table and obediently walked over, took the pizza out of his bag, and set it down. He snapped the stapled bill from the box and walked back toward the woman who had been watching him closely. He was getting a creepy feeling about this delivery.

The woman sipped from a drink of a brown liquid jiggling with ice as he approached. She hadn't said another word. Despite the poor light, he figured out that she was younger than he first thought—early twenties at most, and not all that bad looking. Her silky pink bathrobe rode considerably up her bare crossed legs. When she leaned forward to set her drink down, the top of her bathrobe peeked open, revealing the round mounds of her large, unincumbered breasts. He tried not to peek, or at least be obvious about it. His quick call was that she had just come home from work, shucked her clothes, and was relaxing before dinner. He hoped that was the case and didn't want to know more.

"That'll be $17.50, please," he said, handing her the bill, which she reached out to grab, making no effort to hide her bouncing chi chis.

"Say, don't I know you?" she asked, totally ignoring the bill. Before he could reply, she answered her own question. "Sure, I do. You played football for Justice High. Right? You were the quarterback, halfback, or maybe the tight end?" She giggled, apparently amused by her unintentionally suggestive reference.

Marshall was very much a red-blooded young man, and it was getting more and more difficult to ignore the come-on from this attractive woman. Given a chance to consider a situation, he almost always chose the correct path. It was only when he reacted instantly that he got himself into trouble. He had other deliveries to make, and he quickly decided that he wanted no part of where this deal might go, although it would make a delightful story for his friends. All he wanted to do was to scram ASAP.

Still, he was easygoing and always concerned about other people's feelings. The lady probably had a long day at work and was just making conversation. Maybe he was just getting the wrong vibes from her. Nothing more on her mind, he hoped. He didn't want to be rude.

If only this delivery had been on a credit card, he could just smile and leave. Unfortunately, it was a cash order. His store, Cow Paddy Pizza, still permitted customers to pay cash to the delivery boys if they preferred. Justice Texas was small enough and friendly enough for a little neighborly trust to encourage business. Actually, the delivery crew usually liked cash orders better because there was almost always a tip, which was rarely the case on credit card orders. He had to collect from her—hopefully with a tip.

"Yes. I played football there, but I was a wide receiver. Now, I hate to rush, but I am late for other deliveries. Could you kindly pay me? Please."

She ignored his request. "I thought so. You are so big and strong with those wide shoulders. I just figured you had to be an athlete. I went to Justice High for a while a few years back. So, what's your name? By the way, I'm Lucy."

Marshall was getting flustered, but he still had to be nice, and he didn't want to have to explain to his boss back at the store why he was stiffed on a twenty-dollar delivery. "I'm Marshall," he responded.

Something was triggered in his head. *"Lucy," a few years back at Justice High?*

She could see he was uncomfortable standing there. "Okay then, Marshall. Nice to meet you, and thanks for being so prompt in your delivery, bringing it in here, and especially for putting up with little old me. It's been a long day, and I'm just happy to have company, even for just a few minutes, with a big, strong, handsome man. I've been so lonely lately," she lamented in a woeful voice just this side of tears. She seemed to sense she had to make her move soon, or he'd just run out. "I'll have to go get my purse in the bedroom. It'll take just a minute." He looked visibly relieved, until she followed up with, "Say, how about something to drink? You must get awful thirsty running around on your deliveries? Or better yet.." She smiled and glanced over at the smoldering ashtray.

"Thanks, Lucy, but I really have to run. Maybe next time," he blurted out, amazing even himself.

She smiled. "Look, I understand. I'll be just fine after a while." The woman actually had the gall to play a sympathy card to a pizza delivery boy. Marshall wasn't buying it, although he felt sorry for her. It always upset him when he believed he was at all responsible for someone else's unhappiness. So, when she asked him to sit on the couch for just a second while she fetched her purse, he did, assuming it would help him collect.

As soon as he sat down, however, she eased in his direction, making a deep cooing sound. He noticed the black devil tattoo she had on her neck, and that was it. He jumped up and was about to bolt for the door.

"Stop. Hold on, kid. That's enough!" she ordered him now in an abrasive, scolding voice, totally different from the seductive one seconds before. Her oozing sensuality and desperate need turned instantly into frigidity and formality. "Stay right there. I'll get your money." She got up and disappeared down the hall.

He froze. Maybe he'd get paid after all. *Lucy? Devil tattoo? Oh, my goodness! Sure, I remember her. She's Lucy "Morals". That wasn't her actual name at Justice High a few years before us. She had the reputation for chasing anything in pants and being the loosest girl ever. She never graduated and left because she was pregnant. I've been cavorting on the couch with Lucy Morals. Oh, boy. Let me out of here.*

He was just about to leave when she reappeared with a twenty-dollar bill in her hand. He stopped, but she kept coming and bumped right into him. Marshall, who was renowned for his clumsiness, grabbed at her and they tumbled together onto the carpet. He tried to push her away without touching any sensitive parts and get to his feet. In the meantime, she was screaming, "Get off of me! Get off of me!"

When Marshall finally got up, he glanced toward the hallway. His heart dropped to his feet. Standing there was an enormous brute of a man in a tank top shirt and tight gym shorts. The guy's huge biceps and bulging calves were bristling with ugly black hair, and yet he had only a few stray strands on his head. Stubble covered his multiple chins, which hadn't seen a razor in some time. Marshall could feel the contempt in the creature's beady, black eyes. An unmistakable growl came from his throat.

"Brutus, protect me! This nasty kid just attacked me!" came the wounded cry from miss Lucy.

Marshall could handle himself, if need be, but not this time. He was out the door and down the steps. He never looked back. Why did he always stumble into these kinds of predicaments?

Perhaps there was some justice in the world beyond the town of Justice. A week later, during a slow period, Marshall was sitting around with some of his fellow delivery guys having a coke. One thing led to another, and Marshall described his experience with the notorious Lucy. He was shocked to learn that one of the other guys had gone through a similar experience there. It was apparently a game with her and her goon boyfriend to get a free pizza now and then. They relied on the assumption that the delivery boy would never bring up the incident for fear of being accused of making advances at her.

This time, though, they had picked the wrong kid to mess with. Lucy couldn't believe her eyes when she answered the door one evening and there stood a humble and apologetic Marshall Morris. He was so sorry for what had happened and begged her forgiveness. He handed her a Super Supreme pie with all the toppings as a small token of his condolences. She eagerly grabbed it and slammed the door. As he drove away, Marshall sincerely hoped that the couple enjoyed their pizza—especially the liberal application of an Ex-Lax topping. Marshall Morris went all out for his customers. Now two of his customers would go all out for him.

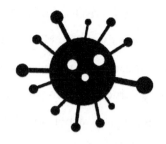

CHAPTER 2

While much of the southern United States and Texas is noted for blazing and sizzling heat in the summer, it surprises some people to discover that it can get chilly during the winter months. There is no sustained cold like in New England or Colorado, but a person can get uncomfortable filling a car's gas tank in February in Austin with a twenty-mile-an-hour wind whipping with fifty degrees on the thermometer. The adage about blood thinning out in the south may have some truth to it. That said, no matter what the weather in Texas is doing, some folks never vary from the standard dress of shorts and T-shirts year-round.

The high school kids in Justice, Texas, which is close to the Gulf of Mexico, moved their hangouts around based on the seasons. When the weather was warm, everyone flocked to the Bigaburger, a drive-in joint with several wooden picnic tables arranged at the rear under a group of stately old oak trees. In the fall, when the weather cooled, they swarmed to Papa Juan's, an indoor restaurant that was divided into a family side and a kids' hangout side. Never the two shall meet. Papa Juan's had been the chosen after-football game destination going back several decades. It was originally a pizza place, but with the competition from Cow Paddy Pizza and others, it now specialized in Mexican food, which was hands down the most popular type of food in South Texas.

Even though it was still August, a lingering taste for Mexican food had drawn Marshall and some friends to Papa Juan's on a Friday evening. The summer break was about to end, and the kids would return to classes at Justice High in just a few days. Marshall and his best friend, Graham Brown, had graduated in the spring. They both would be off to college and pre-season football practice shortly at Central Texas University in Austin. Marshall was vigorously assaulting an enormous plate of Tex-Mex. Next to him in a booth were his girlfriend, Mallory Jollen, and her younger sister, Paula. Across from them were Graham and his girlfriend, Jennifer Wilson. The decor at Papa Juan's had changed little throughout the years. It remained sixties all the way, with a jukebox and tired old movie posters, but no one seemed to notice. That evening, the place was packed with kids who'd been chomping on burgers all summer and wanted to cram in a few tacos and tortillas before heading back to school next week.

Marshall, known for his voracious appetite, was finishing up his first course, having vacuumed up four beef tacos, a couple of chalupas, mountainous helpings of rice and charro beans, and an entire basket of tortilla chips all by himself. He was on his second enormous glass of sweet tea. "You know, I think I might try a chimichanga for my next course," he announced.

Mallory, who was used to his eating habits, rolled her eyes but couldn't let that announcement pass. A chimichanga is a huge bloated tortilla filled with meat and spices that resembles a massive baked potato. Most humans have trouble finishing one. Mallory smiled. "Eat up. We wouldn't want you to leave hungry. We'll have to call you Burrito Boy."

"Hilarious," he said between bites. "Say. Could you please slide the chips my way?"

"Burrito Boy? I like that. How about Burro Boy, since he can be so stubborn sometimes? He never knows when to quit," Graham suggested. All four of them chuckled at that suggestion. "Speaking of burros, have any of you ever heard about Marshall's run-in with a donkey?"

Between bites, Marshall mumbled. "Hey, Graham, put a lid on it!"

The objection, of course, only emboldened his friend.

Paula, Mallory's "little" sister by two years, who was never afraid to speak her mind, especially when it was least appropriate, immediately chimed in. "Donkey? Marshall? Tell us. I can't wait!"

There was no stopping Graham. "It was a few years ago. I think when we were juniors. Marshall and I headed out south of town toward Galveston to check out a place for bird hunting. It was mostly flat, with open rice fields and canals with patches of trees here and there. We had permission from the landowner if we promised to close any gate we went through. He didn't want his livestock to get out. It was muddy, but not too bad as long as we stayed on the dikes between the canals. We kept looking for birds but didn't see any. We had walked for maybe a half-mile or so. Of course, you know, our friend here. He gets bored, quickly. His mind wanders."

Mallory added, "Oh, yes. I'll second that remark."

"Anyway," Graham continued, "we kept walking and came up to a little rickety corral, out there in the middle of nowhere. And wallowing in it was the most bedraggled, skinny, scruffy donkey I'd ever seen. He was a mottled brown color and was just standing there with his bowlegs knocking together totally still. He didn't even swish his tail. We assumed he was asleep. Marshall decided to liven up the day. For years, he'd been bragging to me that even though he was born in Brooklyn, New York, he has adapted to the ways of Texas and was quite the horseman. I'd witnessed nothing to back up this claim and, frankly, doubted his boasts. Here was a chance for him to put up or shut up."

Marshall tried to interrupt, but Graham talked right over his protests. The girls were all biting their lips, holding back smiles, anticipating what was about to come. "As I stood and watched, the converted cowboy unlatched the gate, entered the corral, and walked through the muck up to his chosen steed. The donkey still hadn't moved a muscle. Since the animal wasn't much bigger than a large dog, and lanky Marshall was pretty tall with long legs, it wasn't much of a problem for him to scramble up onto the back of the ugly-looking beast. So far, I still wasn't impressed, and apparently, neither was the donkey, who finally opened his bulbous bloodshot eyes and flicked his long floppy ears. Otherwise, he remained still."

"Our born-again cowboy was quite proud of himself at that point, perched upon the bony back bone of that lethargic animal. He also realized I still wouldn't believe his riding claims unless he got the creature to move at least a few steps. At that point, it didn't look like the animal had any interest in moving a muscle. Marshall then did a 'giddy up' thing and rocked forward, hoping his steed would move. Nope. Nothing. He was apparently stuck in the mud. Marshall's most consistent quality, which often leads to his undoing, is that he never gives up. When his cries and forward lunges failed to impress, he tried another approach. He grabbed the donkey's ears and yanked. Guess what happened?"

"Hurry. Tell us!" Paula giggled.

Graham chuckled. "At first, nothing, but then the animal turned his shaggy head around and gave Marshall what had to be the donkey evil eye. He'd had enough of this jerk on his back. Without warning, he let out the loudest 'HEE-HAW, HEE-HAW' I've ever heard and took off like a thoroughbred racehorse. He zoomed around that corral, bucking and jerking like an equine rollercoaster."

The three girls were in stitches picturing the situation.

"Now, I have to be honest and give our Ty Murray wannabee credit where credit is due. For the first couple of trips around, our boy somehow hung on. Of course, both the donkey and Marshall knew it was only a matter of time. The animal had a few tricks up his tail, and he finally ran right at his watering trough, filled with smelly scummy water, and then jammed on the brakes. That solved his problem when Marshall went flying over his head and executed a perfect swan drive head first into the slop. Then, to make matters worse, the donkey saw the open gate Marshall had forgotten to close when he entered the corral. In a flash, the animal was out the gate and galloping for all he was worth across the rice paddies. Now we were all in trouble."

"Coughing and wheezing, the mudnight cowboy removed himself from his swimming pool. He was soaking wet and covered in slop, but otherwise uninjured, his pride aside. I enjoyed the display and had a merry laugh, but I was now more concerned about finding that animal who we had let loose. We tromped out across the rice fields to find him."

"Did you ever get him?", Jennifer asked.

"Nope. Never saw hide nor hair of him. No idea where he'd gone. We must have walked for miles looking until it was almost dark. We were sure the property owner would not be happy with us and dreaded having to own up to what we'd let happen. Texans are quite protective of their livestock. We had circled all the way around and had to pass by the corral on the way back in. Guess what? The ugly scruffy critter was snoozing right in the middle, just as we'd found him, although I swear, I could see a slight smile on his face. We closed the gate and headed out of there."

Paula added, for good measure, "Well, I guess we know who the real ass was in that story. Right, Burro Boy?"

Marshall had one brief reply. "Hee! Haw!"

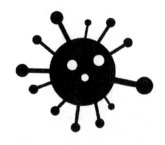

CHAPTER 3

After tucking away mountains of burritos, enchiladas, and other Mexican delights, Marshall topped off his meal with five or six scrumptious *sopapillas*—fried dough dipped in powdered sugar and filled with cream—which the restaurant served for dessert. To redirect the conversation away from his escapades gone awry, he brought up a new topic that soon had everyone concerned. "This Asian flu thing. Do you guys think it's going to get bad? I keep hearing stuff around town and on the tube about it spreading and maybe becoming an epidemic. I can't imagine it could affect the country, Texas, or even Justice all the way from the other side of the world. Do you?"

"I don't really know, but I heard yesterday that a pro basketball player in the NBA caught it, and they called the game off on the spot. There is talk they may suspend the entire NBA season. I don't know how true that is." Graham responded.

"Maybe," Jennifer added. "I suppose it could be like the flu that goes around every year. A lot of kids catch it and miss a few days of school. You can get a shot for it. It might be like that. I can't imagine it would affect our classes, sports, and everyday life. No one wants to catch the flu, but unless you're really old or already sick, it isn't usually a big thing."

Paula wiggled in her seat, eager to make her contribution to the conversation. Even though she was younger than the others and wouldn't even start high school until fall, she considered herself the social and intellectual equal of anyone at the table. She was never reluctant to speak up and was always delighted to stick her nose in her sister's affairs. She adored Marshall and wouldn't have hesitated to pursue him, had her big sister not claimed him first. All of her perpetual pesty qualities aside, she was a brilliant student who kept up with current events as a voracious reader of books and internet offerings. This new virus? Obviously, she knew a lot more about it than anyone else in the booth.

"Okay, okay, kids, slow down," Paula scolded. "This virus thing could just blow over, but from what I've read, many of the so-called medical experts are very concerned. Although no one is absolutely sure, it seems likely that the disease started in China and came from a market where there were sick bats sold for food."

"Cut it out. You've got to be kidding. Bats! Yuk. It makes me sick just to think about it. I can't believe that. Go back to your coloring books," Jennifer fired back.

For once, Paula held her tongue and ignored the demeaning remark, continuing to expound upon what she knew. "Already hundreds of people in China have caught COVID-19, which is the name they have given it. Within the past couple of weeks, it has spread to the United States, probably from infected travelers who arrived here from China. Cases are popping up all over the country, even here in Texas. Maybe it will just die out, but it might spread around."

"Could it become an epidemic?" Marshall asked

"Maybe. It could become a pandemic, which is when a disease spreads over several countries. A virus germ causes COVID-19. When we get sick often, it's because of bacteria germs, which are cells that get into us and cause trouble. Viruses can be even worse because they're tiny and harder to treat. This virus gets into our lungs and sticks to them."

"And to think all those years I assumed my baby sister wiled away her time watching *Dora, the Explorer*. You were working on your medical degree." Mallory just had to tease this half-pint, know-it-all.

Paula tried her best to look disgusted and rolled her eyes toward the ceiling. Mallory could not let her sister know how impressed she really was with her knowledge. Having gotten into her jibe, she asked a serious question. "So, doctor, all this sounds bad, but if all we're dealing with is another flu, as Jennifer said, who cares? There must be a shot, pill, or something for it."

"Nope. Not yet. The big problem is that COVID-19 affects different folks in different ways. Some people don't even know they have it, while others suffer extreme symptoms and even die. The experts know little about it yet. If there was a cure, I guess the threat wouldn't be so bad, but there isn't."

"How do you get it?" Graham asked.

"From what I've read, by contact with others who are infected. It spreads easily through close contact." She couldn't help herself. She looked directly at Mallory and then at Marshall, trying to control her grin. "So kissing is banned from this moment forward."

A huge laugh erupted from them all.

"The symptoms vary from patient to patient. In most cases, a fever, cough, sore throat, muscle soreness, tiredness, and a loss of taste and smell can be indicators, although you have to be tested for it to be sure. Here in Texas, allergies alone lead to many of those symptoms."

Marshall yelped. "No. No. Loss of taste. How can I survive? I live to eat."

"The way you shovel it in, big boy, you probably don't taste it much anyway," Mallory teased. Marshall looked unconvinced.

While his buddy would follow his heart at a moment's notice, Graham Brown was much more of a grounded, practical sort of fellow. After thinking about Paula's comments for a bit, he asked the logical question, "So, Paula, what have you read about preventing someone from catching this Invalid-19 stuff?"

"COVID," she corrected. "It seems to be transmitted through tiny droplets from sneezing, coughing, talking, and even breathing on each other. Keeping a safe distance from others. Wash your hands a lot. Don't touch your face or eyes, if you can help it. The new buzz term is going to be *social distancing*."

"How about masks?"

"I don't know, Graham. No one is saying to wear them yet. What I've read is that masks protect the surrounding people from catching it from you, but do little to protect the wearer."

"Well, that's a relief. Can you imagine me having to hide this gorgeous mug behind a mask? Why my public would raise a ruckus." Marshall kidded.

"Somehow, the rest of us would struggle by not seeing your grinning puss every day," Graham responded. "Although, as I think about it, I would bet that there would be a lot of resistance if they ordered everyone to wear masks. Young people, especially, don't like to be told what to do with routine personal liberties. Maybe it's a good thing that masks don't seem to help. Thanks, Paula, for all the information. You have now ruined all our days."

Paula was beaming with pride, but suddenly plummeted when she thought Graham was serious. Thankfully, his wide smile convinced her he was just joking. She really had done them all a great service. As they would all discover in the weeks and months to come, rumors and disinformation about the virus would run rampant throughout the entire country. Little straight useful information ever came down from the government at any level. Her diligence in providing accurate information was invaluable.

"Well, folks, I sure hate to say this, but COVID aside, this meal may be the last we have together for a while. Graham and I are off on Monday to Austin, and preseason football camp before classes start in about three weeks after Labor Day." Marshall lamented for just an instant. "Of course, we'll only be a couple of hours away. I'm sure we'll be home, and you all will visit us there." He and Graham were to start their college careers at Central Texas University. They were both going to play football and report in a few weeks before classes started. The three girls would all be at Justice High. Jennifer would be a senior, Mallory a junior, and Paula, MD, a freshman.

Paula had opened their eyes to a virtually invisible virus from the other side of the world. Even after digesting her information, none of those kids felt at all threatened by the ominous overtones of a pandemic hidden right there in front of them. They were much more concerned about embarking upon a new school year and adjusting to life without a daily dose of Marshall Morris. Being kids, they were perpetually optimistic, with no way of knowing or worrying about what lay ahead.

CHAPTER 4

He could hardly believe that four years had flown by since he walked down the polished marble floors of Justice High as a brand new freshman eager to get to high school but still nervous about what to expect. It didn't take long for the lanky teenager to adjust to the big school and figure out how things worked. In short order, without even trying, he established his own reputation as a student with unique traits that set him apart from most other teenagers. Marshall's personality came with an all-encompassing sense of mischievousness that led him into one complicated escapade after another. The young man harbored not one ounce of evil and never set out to make trouble or harm anyone. Yet, if something unusual happened around the school, he was probably involved.

When he first arrived as a freshman, no one would have believed that the rail-thin youngster, who couldn't seem to get out of the way of his own feet, would mature enough to earn a precious scholarship to play football at Central Texas in Austin. Marshall was full of surprises. He had grown to just over six feet and had added solid, lean muscle to his still gangly build. He realized that the path to playing football in college most often ran directly through the gym, but he found that pumping iron bored him silly. He was a naturally gifted runner who relied on speed rather than power to succeed in the athletic field. He was exceedingly bright, sometimes to his own disadvantage, when his hands and feet moved just a little slower than his brain. Marshall Morris was clumsy with a capital C and was prone to bump and stumble in the most routine situations.

His light brown hair was never really long or unkempt, but his natural curls always made him look like he'd missed a haircut or two. He wore a perpetual smile that revealed gleaming white teeth. His sparkling brown eyes hinted at his deep intellect. He was easygoing and instantly likable, with a swift sense of humor. He was the first to laugh at his pratfalls and booboos. He was the ultimate blithe spirit, always on the go, planning, scheming, and thinking about what would come next, often ignoring what was right in front of him. Trends and styles didn't interest him in the least. Few folks could remember seeing him in anything other than jeans, a T-shirt, and his well-worn pair of Keds. No Air Jordans for him.

Unlike many teenagers today, Marshall Morris didn't have a selfish bone in his body. He had a genuine concern for others and was always on the lookout to help the little guy, even if it was at his own disadvantage. He avoided the spotlight and calling attention to himself. He'd gladly give up his own lunch money and go hungry so someone else could eat.

Though a good-hearted person to his core, his intended good deeds didn't always work out the way he planned. There was the time he helped those nice men load up their trucks with all the high school computers. How was he supposed to know they were stealing them? Or the time the school lunch staff was shorthanded, and he volunteered in the cafeteria with the food preparation. Well, they should have marked the regular and hot chili pepper better. If Marshall was around, something unexpected was bound to happen.

Marshall excelled in sports and the classroom, where he worked hard to make the academic honor roll every term. He was among the most popular and well-recognized students in his class, enjoying a healthy high school social life, so long as he could stay out of the spotlight. His first meaningful relationship began when he literally ran into Nancy Hooper in the school library. Nancy, who was to become the valedictorian of their class, was a bookish, introverted academic genius who seldom dated. Even though she and Marshall would seem to have polar-opposite personalities, they hit it off and dated for several months. They got along fine and enjoyed each other's company, but the burning hot embers of passion never quite kindled. Nancy was now headed way back east to MIT, Harvard, or some other prestigious eastern school.

Then, just this summer, Cupid's aim was a little more accurate when a tiny African American server at Bigaburger began doing cartwheels with his heart. It took a push from Graham and some assertiveness from Mallory herself to get the big lug to ask her out. Mallory Jollen would be a junior in the fall at Justice High, where she'd earned straight A's and was a member of the cheerleading squad. She first noticed Marshall Morris as a player on the football team, although she was sure he had no clue she even existed. She had fled New Orleans and sought refuge in Texas with her mother, a single parent, and siblings during a horrible hurricane and flood disaster. Her older brother, Marques, had spent two years at Texas Southern University in Houston before dropping out. Younger sister, Paula, a meddlesome, pert, and decidedly opinionated teenager, was still in junior high.

Mallory was shy and reserved rather than forward or bubbly, which probably explained why her social life at Justice High had been almost nonexistent. The boys had certainly noticed her. She was only a few inches over five feet, but had an athlete's compact and well-toned body. She had never tried gymnastics and might have excelled in that sport. In fact, a large picture of Olympic super gold medalist Simone Biles graced one wall of her bedroom. She liked to wear her jet-black hair pulled back, much like the famed local gymnast. Her large dark eyes, turned-up nose, and tiny mouth perfectly complimented her flawless caramel skin. Mallory saw herself as perhaps cute but not attractive. She couldn't quite throw off a lingering sense of insecurity brought on by the major disturbing family life events she'd endured back in Louisiana. That said, once she opened up, Mallory was sweet, upbeat, and fun to be around.

There was just something about Marshall Morris that attracted her to him. His reputation ranged from "Mr. Wonderful in Keds" to "the biggest goofball at Justice High." As she got to know him better, she soon realized that his appeal wasn't that he was different, but that he was so uniquely genuine. He never tried to feed a girl a bunch of lines. Still, she surprised herself by being so forward with him that day with his friend at the burger joint. She almost died when he asked her out.

Mallory loved music, including the popular teen stuff, but she also enjoyed choral and even classical genres. She was a member of her church's youth choir and had already sung solos at the regular Sunday services, where Marshall's mother, Sally Morris, had noticed her. It was a little early, but Mallory was already thinking about making music for her career. Once they started dating, a spark flared. They both enjoyed each other and had lots of fun on double dates with Jennifer and Graham.

Society being what it is, the possibility of issues arising dating an African American girl crossed Marshall's mind. He had no qualms about it but was curious about how others might react. He was very close to his mom, whose only concern was that he had cleared the way with Nancy, who was a non-factor at that point. She encouraged him to go for it.

Their relationship was going strong when an unexpected bump threw it off the rails for a while and could have ended things for good. It did, in fact, deal with race. Marshall had become involved with a group of old local veterans who were fighting the teardown of a statue of a local war hero. Marshall Morris never did things halfway and vigorously joined the fight. In doing so, he jumped right on the bandwagon of those who believe that eliminating public statues anywhere in the United States is wrong and should be stopped. Unknowingly, he bruised Mallory's feelings so much that she broke off their wonderful relationship. Her action caught Marshall completely unawares. He was clueless about what he had done to upset her. He had been shortsighted by failing to realize his opposition to the tearing down of statues implied he was endorsing the horrible human rights and slave-owning policies of many Confederate generals whose likenesses abound throughout the South. As an African-American, whose ancestors had been subject to the cruelty of those "heroes", she found Marshall's blind spot too much for her to tolerate.

Marshall was dumbstruck and very upset with himself, thinking of how much he'd hurt her. When he'd rushed to join the anti-demolition crowd, he hadn't thought through all the implications. When he finally considered the wider scope of his predicament, he realized in no way had he intended to endorse the actions of former slave owners. It took a long heart-to-heart discussion with Mallory to win her back.

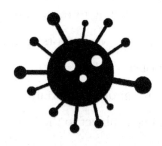

CHAPTER 5

Things between them became great again quickly. Mallory was very upset when their relationship cratered over the statues, but she simply couldn't accept a person who ignored the plight of people of color. In the end, it was yet another case of Marshall barreling into a situation, only to find out later things weren't quite what he expected. Their relationship, still only a few months old, had barely survived that crisis when it suddenly faced another major stumbling block. Marshall was heading off to college a few hundred miles away, and their separation was imminent.

Mallory's life had stabilized considerably after her mother moved her family from Louisiana. The first five years of her life were spent in a tiny white clapboard shotgun house in Jefferson parish close to downtown New Orleans. The neighborhood was poor and rough. Drug use was rampant, and crime rates were high. The family never had a lot, but money was only a part of the problem. Barbara, Mallory's mother, was determined to do her very best for her children, but life was difficult. Against all odds, she earned her associate's degree from a junior college and held a steady job in the accounting section of a local department store. Unfortunately, her marriage to Mallory's father, which had never been very strong, completely fell apart when Paula was born. Her husband was a heavy drinker and routinely abused her, often with the children present. She got a temporary restraining order and finally a divorce to keep the man away, but he still showed up from time to time to wreak havoc on the family. The divorce decree called for him to pay child support, but he barely ever paid a dime. Whenever Mallory's father was around, the children would do their best to hide, which was hard to do in such a small house.

Mallory shivered when she thought back to her former life in Louisiana. Issac Jollen worked on the docks at the port along the Mississippi. She remembered him coming home from work in clothes that were totally black and reeking of coal dust from loading and unloading freighters. Dead tired, he would sit down at the kitchen table hammering down Dixie beers while her mother fixed dinner. During her toddler years, other than yelling at Marques, who was entering his teens, he paid little attention to the kids. There was little love or affection in the family, but at least he rarely fought with Barbara. That was to come later. Mallory attended pre-K classes in a small turn-of-the-century red brick schoolhouse two blocks away. She knew no other life, and her family seemed much like all the others in their neighborhood. Things were okay.

Even though she had still been very young, she clearly remembered the day when everything fell apart for the Jollen family. She came home from school to find the lady next door waiting for her.

There had been an accident. Her mother was at the hospital where they took her father after a coal chute fell on him at work. His legs were crushed, and he was badly injured. After a week in the hospital, Issac came home to spend most of his days lying in bed under the influence of strong pain medication. Gradually, with the help of a walker and usually steadied by his wife, he spent a few hours each day at the dining table and sitting on the small front porch of their tiny house.

While doctors had assured him that his legs should eventually heal enough to permit him to get around with a cane, he would never walk naturally again. At age thirty-two, they branded him an invalid for life. As the months went by, his physical condition improved, although his right leg was useless. Unfortunately, his attitude and outlook on life darkened as he healed. It was apparent that he could never again perform physical labor, and without even a high school education, he qualified for little else. To complicate matters, an investigation of the accident on the job revealed he had been drinking at lunch that day and his inebriation likely contributed significantly to the accident and injury. While his medical bills were covered, they ruled him ineligible for disability compensation. He could scarcely control his anger over that decision. His bitterness grew. It had been tough enough for the Jollen family to struggle by when both he and Barbara were working. Now they'd have to make it on her small salary alone. The fortunes of an already dreary, poor black family in the New Orleans ghetto had taken a serious downturn.

Mallory tried to block out memories of those days, but the images were still so vivid in her mind that she found it impossible to ignore them. She struggled to cherish some good things about her father, but there just wasn't much. He ignored his children as if he resented their existence and they imposed an unfair burden on his life. She vaguely remembered the family going to a carnival once. He won a teddy bear by throwing baseballs at bottles and gave the cheap fuzzy little toy to her. She loved it until a few days later it disappeared from her bed. Daddy had taken it. She never saw it again.

Their little shotgun house had two small bedrooms. The walls were paper-thin, and privacy was non-existent. She shared one bedroom with Marques, and her parents had the other on the other side of a common wall. After the accident, when Barbara was at work and the kids were at school, Issac passed his days sitting on the front porch with a Dixie beer in his hand, napping a lot, and sometimes listening to baseball games on the radio. When his legs healed enough for him to walk, he'd head down the block to the "He Ain't Here Club" where he sat at the bar and babbled about his bad luck to anyone who would listen to him. He wallowed in his own sympathy, but never tried to improve his circumstances.

When he was around the house, he was usually in a foul mood, finding fault with everything. His rantings often turned to rage. Everyone tried to avoid him, which was impossible in that house. At least when he was off bingeing at the bar, it was still tense but much more peaceful, although they dreaded when he came home.

As a teenager, Marques stayed out of the house as much as he could. He hung out with his friends in the hood every day. The kids he associated with had little to do, and opportunities to get into trouble were everywhere. Drugs were available on any street corner. Shoplifting and petty theft were accepted and expected routines. It was only a matter of time before he would get mixed up with an organized gang and in really big-time trouble. When Marques was at home, his father was constantly on him about every little thing, from his baggy pants to being lazy. Marques was still growing but had experienced his growth spurt. He was already taller than his father and had played enough basketball and lifted enough weights to develop a rugged build. Constant bickering with his no-account father didn't help his disposition. The young man had gained a serious attitude problem and a chip on his shoulder. Mallory worried that one day they would come to blows. She was afraid of what might happen if they did.

Mallory avoided her father as much as possible, and he mostly ignored her, anyway. Still, there was no place to hide. When the daily arguments began, she would run to her room, jump on her bed, and pull her pillow over her head. She tried to block out the raised voices and yelling but could not. She would lie there terrified for her mother, whimpering, unable to escape the terror in the next room. Those days were impossible for her to forget, even many years later.

She was working on a coloring book one evening around 6:00 p.m. Her mother had just gotten home from work and was preparing pasta for dinner. Marques wasn't at home, but her father sat at the kitchen table with his can of suds, talking to Barbara as she cooked. The conversation started off civilly, although it was apparent that Issac was drunk, and Barbara, who'd had a long day, was tired. All the ingredients were there for a blowup.

Barbara tried her best to steer the conversation to the kids, local news, or even the weather, but Issac wasn't interested. After a few minutes, having failed to ignite a conversation, she just gave up and went about the business of cooking spaghetti.

"So, what's wrong with you? Cat got your tongue?" he asked.

She ignored him.

"Say, where have you been eating for lunch? You look like you've gained ten pounds." His voice level ratcheted up. "Oh, so that's it. We can barely make it day by day, and you are stuffing yourself at lunch with expensive restaurant food. That's selfish of you. Got you, don't I, Barb?"

Long ago, she promised herself to remain cool in these potentially combustible situations and to ignore his ridiculous accusations. Inevitably, though, she could stand only so much, and eventually, against her better judgment, she would snap back at him in kind, even though she knew that would set him off and the battle would be on. "No, that's not right," she replied. "I bring my lunch, which is one sandwich, every day in a brown paper bag. I eat at my desk."

He took a second to consider her words as the alcohol numbed brain cells rattled around in his head. Then suddenly he erupted. "Aw, shit! Your chubby butt better not be from what I'm thinking, you bitch. You've already done that to me twice. Is it because you're pregnant again? I'm not standing for it. And if it is, who did it? Have you been sleeping around out there when you're supposed to be at work? Who is it? You tramp! That white boss of yours, I'll bet. I've got a mind to go over there and kick his ass!" he ranted at the top of his voice. His agitation was at max. It was the worst and most dangerous time to be around him.

She had been there many times before and knew there was no way to win this conversation. If she reacted in kind, he'd blow up. If she was quiet, he'd blow up. She was just about to drop the spaghetti into the boiling water but turned and looked straight at him. She swallowed hard. "You got one thing right this time, Issac. You're going to be a father again. But you missed the other part. You, you fat ass drunk. The father is you. You're so drunk most of the time, you can't remember anything from one day to the next."

"Another kid! Another little brat to feed and pay for! Do you think I'm made of money? Struck down by this horrible accident, I don't need more pressure. Why in the hell did you let this happen? Three times you've tricked me. I'm sick of it. I am sick of you, all of you." With effort, he raised himself to his feet and started across the room toward her.

"It took two of us." She knew what was about to happen but wasn't about to back down. Her anger was flaring. In fact, as he staggered toward her, she grabbed the glass of red wine she had been sipping while she cooked and flipped it right in his face. "There you go, Issac, a toast to our growing family."

That incensed him, and as he moved to swing a balled fist at her, he bumped into the stove, causing the boiling pot of scalding water to slosh down his side and leg. He was so bent on grabbing her, he ignored the pain. He snatched her wrist as she twisted to get away from him.

A voice yelled at him as he drew back his arm and prepared to punch. "Let go of her, you son-of-a-bitch!" Marques stood there, glaring at his father. There was deep hatred in his eyes. "Do it!" he screamed.

Issac hesitated and dropped his wife's arm. He turned his attention to the newly arrived challenger. "Well, looky here. The cavalry has arrived. A little punk just out of diapers, who thinks he's a big man."

Marques flew at his inebriated father, slammed his fist directly into the man's jaw. The unexpected blow rocked Issac, who fell back against the stove where his hand contacted the flaming gas burner. He screamed in pain. Issac Jollen was lazy and no family man, but he knew how to take care of himself out on the streets. He'd be dammed if he'd let a young kid get the best of him. Burned hand or not, he rushed toward Marques and bowled him over with his bulk. His two hundred twenty pounds were at least eighty or ninety more than his son. Both were lying on the floor with Isaac on top. The crazed man grabbed his son's neck with both hands and began choking the boy.

"Issac! Let go of him!", Barbara screamed, "You're going to hurt him.

If he heard her, he didn't let up. He was obsessed and seemed intent on killing their son. She was frantic. She grabbed him around the neck to pull him off, but he was too big and strong for her to move. If she didn't do something, it would be too late. There was a knife rack on the counter. There was no choice. She leaned across the bodies on the floor and snatched a carving knife. How did this get to be so horrible? Her rotten husband was about to kill her precious son. The choice was simple. She raised the knife, closed her eyes, and was just about to plunge the blade down into Isaac's back when the door flew open and two black-clad New Orleans PD officers ran into the room. One pushed her away and took the knife. The other smashed Issac across the face with enough force to make him release the choke hold. Within minutes, both Issac and Marques were in handcuffs. Barbara sat on a kitchen chair sobbing with her hands covering her face. Mallory, who was also wailing, was hugging her mother. Thank goodness some neighbor had called 911.

The police released Marques, but they threw Issac into a police cruiser. They took him to the station where he was booked and thrown into the drunk tank with a few dozen other stellar citizens.

CHAPTER 6

Her father's failures made Mallory even closer to her mother. She'd been too little to understand what was going on. She seemed to remember being happy to hear she was getting a new sister or brother. In looking back, though, she had always wondered why her mother hadn't immediately been done with her father. Why hadn't she dumped him? Gotten rid of him? Look what almost happened. Marques aside, he'd been abusing her for years. There must be something she could have done. The police? A lawyer. Even as a tiny child, she feared him and begged her mommy to keep the man out of their house.

Strangely enough, Barbara took no action against her abusive husband. Despite the strong urging from the police, she refused to even press charges against him. Young Mallory, of course, didn't understand any of what was really going on but wailed for hours when her mother told her that daddy was coming home again. It wasn't until years later when Mallory was old enough to understand she explained why she didn't get rid of him after the incident with Marques. Mallory was in junior high school in Justice, where they had been living for several years. The two were eating dinner, and neither Marques nor Paula were around.

"There's something I've been wanting to talk to you about for a long time, but I wanted to wait until you were old enough to understand," Barbara began.

Mallory looked across the table at her mother and immediately knew what she had in mind. "You mean about why back in New Orleans after daddy almost killed Marques, and I screamed my head off you let him back in the house?"

Barbara smiled. This kid is so smart. "Yes. You were very young and couldn't have understood all the implications of the situation."

"You will not tell me it was because you loved him. I'd have a tough time believing that. Not the way he treated you."

"No. No. there was no love left between him and me. In fact, I'm not sure if there was ever any genuine love between us. I guess you should probably know that we only got married in the first place because I became pregnant with Marques." If Mallory was surprised by that admission, she didn't react to it.

"I will say that he was much easier to live with before the accident. We could get along day by day, and things weren't too bad. After the accident, everything changed. He lost everything physically. His pride was shattered. He couldn't even work. He turned to booze and then vented all his frustration on me as the reason all those bad things happened to him. I was convenient and easy to blame. He took out some of it on Marques, who was at exactly the wrong age as a know-it-all teenager. Luckily, he mostly ignored you. If he had ever taken one step in your direction for any reason, I probably would have killed him on the spot." Barbara stopped and looked closely at her daughter. She had been absolutely sure that bastard had never touched her, but maybe she had missed something. She shuddered to think about that possibility, but now would be the time for Mallory to tell her. She held her breath.

Tears welled in Mallory's eyes. "No, Mama. He did nothing like that. He mostly just ignored me, like I was an extra piece of furniture or something."

That relieved Barbra.

"After the police incident, I knew in my heart that our marriage was over, but for the first time, your father showed remorse for his actions. He apologized and begged me to take him back. He knew he had no other place to go. He promised to straighten up and even find a job. I didn't really believe him, but it wasn't like we had anywhere else to go, either. I was pregnant with Paula. Maybe he could be helpful, and any money he brought in would be a plus. I understood why so many battered women refuse to prosecute their abusive husbands. Going it alone with three kids is scary. There was no one else I could turn to for help. Down deep, I was sure the SOB would never change, but I suppose he deserved one last chance."

"So, you let him come back. I remember being so scared of him, but after a while, I guess things settled down?"

"Yes, they did. He actually remained remorseful and grateful for a while. He seemed to appreciate how bad he'd become. He found a job, working the late shift at a convenience store, which at least kept him away from the house for part of the day. Between there and the bar, he was gone a lot more than before the blowup. A few times, he actually handed me a little cash, which I desperately needed. Of course, all this time I was getting bigger and bigger with Paula."

"I can remember a little what you looked like. What about Marques? How did they get along?"

"They didn't. I tried hard to control your brother at least a little, but I really couldn't. He spent most of his time with his friends in the gangs. He and Issac never spoke again, as far as I know. They seemed to have weird mutual respect for each other. Issac, in particular, seemed almost proud that his son stood up for his mother, even though it was against him."

"Did Dad ever take more interest in his family? How about the baby on the way?"

"None. I got myself to the hospital just in time, by the way. I don't know where he was. He never came to the hospital at all. Never heard a word from him. I managed okay. We had some wonderful neighbors, thank goodness. Once I had Paula on a kind of schedule, I contacted a local lawyer and started the divorce proceedings. When your father heard about that, he appeared at the house and was very upset I had filed. Right then, I saw some of the old Issac coming through. That worried me. I asked the lawyer to do something, and he had a temporary restraining order issued by the court which was supposed to stop him from coming to our house."

"Did it work?"

"Not really. He still came over. I had to threaten him to get him to leave. He had lost his job at the store for drinking while on duty. No surprise. He had lots of time on his hands."

"Were you afraid of him?"

"Yes. More and more, I was. The funny thing was the liberating event that changed all our lives was the horrible hurricane and flood. Our house had over ten feet of water in it. We spent a few dicey days salvaging what we could, but eventually, we came to Texas and never looked back. Without that storm, I hate to think where we might be today."

Mallory grabbed her mother and smothered her in a magnificent hug.

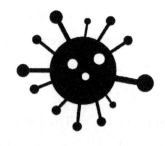

CHAPTER 7

In Katrina's aftermath, the Crescent City was a mess. With little alternative, Barbara loaded her three kids on a bus and ended up sheltering with a few thousand other New Orleans refugees on the floor of the Astrodome in Houston, Texas. Louisiana had always been home, and despite their domestic problems, she intended to return there as soon as they cleaned up the city. What they hoped would be only a few days became weeks. Barbara was completely out of cash. Her family was living off of handouts from relief workers. She knew they couldn't last indefinitely and looked for work in Houston. It turned out to be one of the best decisions of her life. She immediately caught on with Exxon as a petroleum analyst assistant with wages several times higher than she'd had back home. Beyond that, she loved the work.

Having finally gained a bit of stability with a regular income stream, Barbara seriously considered her options. Yes, Louisiana was home, but it just didn't make sense to think about not going back there now. Her ex-husband and all the problems he caused were back there. She was not eager to start that misery up again. And then there was her son, Marques, a teenager who had already fallen in with a dangerous crowd in their old neighborhood. She knew he'd go right back to them as soon as they returned. She became friendly with a coworker at Exxon, who lived south of downtown Houston in the suburb of Justice. Her friend loved that community and said it was a great place to raise kids. That weekend, Barbara rode down the Gulf Freeway to check it out. On an impulse, she visited a local apartment project and signed a six-month lease for a three-bedroom apartment. If things didn't work out, they could always return home later. They never did. The family flourished in their new setting.

The girls were pleased with Texas. Neither of them had been old enough in New Orleans to establish friends or ties there. Still, Mallory's memories were anything but good. Justice, Texas, was a suburb of the huge Houston metropolis to the south on the way to Galveston on the Gulf of Mexico. Justice was a true bedroom community without a lot of business or industry actually in the town. Many of the wage earners who lived in Justice held jobs in downtown Houston or at the NASA headquarters complex located across the Gulf freeway. Extensive shopping, excellent schools, libraries, and other recreational alternatives were readily available for young families. Most importantly, unlike the New Orleans inner-city parishes, Justice was safe. Crime rates and drug use were much lower than back home.

There was one aspect of Justice that gave Barbara some pause about relocating her young family there. The place was very white, which didn't mean that her black family would be ostracized or resented. It was dramatically different from their old neighborhood where even seeing a white face was a surprise. In Justice, it would be the other way around. One reason she signed a short-term apartment lease was so they could be flexible if they were uncomfortable there. Fortunately, issues of color never surfaced as a problem among the kids. Justice had a high average level of education, at least partially because of NASA and the demand for educated people from around the world. Not that there were not plenty of cliques and factions in the upper levels of schools. Such groups are commonplace almost anywhere and were based on income levels as demonstrated by cars, clothes, or other reasons for kids to envy one another.

Mallory enrolled into an elementary school in Justice. She was still young enough not to have much else to compare with her new school or schoolmates. The transition from Louisiana was easy and seamless. She loved school and immediately fit right in. She discovered music early on and continued to pursue it as she passed upward through the grades. Petite of stature and naturally quiet, she was well-liked and blended in rather than being known for her unique ideas or opinions. She was the type that had a few very good friends rather than bunches of them. She would much rather go with the flow than go against the grain. Her mother always suspected that her desire not to make waves came from lingering fearful memories of Issac.

Her sister, however, had no such qualms. In fact, she had never met her father, although she had heard about him and the terror he created. Paula could claim to be a Texan through and through. She hadn't been born there but arrived before she was even a year old. If terrible memories haunted Mallory in some ways, Paula had no such inhibitions. As a toddler, she was never reluctant to approach anyone about anything. She was very active as an infant and gave her mother fits about sleeping through the night. She hatched daily major meltdowns. She craved attention and was determined to get it. While Mallory was the inveterate team player, Paula was the fifth wheel, whose activities resulted in several parent-teacher conferences. Her grades were good, but she just had to do things her way. It wasn't that she was a troublemaker, only that she was convinced that she knew best.

In Paula's view, her "little sister," Mallory, should report everything she said or did to her every day. Paula understood Mallory was sweet and would always turn the other cheek to avoid confrontation. Paula took full advantage of her sister's vulnerability and thought nothing of nosing into her business. She was outgoing, likable, and invariably amusing. It was impossible not to like Paula unless she was your younger sister and always reading your personal diary. At least when Mallory crashed head over heels for Marshall, she had enough common sense and decency not to horn in on that relationship. As far as she was concerned, though, even though she was only thirteen, an eighteen-year-old boy was fair game. Mallory better not trip up. Marshall got a kick out of Paula, much to Mallory's irritation.

Marques was disappointed about not returning to New Orleans, mainly because he missed his buddies, although he benefited more than any of them by staying in Texas. After two years at Texas Southern University, he dropped out. He was bright enough but simply didn't care for schoolwork. He took a job as a gofer for a non-profit group that advocated the end of worldwide warfare. Although he never bought into the ideas professed by the group, it was his job to help set up rallies and meetings. When he took the job, he did not know he would end up literally butting heads with his sister's new boyfriend. Marques became a key player in the attempt to steal a statue. He was very fortunate to have avoided arrest and jail time.

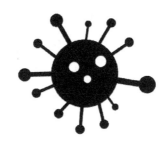

CHAPTER 8

The summer was nearly over, and Marshall would soon be off to college, leaving Mallory behind at home. On that last Sunday afternoon, the two sat alone in the bleachers at the Justice High football field where Marshall had played so well, urged on by Mallory and the cheerleading crew. That spot had become something of a special place for them. It was where they had reconciled after their emotional breakup over the confederate general matter. Marshall was excited about college and hadn't focused on how his absence might affect their relationship. Little else had consumed Mallory over the past several days. Her mind monster had been working overtime as she hashed and rehashed their looming separation in her head.

"You know, Mal, Justice is a really neat place. My mom and I were so lucky to have landed here from back east. It's a great place to live. Justice High was fun and there were so many nice kids here. Right?" Marshall offered.

"Yup."

"I've only been to Austin a couple of times, but it seems to have everything. Graham and I went there on a football recruiting weekend. They laid out the red carpet for us. They had these escort girls show us around campus and take us to a football game. We went to a frat house party that night. It was amazing. The facilities are impressive, too. You should see the locker rooms. First-class. Every player has his own little dressing space. There are TVs everywhere, video games, and a lot of other stuff. There are no athletic dorms anymore, but they require us to live on campus, at least for the first year. The rules now allow us to get free unlimited meals and snacks, and the food there is incredible."

"That sounds perfect for you."

"You bet. I'm a little worried about how well I'll do against those huge recruits they pull in from all over the country. Graham heard they'll probably ask us to red-shirt for the first year."

"Red-shirt? What is that?"

"It's what college teams do to manage their squads. It depends where they need players at what positions. You have five years to complete four years of playing eligibility. The coach can ask you to sit out your first year. You practice with the team but never actually play in a game. When you start your second year, you still have four years left to play. It's done all the time."

"You mean you go out there every day, knock heads with other players, sweat, freeze, and bleed, but never play in a game? That sounds crazy. Why would you do that? It also means you have to spend five years there instead of four. Right?"

"Yes, it does, although by spreading out your class load, it can be easier on your studying. In fact, there have been many players who actually graduated and still played in games for the team, as long as they were enrolled and taking some classes. I don't know if they would ask me to red-shirt or not. I don't care. I can't wait to get there. It should be so much fun. You know..." He looked over at his tiny girlfriend, who spun her face away from him, but not quickly enough for him to miss the glistening in her eyes. He stopped short. "Hey, hey. What's the matter with you?"

"Nothing, Marshall. Nothing. You're excited and should be," she said with a sniffle.

As usual, Marshall had run off a hundred miles an hour in one direction, bent only on getting to his destination, ignoring how he would get there. The biggest, roughest recruit he would meet on the football field in college couldn't have shaken him up more. "Oh, no, Mal. I'm so sorry. All I was thinking of was myself. What a dumbo I can be."

"Yes, the 'amazing parties' and 'girl escorts.' Sounds great. Have a delightful time," she shot back. He tried to reply, but she cut him off. "Marshall, I understand. I really get it. You're about to do something wonderful and exciting. I'm happy for you. I've thought about your leaving for a while and what it would do to us. You know, you and me."

"Nothing," he said, "except we'll be physically apart."

"Hush!" she ordered with a quavering voice. "My conclusion is that it would be unfair for me to hold you back in Austin. You should be free to do whatever you want without strings attached. Among the amazing parties, coeds, whatever, I can't expect you to be tied to some little high school girl way back home. I just can't." Both were quiet, in deep thought.

As much as I care for this guy, it's so hard for me to forget our life in New Orleans and what my rotten father put us through. I suppose I'm gun shy about long-term relationships that call for devotion and faithfulness. I'm just so afraid that he'll dump our relationship on the rocks when he gets to college and Justice fades away in his mind. I'm just not ready to face the hurt I'm sure will come. As much as it kills me to push him away again, it's better to face and deal with it now. It's so hard because I know in my heart that I love the guy. There, I've said it, but I just have to be fair to him.

"Are you kidding me? Do you think once Graham and I hit the interstate driving west tomorrow that I'll just forget all about Justice, everyone here, and you? No way. Come on, Mal, give me a little credit. I know I'm flaky, but I am not completely nuts."

"Yes. I knew you would say that, but you haven't left yet. Austin will be amazing. High school romances almost always evaporate when people go to college. It just happens. The girl left at home gets jilted. I'm not sure it's anyone's fault, really. New worlds open up, and people move on."

"Sure, you're right. That doesn't mean it has to happen to us."

"I'd love to think that. I really would, but I know you only too well. Of course, you'll get totally involved over there. That's what you do. You're not a halfway person. Once you decide to jump in, it's all the way. Justice and Mallory Jollen will soon be in your rear-view mirror." She snuffled, fighting back tears.

No one spoke for a moment. Finally, Marshall turned and placed a hand on either of her shoulders. He looked down as tears fell onto her lap. "Look at me, Mal," he asked. She slowly raised her head until she was looking into his deep brown eyes. "You just said the word. *Love*. Although I'm excited about what lies ahead, don't sell me short. I've done a lot of thinking about us as well. How much I'm going to miss you. How excited I'll be to come home and see you. Two-some hours. That's all it is to drive. We have our phones. And how much fun we will have when you come up to Austin for a weekend. Just think about that. You're not the girl I used to date back home. You *are* my girl. And, Mallory, I do. I love you." He pulled her tight. He didn't lose it, but there was a humongous lump in his throat.

Half smothered by his bulk. She looked up at him. "Me too. Of course, me too. I can't imagine losing you. I just have this thing about getting hurt. As hard as it is now, it might be better than later when I see a picture of you dancing the frug at a fraternity party with some debutante!"

"The frug? What the heck is that? Some kind of toad?"

She giggled. "No clue. I think I read it in an old magazine."

"Well, here's the deal. Miz Jollen. Just a few weeks ago, you gave me a divorce. It didn't work. You are not giving me another one. Am I clear about that?"

"Very clear, sir. Very clear."

"So, are we good, you and me? No more of this overthinking nonsense?"

"No, we aren't good. We're great. Say, when's the first week I can come up there?"

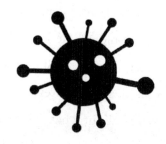

CHAPTER 9

While it had been their plan to set out bright and early on Monday morning, it was almost noon before Marshall and Graham took off for Austin in Marshall's 1971 orange Jeepster Commando. Graham had serious reservations about the ancient clunker making it the entire 150 miles to Austin. Often, the first day of college is a special and stressful occasion for families as a child leaves the nest. Here, since the boys were reporting early for football practice, they somehow convinced Marshall's mother and Graham's parents to wait and come up two weeks closer to the start of classes. That way, they could bring most of their stuff later and also include anything they had forgotten. Marshall had to go by and see Mallory, who kept things together very well. Of course, Marshall's thoughtful move meant that Graham also had to drive by Jennifer's house, or there would have been hell to pay, even though Jennifer was headed to CTU herself in a few days.

The drive along Interstate Highway 10 and State Highway 71 to Austin was uneventful, other than the boys having to stop for lunch along the way at a barbecue restaurant. Though they still had a hundred miles to go, Marshall decided he could probably make it the rest of the way without stopping for a snack. The city of Austin is near the middle of the state on the western side of a triangle between San Antonio to the south, Dallas to the north, and Houston to the east. It is the capital and a popular destination for high-tech companies which flocked there in great numbers. The population had grown tremendously in recent years, and the city was fast transitioning into a major metropolis. Besides Central Texas University, there were ten other institutions of higher learning scattered around the city.

Buoyed by youthful enthusiasm and the excitement of entering college, it was not surprising that the boys never bothered with maps, GPS, or written directions to figure out where they were going. After all, they had been there once already, hadn't they? It was easy to follow the roadside signs to the outskirts of the city, which they identified with dead certainty by spotting the beige state capitol dome. So far, so good.

They weren't sure what exit to take off the elevated highway that crossed the city. They were whizzing along when Graham yelled at Marshall, "There it is! Next exit. I just saw a sign that said 'CTU'. That has to be it. Do it!"

"Sounds good to me," Marshall said as he quickly cut over three lanes. An ear-shattering blast of an eighteen-wheeler air horn directly behind them let Marshall know he had just cut in front of a truck, and the driver wasn't pleased. He had little time to worry about it because he had to swerve again to make the exit ramp, which they rolled down to a stoplight. Graham pointed across the intersection where there was a "CTU" sign with a left arrow. Reassured they were headed correctly, when the light changed, Marshall made the left turn unto congested downtown Austin traffic. After traveling several blocks and not seeing any signs, a smidgen of doubt crept into their conversation. Nothing looked familiar until Graham noticed a group of older gray stone buildings surrounded by a brick wall and gigantic oak trees. There was a large monument sign in front that was obscured by heavy bushes and landscaping in the center of a circular entrance driveway. They couldn't see a large "C" on the sign, but just as they tried to read the rest, a city bus drove by and blocked their view. To complicate matters, there was an impatient taxicab driver right behind who kept leaning on his horn to let them know he didn't appreciate their sightseeing.

"Got to be it", Marshall decided and hooked into the driveway. Sure enough, he spotted a "CTU" sign, and two or three cars parked there with their trunks open, obviously dropping off incoming students. "Well, we made it, Graham. I wonder where the dining hall is?" As they parked at the curb, they noticed two girls, dressed exactly alike, standing near the entrance to the building and pointing at them. Both boys smiled and stood a little straighter, but then looked away.

"Why don't you unload? I'll go in and get our room assignment," Marshall suggested.

"Okay, that's cool," Graham replied as he watched his friend disappear inside the building.

Marshall was surprised at the solitude of the dorm building. He expected more activity, hustle, and bustle, especially on the first day. He looked around and finally spotted a table with the two girls sitting at it. They had some papers and computer printouts in front of them and were obviously checking students in. Just what he needed. He walked right over.

The girls looked up at him. They were smiling about something. He stood there for a moment until, finally, the one with blond hair and glasses asked, "Can I help you?"

"Sure can. My buddy and I need our room assignment. We just drove here from Houston. Say, where is the dining hall?"

The other girl, a brunette, then said, "So you're checking in, are you? You're enrolled at CTU?"

"Yes. In fact, we're on the football team." Marshall had always heard that most coeds fawned over jocks and football players in particular. He was more than surprised when both girls broke into laughter.

Graham had made excellent progress in unloading a lot of their stuff out onto the sidewalk. He was happy to see Marshall headed his way at a good clip. How had he gotten stuck with the manual labor while Marshall talked to the girls?

"Okay. Okay. Let's get this stuff back in the car and get out of here pronto. Come on. Come on. Hurry."

"I take it this is the wrong place, then."

"Yep, unless you're a young woman who wants to become a nun. This is the Carmelite training school for girls. The Mother Superior was not amused. She's watching us through the doorway."

CHAPTER 10

After quickly deciding that taking vows into a convent wasn't for them, the pair wandered around the city for a while more before they finally found Blanco Hall on the Central Texas University campus. This time, Marshall stayed with the car and Graham went inside. Surprise. Surprise. They had found the right place. After checking in with the front desk, they found a luggage cart. Blanco Hall was a twenty-story high-rise dormitory building with several banks of elevators. With their gear loaded, they pushed the cart on an elevator and rode up to the nineteenth floor. Their room, 1910, was set up for roommates with two of everything: beds, desks, bookcases, and chests of drawers. They shared a bathroom. Both the laminate tile floors and the sheetrock walls were a light gray. The room wasn't exceptional but perfectly suitable for two incoming freshmen. After dumping their stuff on the beds, Graham walked over and pushed the curtain aside to look out the window. "Wow. Marshall. Come here. Look at this."

Marshall came over and peered out, looking down from some nineteen stories. The entire university campus spread before them, but what caught his attention was the amazing, glimmering football stadium right next to their dorm. Surely, the coaching staff had chosen these rooms with that view to inspire their recruits. Marshall was a bit more stoic. "Well, if we don't make the team, we can at least watch the games from right here."

The welcome packages they were given when they checked in included a notice that there was a meeting of all football squad members that evening at 7:30. Since it was already almost 6:00, Marshall was getting very nervous about dinner. Luckily, they could go through the line (but only once) downstairs at the dorm's dining room. Marshall would have to make do with one helping or risk being late for their first football meeting. He reluctantly agreed to forgo seconds in the team's interest.

They walked right next door into the football complex and followed several other boys toward a conference room with tiers of amphitheater-like seating. There were close to a hundred young men in the room, which was abuzz with anticipation and nervousness. For many, this session was the start of what they had been working for and dreaming of for at least the past four years. They were well aware of how fortunate they were to have been recruited. There were hundreds of other high school players who would love to have been there.

There is a universal tendency for students to fill up a classroom from the back to the front as far away from the instructor as possible. Graham and Marshall quickly realized the rear of the room was reserved for upperclassmen and established team members. The front rows were for the newbies. As they took seats in the second row, they glanced around the room and recognized several of the players they had watched in games on television last year. Neither of them could believe they were actually in the same room with those guys whom they idolized.

Marshall enjoyed playing football, and despite his clumsiness, was very good at it. As they waited for the coaches to arrive, he looked around the room and couldn't help but thank his good fortune for being there. With the modesty of his mom's resources, there was no way he could have afforded to be there without his football scholarship. When Head Coach Jack Crown called him last spring to tell him they were giving him the award, he couldn't believe it. It surprised everyone. The National Collegiate Athletic Association (NCAA) had strict limits on football scholarships. They were handed out sparingly by coaches, and only to players they thought had the potential to help their team. The full squad included scholarship players and a few "walk-ons." Graham was a walk-on and didn't have a football scholarship. His parents could help him through college, so the financial aid wasn't critical. The coaches knew Graham was an excellent player and encouraged him to walk on. They might give him a scholarship later. *I like football, but I could live without it,* Marshall thought. *It's Graham's life, and he's terrific at it. He deserves a scholarship more than I do. I hope he gets one.*

The entrance of a small but sturdy-looking man wearing an orange CTU Brahma Bulls hat and muscle shirt interrupted Marshall's reverie. A thunderous "Snort! Snort! Snort!" exploded from the players. Coach Jack Crown flashed a quick smile at the reception and then got right down to business. His cap totally hid his close-cropped silver hair, but it was his intense gray eyes that immediately captivated everyone. He had a ruddy complexion, and for once, his mouth didn't have a whistle hanging from it, which seemed to be a part of him most of the time. Well under six feet, he stood ramrod straight, scrutinizing the assembled players. There was no question from anyone that this man was a leader. His exemplary record at CTU spoke for itself. Everyone was eager to hear what he had to say.

The coach took his time looking around the room, almost as if he was taking attendance and could name them all on sight. He leaned forward, grabbed either side of the podium, and began in a steady monotone of clipped but forceful words. "Welcome to everyone. Last season, we won twelve and lost two. We were second in the Elite Eleven Conference and won our bowl game. That wasn't good enough for Central Texas University. But that was last year. This year we're going to run the table. We will not fail. The amount of football talent in this room is more than we have ever had at this university. All you have to do is look around the room and you see what I'm talking about. Just wait until you bump heads on the practice field. The only thing that can hold us back this year is ourselves. I'm glad you're all here."

"And now there is the other thing." He stopped for a moment to let those words sink in. Several players looked at each other, wondering what was coming next.

"It has always been my practice to shoot my teams straight. I tell it like it is. Honestly, men, right now I'm not sure what lies ahead. I know you are all aware of what they are now calling a pandemic. A pandemic is a worldwide epidemic. This one started somewhere in Asia and is now sweeping across our country. COVID-19 is a mean virus that can kick your butt. Many people have already died from it. It's very contagious, and you catch it by being close to someone who is already infected. One of the worst aspects about it is that the expert doctors don't seem to know much about it yet. It could spread through this room overnight. We will definitely have to take extreme precautions against it here on the team. I'm not sure exactly what measures we will implement yet but be prepared to obey whatever rules come down. Most of it is common sense. Don't get too close to others. Wash your hands a lot. And other things. So far, they say masks aren't necessary because they don't protect the wearer very much. Only the person you might sneeze on. They have a test for the virus, which I'm sure we all will be taking."

"Also, it might be even worse."

They glued every eye on Coach Crown.

"We may not play any football here this year. The league and the athletic directors are meeting this week. We don't know what they'll decide. They might determine that the virus makes it too dangerous for us to play. I don't know what they'll come up with. I know one way or the other, this situation will affect us. Until we hear otherwise, we will proceed normally. Get in here tomorrow, get your physicals, take your tests, and I'll see you on the practice field tomorrow afternoon." He raised his right hand and pumped it three times. The room reverberated with "Snort! Snort! Snort!" Coach Crown pivoted and left the room.

Seldom was Marshall short for words, but this was one of those occasions. The crowd of enormous football beefsters filed out as silently as if they were leaving Sunday morning services. Any other time, it would have resembled a stampede. No one had even remotely considered they could cancel an entire season.

CHAPTER 11

After the meeting ended, the boys headed back to the dorm to unpack their gear. Graham was a brooder who kept running and re-running matters over and over in his head. "That is the last thing I would ever have expected to hear from the head coach. We could scrap the entire season. I can't imagine Texas without football. I guess we need to take this virus seriously. I thought it only affected really old people." Graham prattled on while he unpacked his clothes and neatly folded them into the drawers in his dresser.

Marshall had crashed on his bed. He lay there on his back with his legs looped over his unopened bags. He was thinking about sitting with Mallory at the football field on Sunday afternoon. They had both dropped the "L" word, and while he didn't regret saying it, he now felt a little sheepish. He composed a text to her describing their day but didn't mention the coach's meeting. It pleased him to discover that there was a perfect little heart shape emoji he could add at the end of his message, which conveyed his feelings without having to type out that magical word. He had been ignoring Graham. His girlfriend obligation completed, he tuned him in.

"I agree. It really surprised me too. I don't see any way we don't play, but if it happens, we just ride it out. We don't have a choice unless you want to go back to the convent and sign up for field hockey? Did you notice the size of some of those dudes in that room? They made Big Daddy Boyd, our biggest player, look like tater tots."

"Tater tots?"

"You know what I mean."

As instructed, they reported in at the complex the next morning for physical exams and aptitude tests. There was a group of doctors who weighed, measured, and prodded them. They recorded Marshall as being six feet two inches and 202 pounds. Graham was two inches shorter at an even six feet but weighed in at 228 pounds. After the physicals were over, they took a multiple-choice Wunderkid aptitude test. Graham, of course, approached every step in the process as a personal challenge. He was interested in performing to the best of his ability. Marshall preferred to pick his shots where he would bear down and concentrate. He simply didn't see why a multiple-choice test was needed to play football. The assistant coach who was acting as the proctor for the test was more than a bit surprised when Marshall handed in his test after only five minutes of the thirty allowed. Marshall smiled and went out into the hall to wait for Graham, who took the entire thirty minutes.

After attacking the healthy cold cut lunch spread that was laid out for the team, there was a highlight video run of last year's season. It gave the squad a chance for their meals to settle before actually taking the field for the first time in sweats and T-shirts. The first practice was mostly calisthenics and wind sprints. The coaches broke the squad down into position groups, with a specific coach assigned to each. Graham was with the linebackers and Marshall with the wide receivers. During the two-hour session, Marshall lined up next to several other wide receivers for a one-hundred-yard wind sprint. There were about ten of them and Marshall crossed the finish line in third place, which was impressive given the high quality of players that were there.

As he was catching his breath after the run, he looked over at one of his teammates, who was a well-proportioned African-American and one of the two that had beaten him. There was something about that fellow that looked familiar. *Aha! I know that guy. It's Zack. Zack Middleton from Bayside High.* Bayside was Justice's biggest rival, who had defeated them in the biggest game ever between the two teams. Zack had been their quarterback back then.

Marshall walked over to him and stuck out his hand. The other boy had been bent over with his hands on his hips, catching his breath. Sweat was dripping from his brow. He looked up. "Well. I'll be. Marshall Morris. I saw your name on the list. How are you doing? We're a long way from the Cougars."

"I'm doing fine, Zack. A lot better than the last time I saw you. You knocked us right out of the playoffs, and then your team made a good run, didn't it?"

"Sure did. We went all the way to the state championship before we lost."

"Maybe we can improve that together here. You were a quarterback back in high school. What are you doing with the receivers?"

"Have you seen who they recruited at quarterback? Ed Fisher from Florida, the number-one-rated high school quarterback in the country for one. And there are three or four other ones who are also excellent. As much as I love that position, if I have any chance to play, it won't be there." The coach was whistling for them.

"Right. I get it."

"Say, Marshall, how about joining a couple of buddies and me tonight after practice at the Broken Spur over on 6th St. They're lax on checking ids, and they love CTU players."

"Sounds great, so long as you don't bust my chops about that game!"

Zack grinned, and they both jogged over to the coach.

Anyone in their teens and twenties who ever visited Austin knew about 6th St.—a four-block downtown area crammed with bars, honky-tonk places, and eateries. CTU students and kids from all over the state flocked there nightly. From the look of things, the pandemic hadn't scared off very many people yet. The Broken Spur featured a long bar and large open area with dozens of individual tables and chairs spread around the room. When the Spur got busy and crowded in the evenings, the servers, many of whom were CTU students themselves, got lax about checking identification to be sure everyone was twenty-one, the legal drinking age in Texas. They served beer in big pitchers dropped on the tables. If one person at the table was old enough, everyone sitting there was good.

Marshall and Graham walked into the crowded joint and spotted Zack and a buddy sitting against the far wall and waving. Graham noticed that a few of the customers were wearing masks as protection against COVID. So far, though, guidance from the government and even the coaches was that you didn't need one. The boys worked their way over and sat down with Zack, who shook Graham's hand. He peeked over at Marshall to make sure he was watching and started in about the Justice-Bayside game. Once he detected Marshall's scowl, he broke out into a big grin, and they all had a big laugh. Zack introduced his friend, who was an offensive tackle from Dallas. He then filled two glasses from the pitcher of beer on the table and pushed them to Marshall and Graham, who nodded their thanks.

Neither of the Justice pals were big beer drinkers, although they both knew that social pressure often dictated some compromise. Graham's biggest objection was that he was a workout warrior. Beer didn't go with his training, especially during the season. Both sipped their mugs. The stuff was pretty good. Before long, they were enjoying themselves. They'd always heard that college life would be just like this. The four had a great time swapping football stories from high school and also speculating on what the CTU coaches would be like. Unlike the Justice boys, Zack was an experienced beer drinker. He liked to chug his quaffs, and when he did, he ended up sputtering and coughing for a bit until the liquid went down. He blamed his coughing on beer going down bad pipes, although that seemed to happen even when he wasn't drinking.

After a while, a country-western band fired up. Now the place was rocking. None of the four boys were sure, but they suspected that the girls at the next table had figured out that they were CTU football players. On their drive over, Marshall had discovered that these credentials didn't impress convent-bound girls, but not so with the local coeds. An attractive blond, who'd been tapping her feet to the music, leaned over and caught Zack's eye, which wasn't much of a problem since he had been scoping her out for at least a half-hour.

"Boot-Scooting Boogie," she said. "I love it. Come on, let's dance." She held out her hand, and Zack grabbed it. They took off through the crowd for the dance floor. The other boys tried to make out like they weren't envious, but it didn't work. Still, none of the other three dared peek over at the girls' table.

Zack was having a great time. When the song ended, he and the girl returned to their tables. Before they sat down (and asking no one else), Zack and the girl pushed their tables together. The girls had joined them, which was what the other boys had been hoping for but were afraid to suggest. They were all cute and had been hitting the beer pretty hard. Marshall was next to a tall redhead from Wichita Falls, Texas. She was a chatterbox, and when the subject of pizza came up, Marshall expounded on his favorite subject. Somehow, his glass of beer ran dry, but someone promptly refilled it.

Had the lady from Wichita Falls had known about her new friend's dance prowess or lack thereof, she might not have dragged him out on the dance floor. Somehow, she avoided Marshall's shakes and wiggles and got through a number with no cuts or bruises. Marshall was amused to see Graham out there with a new friend as well. They had a blast as a group for the next couple of hours. Finally, Graham looked at his watch and saw it was past midnight. They had practice in the morning. The others greeted him with sad and regretful looks when he stood up to leave. Marshall was deep into a discussion about types of pepperoni when Graham smacked him on the shoulder and jerked his thumb toward the door. He shrugged but didn't move as Graham walked across the restaurant toward the door. Marshall couldn't decide what to do.

Graham was halfway down the block before Marshall caught up to his friend. Graham looked over at him and smiled. "Excellent choice. We have practice tomorrow."

"Yup. As usual, you're right, padre. But," he patted his pants pocket, "I have her number."

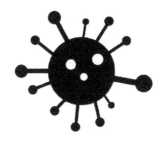

CHAPTER 12

Marshall crashed into bed in the dorm room. It had been a long day. He was just about to draw the imaginary curtain that permitted him to fall asleep anywhere when a shocking thought jolted him. *Mallory!* He had totally forgotten about her for the past several hours while he had been out drinking and carousing with other girls. He hadn't lasted even one day. It was all in good fun, and he certainly hadn't crossed the line. Yet. He felt terrible. Low and guilty. Sure enough, he checked his messages, and she had texted him around 8:00 PM. He had missed it. It was now past 1:00 AM, much too late to call her. He sent a text with no words, just a series of heart emojis. In the morning, he would figure out how to explain missing her message.

Normally, when the boys arrived at the football complex in the morning, they would go straight to their lockers and change into sweats, then head out to the field to stretch and await the start of practice. It was Monday and the beginning of their second week. So far, all they'd done was exercise and run drills. There had been no serious blocking or tackling. That was to change shortly. They would be in full pads from this point forward until further notice. Marshall wasn't pleased with that prospect. These guys were bigger and rougher than back at Justice High. He wasn't keen on getting knocked around. Graham wasn't upset. In fact, he relished the chance to make some serious contact, which is what he was built for and enjoyed. He wanted to win a place on the team and a scholarship. He couldn't accomplish his goals by tip-toeing around with drills. He was ready for some action.

Unfortunately, fate suddenly intervened, and everybody's schedule was derailed all at once. Instead of going to their lockers to dress for practice, the coaches ushered the team into the tiered meeting room, which was buzzing as usual. Something was up, but no one knew what. Everyone was guessing. Maybe the season had been scrapped? What would that mean to them? If there was no football, would the school take away their scholarships? This situation concerned everyone. Coach Crown stepped in and provided the answers.

He scanned the room, as was his custom, to make sure he had everyone's attention, which was entirely unnecessary that morning. The only sound that broke the silence was a raspy cough from Zack Middleton. "Men, I've been in this coaching business for over forty years. I thought I had seen everything until now." he paused, looked down at a piece of paper in front of him on the podium. He shook his head and read. "All offices and departments of Central Texas University are notified that all athletic activities for all sports, intercollegiate or club, are immediately suspended until further notice. Department heads, coaches, trainers, and other supervisory personnel shall immediately implement the precautionary pandemic virus protocols as outlined below in their offices and spaces. This is a directive issued by the Chancellor of the University this morning." He stopped reading and looked up at his team and sensed collective shock.

"Coach, what does this mean to me? I would have been a high NFL draft choice last spring, but I stayed in school to give it one more shot to win it all. It could screw me with no football." a voice asked from the very back row. It was Errol Stump, a senior All-American running back.

"Son, I'm just not sure how to answer you right now. We have to see how this deal plays out. From what I have heard, this memo aside, no decision has been made yet on the season. The situation is very fluid. No one really knows how much this virus will affect university sports or our team in particular. What we have to do is shut down practice for right now. All of us have to be tested for the virus to see if it's even present here at all. We have to implement the protocols around the team and the complex to minimize the spread of the disease. I hope it's not here, and we can soon get right back to business. Coach Wilkinson will take things from here about the protocols. One more word from me. I'm sure none of you will enjoy some of the safety precautions they require. To that, I say, too bad. If you want to stay on this Brahma Bull's football squad, you *will* comply. If not, you will be gone. No exceptions. This is serious business. Am I clear on that?" He looked around the room to nodding heads. "Fred."

"Snort! Snort! Snort!" thundered from the seats as the head coach left.

Fred Wilkinson was the assistant head coach, who had been at coach Crown's side for many seasons. While the head coach was aloof, formal, hard-nosed, demanding, and polished, Fred was laid back, personable, and easygoing. His personality was disarming, though. Some players had assumed they could take advantage of his nice-guy demeanor, only to discover he had a tough side you did not want to deal with should he become aggravated. Coach Crown had approached this situation head-on in a factual, machine-gun style. Fred came at it from a more practical, "it's not the end of the world" perspective. "Okay, men. I really don't think this is going to be that tough to deal with. After all, you are all full-grown mature college students by now. Right?" he said with a sly grin on his face. He might have been looking directly at Marshall as he spoke.

"This COVID-19 is terrible stuff. Do you fellows want the bottom line? Listen up. There is no cure for the virus. You get better or you don't. No one knows what long-term effects there may be from it. You don't want it, and you don't want your families to have it, including your football family right here in this room. It spreads from person to person so easily. No one is sure exactly how, but it's through contact with others who have been infected. The idea is simple: stay away from that infected person and you will be fine. The problem, of course: actually doing that is difficult. Sick folks don't walk around with badges on."

"Before I get into exactly what we have to do around here, I need to take a second and draw an overall picture for you about this virus. Most people believe it started somewhere in Asia, but as of now, it has spread to every country in the world. It has shown no signs of slowing down. And, honestly, boys, it can kill you. Otherwise, healthy people are dying every day. Before you get too worried, though, the death rate is statistically small. I will give you some very general numbers. About 3% of the population will get the virus. Of those who do, about 10% will be hospitalized and less than half of those die. It seems to affect older people more than younger ones, but that is not a hard and fast rule. Anyone can catch it. Maybe the strangest thing of all is that the severity of the virus varies from person to person. One person will test positive but have no symptoms, while another person will end up in a hospital on a respirator. The doctors don't know why."

"The only sure way to know if you have the COVID-19 virus is to be tested. We are all going to do that. The symptoms are a lot like the common flu, including fever, coughing, sore throat, fatigue, and several other flu-like symptoms. So, to keep our team as healthy as possible, here's what we must do. As Coach said, I reiterate, *must*.

First, wash your hands for at least twenty seconds several times a day.

Second, keep your hands away from your eyes, nose, and mouth.

Third, stay away from anyone who is sick

Fourth, if you are sick, you must isolate yourself for probably at least a week or until you test negatively more than once.

Fifth, cover your face completely before sneezing or coughing.

Sixth, stay away from crowds as much as possible. You must keep at least six feet between you and the next person in lines or in public places. You'll get sick of hearing this one: *social distancing*."

Marshall rolled his eyes back. Social distancing. *If I don't watch myself here, that one won't be hard between Mallory and me.*

"Finally," Fred continued, "it will require you all to wear face masks while you are in this building." A smattering of groans wafted through the team. "Sorry about that, but that is the chancellor's rule. We have no choice. We'll see about the playing field when we get back out there, but for right now, mask up around here. I know there's been a lot of talk about masks being useless as protection. We don't care. Wear them or walk. Your choice. That's pretty much it for now. Come back here after lunch and get your COVID test. It doesn't take long and doesn't hurt." Once again, Marshall was sure the man was looking directly at him when he spoke.

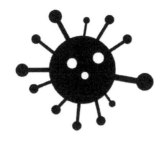

CHAPTER 13

The boys weren't sure what the recent developments would mean, but already their college careers were starting much differently than they expected. The coaches seemed optimistic that practice would resume soon. Maybe. A lot depended on if there was any of the virus on the team. After learning about the symptoms, everyone felt tired and wondered when the last time they coughed or sneezed. Marshall and Graham followed the crowd over to the cafeteria for lunch. They all went through the serving line and piled their plates high. It might be a while before they got all this special free food again. They also knew there was no practice this afternoon and no chance of losing your lunch after the tenth gasser sprint.

Although these teenagers had bodies that most men would envy, it was easy to forget they were still basically kids who were often hard to reach. Lectures from the coaches might get their attention and encourage them to take the matter seriously. Deep-thinking kids like Graham Brown, who absorbed every bit of information, mulled it over, and acted only when he was sure he had considered every aspect of a situation, were rare. Most kids were lucky if the information stayed with them for a day or two. By the time they sat down to lunch, most of the gloom had evaporated, and the collective mood was much brighter. The banter and jokes resumed, almost like a normal lunch. The news had created a sense of unity that pulled them together. It was everybody's problem, unlike an individual who got hurt playing or was cut from the team.

"Well, look on the bright side, guys." Zack Middleton offered, "Much more time for the Broken Spur. I'm headed over there right after the test. Who's with me?"

The same thought had occurred to Marshall, although on further review, he decided to lie low from that place. The temptation was too great. He'd sort of patched things up with Mallory, though he wasn't sure what to tell her. He couldn't blame it on studies, yet. He wasn't about to make up a lie about extra night football practice. In the end, he just told her the truth, sort of. He was out with guys and lost track of time.

Graham looked over at Zack. He was more serious than usual. "Look, it's a free country. You guys do what you want. Maybe you weren't paying attention this morning. I'll just bet partying and bars are a major source of the virus. You won't find me in those joints for a while. I don't want the stuff. You'd best be careful. None of us are bulletproof."

Zack was just about to advise Graham to lighten up when he turned aside and blew off a major sneeze. "Whew," he said, "That hay fever is terrible this year here in Austin. I get it every year."

With the obvious impasse among his friends and not wanting to take sides, Marshall changed the subject. "This test we're about to get this afternoon. What's it like? How do they give it? Do we get a needle? Pee in a bottle? Do they take blood? The coaches didn't tell us much about it. I don't like needles. Never have."

Graham reassured his friend not to worry when he was cut off by Zack, who had a gleam in his eye. Mischief was about. "No, Marshall," he began, "You don't have to worry about a needle. They don't take your blood."

Marshall breathed a sigh of relief. "That's good. I almost passed out during the team physicals when that geeky-looking guy with the frizzy hair in the white coat jabbed me?"

"No, the COVID test is much different. They use a cotton swab to pick up some of your bodily fluids. Basically, they have some cotton on a little stick and they take a rectal swab. You know. Turn around, bend over, and spread 'em. Pretty easy."

Graham's eyes shot to the ceiling. He had to turn away and bite his lip to keep from laughing out loud. Zack was stoic, monotone, and informational. Marshall took it all in like a puppy. He clearly was trying to picture how it would work.

"Does it hurt?" Marshall dared to ask.

"Only just a little, although you might be sore for a few days. Hey, you'll be fine. In fact, it's after 1:00. Let's get over there and get it done."

With a hundred players and maybe two dozen coaches and support personnel, the testing crew had come well prepared. They set up nurses and medical techs in five separate offices. They gave each person a mask to put on immediately. Lines formed behind the doors to each office. The tests only took a few minutes each, and the testing moved rapidly. Zack was directly ahead of Marshall. He went in before him and closed the door. As he left the office after his test, he gave Marshall a half-pained look and rubbed his posterior. Marshall winced.

Marshall reluctantly entered the testing office Zack had just vacated. He was ready to hightail it out of there when he saw the same geeky guy in the lab coat. If the man remembered Marshall, he gave no sign. He turned his back to consult a list on a desk and confirmed Marshall's name. He also reached for a clean swab. He then swung back around and was surprised to see Marshall had vanished. The door was not open.

"Please go easy on me, doc." came a whimpering request.

The man looked down and saw his patient bottoms up, bent over with his pants and shorts at his ankles. Up to that point, the technician had been bored to tears sticking Q tips up all those kids' noses, but this guy made his day. He laughed so hard he almost lost it. Marshall's trepidation, frozen in that uncomfortable position, instantly turned to anger. *What's this jerk laughing at? Let's just get this over with!*

Finally, the man regained his composure. He ordered Marshall to stand up, hike up his drawers, and face him. He then ran a cotton swab up each nostril. It was over in ten seconds and was just a slight bit uncomfortable. The man told Marshall the test results would be available in about a week. He could leave.

Marshall was incensed. He couldn't wait to find that Zack Middleton. He was ready to take him apart, but just as soon as he walked out of the football building, there were six or seven of his teammates, including Zack and Graham, gathered there waiting for him. The jokes came at him from every angle. They all had such a hoot at Marshall's expense that his anger quickly disappeared, and he had a friendly laugh, along with everyone else. It wasn't the first time he'd been the "butt" of his friends' jokes.

CHAPTER 14

His normally bustling office was silent and felt cold, despite the sticky humid fall weather. He knew why. It had everything to do with the unpleasant meeting that just ended. At least the door wasn't slammed when the two people left. He wouldn't have been surprised if it had been. Tommy Kinder sat back in his large leather executive chair and absently brushed his hand under the fuzz of his salt and pepper goatee. He hadn't enjoyed the past twenty minutes when he let his two last salespeople go. Both had been with him since the start and had performed very well. Their effort had been key to the success of his company, Welcome Home Realty. By capitalizing on an outstanding staff, a vibrant and growing community, and pure luck, he had built his real estate sales company into the leading firm of its kind in the town of Justice. In fact, the company had done so well that he could sit back and play "big boss" without having to work very hard himself. He was there to solve problems and glad-hand clients but was not out hustling business, as he did when they first opened. On a typical day, he arrived around ten, and it was an even-money bet that he would return to the office after lunch.

Unfortunately, the COVID pandemic had reversed the business climate and an overwhelmingly negative impact on the local economy. It all boiled down to one basic issue: people interacting with one another spread the virus. There was just no getting around it: the safest measure was to stay home. Retail commerce was hard hit when the foot traffic dried up. It forced companies to reduce staff. Unemployment claims skyrocketed. Welcome Home Realty's primary business was brokering the re-sale of homes. Right now, no one was selling or moving. The future was too uncertain. Virtual commerce was emerging, but it was very difficult to complete the sale of a home to a buyer without physically meeting them at the property and exposing everyone to the extremely contagious infection. Tommy paid his staff from the commissions he received when a home sold. There were a few homes on the market, but even fewer buyers. His cash flow was squeezed like never before.

The success of his company had come rapidly. In the three short years since he opened, the company had become very profitable. A more seasoned and cautious person would have planned for the downturn, which almost always comes. Unfortunately, Tommy Kinder wasn't that type of person. When the cash started rolling in, he geared up his lifestyle and personal spending as if it would never end. He might have been able to survive a slow sales period, but the impact of the pandemic was so severe that he had little chance.

He should have set up cash reserves, but Welcome Home Realty had none. Literally, paying the light bill for the current month depended entirely on commissions earned for that month. His salespeople appreciated things would be tough for a while, but it surprised them when he sent them packing so early. They had observed their boss' spendthrift habits and had been worried about there being enough cash to tide the company over. Besides the boss, the place was left with only one part-time clerical assistant.

Tommy Kinder had come up the hard way. Only recently had he gotten a taste of the good life, and he had no intention of giving it up. Now closer to fifty than forty, he was struggling to preserve his physical appearance as the years inevitably took their toll. His once thick dark hair was quickly abandoning him, forcing a daily comb-over to hide a widening bald spot. Never athletic and well under six feet, he fought a constant battle of the bulge and dressed to masquerade his pudgy build. He preferred expensive Italian loafers with pleated pants and silk shirts in bold, bright patterns and colors. A heavy gold chain adorned his neck amidst a random field of scraggly chest hair. He wore a pricey Rolex Tudor on his left wrist. His nicotine-stained, stubby fingers were ring-free.

A salt and pepper goatee partially hid his jowly neck while emphasizing his full mouth and gleaming white teeth. His skin was deeply tanned year-round, although the telltale orange cast hinted of a spray can rather than basking on the prow of a personal yacht. Shark gray eyes beamed with cat-like quickness under bushy eyebrows. Still, his expensive packaging simply couldn't offset his unavoidable workaday look.

Tommy Kinder had always been outgoing and people-oriented rather than analytical or studious. From his earliest days in Justice elementary school, he spent more than his share of time in time in detention halls. Not that he was slow. In fact, he was exceptionally bright. He didn't take discipline well and felt he had a better way of doing things. Tommy was hardly a bully. Perhaps more of a *Leave It to Beaver Eddie Haskell* clone. He tried to give the outward appearance of being a rule-abiding student while scheming ways to get what he wanted.

Tommy lived across the creek in the poorest section of Justice, which was decidedly different from most of the town. In fact, Apple Town more closely resembled the blue-collar communities closer to Houston than most of Justice proper. Apple Town contained the only light industrial distribution, auto repair, and similar concerns in the immediate area. In Texas, the purviews of school districts are independent of city borders, and Apple Town kids attended Justice schools. His father, who was a truck driver who was gone most of the time. He was the middle child of seven, with four brothers and two sisters. They lived in a tumble-down, two-story brick home with broken shutters and peeling trim. The patchy grass in the front yard always seemed to need cutting.

Mrs. Kinder was a frail woman who suffered from emphysema brought on by a lifetime of chain-smoking, an unfortunate habit that she passed on to her middle son. There was never a lot of anything to go around in the Kinder household. Tommy learned early to fight for his share, even though he sometimes had to muscle over a sibling. It was at home that he learned a lesson, which stayed with him the rest of his life: grab whatever you can, whenever you can, or miss out altogether. It mattered little how you got what you wanted, even if it meant pushing some people aside or hurt feelings.

During his elementary school days in Apple Town, the most desired possession among kids was a bicycle. You had to have your own bike or just forget about having friends. You went to school on your bike. You went to the ball fields on your bike. You went to the arcade and mall on your bike. Most bikes were hand-me-downs with no fenders and bare tires. All the kids dreamed of a new bike at Christmas or on a birthday, but seldom did one appear. They had to make do with what little they had.

One summer afternoon, Tommy and his younger brother were about to start home for supper after messing around down at the creek, which was a few blocks from their house. Tommy was twelve, two years older than Frankie. Since Frankie's bike had a flat, he had ridden with Tommy on his bike to get to the creek. Tommy lifted his bike to let Frankie get on when there a few feet over in the weeds he spotted another bike leaning against a tree. He dropped his bike down and walked over to it.

"Frankie. Look at this. It is a brand-new Schwinn Karate with a cool mountain bike seat," he said as he ran his fingers along the handlebars. "It's bright yellow. Look at the tires. There's not even any tread wear."

"Wow. That's a nice bike. I wish I had one like that instead of the piece of crap I have with flat tires."

Tommy figured that the kid who owned the bike must be down at the creek. Incredibly, he hadn't locked it to a tree or anything. It was unattached. Tommy immediately saw a golden opportunity. He hesitated, but only for a second. "Well, here you go. It's unlocked. Hop on and let's get out of here. Come on!"

"Are you kidding me? Steal a beautiful bike like this? Tommy, get serious."

"No one will ever know. It probably belongs to some rich kid from over in Justice across the creek. Nobody on our side could afford a bike like that. We'll keep it out of sight. You'll have the best bike in our entire gang."

Frankie's eyes got big. Now he really wanted that bike. "But what if some big kid owns it and comes after me? I'm only ten. I can't fight much."

"Stop worrying. I'm your big brother. I'll protect you if need be."

"You will?"

"Sure."

Frankie needed no more convincing. His big brother's assurance sealed the deal, and he really wanted that bike. He grabbed it from Tommy and hopped on. Tommy ran over and got on his bike. Off they scooted as fast as they could pedal. Both brothers were lucky their father wasn't home that evening. He just might have asked where the new bike came from. Their mother never noticed. After supper, they couldn't resist taking it for a spin around the block. It was a fine ride.

Tommy was sitting on the Schwinn in their driveway with Frankie standing next to him. He was breaking it to his younger brother that he was taking the bike for himself. Frankie could have it in a few years when Tommy was done with it. Suddenly, he noticed an SUV headed right toward them. Alarms rang in Tommy's head, and he quickly got off the bike, handed it to his brother, and bolted into the house. He left Frankie there alone, dumfounded but only for a moment.

The SUV pulled right up to their driveway and two big teenagers jumped out. They were hopping mad. "What are you doing with my Karate? You stole it from me at the creek this afternoon. You little thief! We ought to call the cops."

Before Frankie could react, one boy swung his fist and caught poor Frankie square in the eye. The little kid fell over and balled loud enough to be heard up in Houston. Tommy watched the confrontation peeking around the blinds inside the house but didn't help his little brother. The bike and the big kids took off. Poor Frankie had a black eye that would be around for a while.

I guess the little fellow learned a lesson about stealing other people's property, He mused.

That incident was repeated in one form or fashion many more times in Tommy Kinder's life.

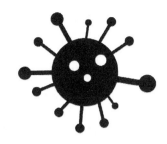

CHAPTER 15

Tommy never enjoyed school and skipped days whenever he could get away with it. His mother would only fall for an upset stomach excuse every few weeks. He got by as an average C student with a minimum of effort. While he disliked all team sports and avoided them like the plague, he enjoyed being the center of attention. He had a deep desire to show off and prove to his schoolmates that he was much more than his nebbish reputation implied. He was initially disappointed when, after joining the acting club, he was assigned to scene building. First, that required some hard physical work, which was against his basic nature, and also it didn't let him show off in front of others. In fact, a central theme in his life was to crave the spotlight, just so long as he didn't have to work too hard for it.

After a few months of nailing together 2x4's and painting background, he was determined to quit the acting club when an unexpected opportunity popped up. The class play year was *Annie Get Your Gun*. Tommy was sitting on the side of the stage one afternoon watching rehearsals. Allison Smith, who Tommy had long had a crush on, played Annie. With long blond hair, blue eyes, and peaches and cream complexion, she was gorgeous and one of the most popular girls in the school. She was a cheerleader, class vice president, and her father owned the biggest car dealer in Justice. Tommy Kinder had a zero chance with Allison.

"There's no business like show business," Allison sang out with a melodious voice in perfect key. Buffalo Bill was supposed to chime in, but there was only silence from Teddy Mayer, who had that part and was standing next to Annie. Everything stopped.

"Teddy. Go ahead, join in now." urged Miss Francis, the teacher in charge of putting on the play.

Still, nothing. And then, "Like no business I know." came from Teddy in a discordant screech that hardly resembled music. He stopped and was red-faced. "Sorry, Miss Francis. I have a really sore throat. I don't know if it is allergies, a cold, or what."

The teacher looked over at him. The show was opening in just a few days. She desperately needed a healthy Buffalo Bill. If he didn't rally, the entire production could go up in flames. What could she do? Teddy had been so rock solid she hadn't named an understudy. "Okay. Let's take a ten-minute break, kids," she announced, not knowing what else to do.

Tommy was anything but shy when he sensed an opportunity. Here was a chance to move in for the kill, and he didn't hesitate. The amusing thing was, he had been fantasizing about singing that song with desirable Allison. He knew the words.

"Miss Francis, I can solve your problem."

The teacher was staring off in the deep in her own thoughts and didn't seem to hear him. Then she noticed he was next to her. "Sorry, Tommy. Please go back to your painting. I'm very busy right now."

"Me. I can do the Buffalo Bill part. Give me a chance. You're stuck with frog-throated Teddy. Let me try. Please." He could apply the sweet approach when needed.

"You? Come on. You've never been on the stage in your life. I don't have time to waste. This is critical to the entire production. "

"I already know the words, and my voice isn't half bad. Let me try. Please. Otherwise, I've had about enough of this acting club. I'm done. I'll just come to the performance and see how it turns out. I'll let my friends know not to expect much, so they won't be disappointed."

"Oh, that's nice. Bad advance publicity. That will help." *Is this little SOB trying to blackmail me? What the heck?* "Okay, give it a shot, but make it quick. I have a big problem to solve. Places, everyone, except Teddy. Stand aside, please."

Tommy bolted up on the stage and stood just a few feet from his heartthrob. Allison glanced over at him. She refused to look at him, rolling her eyes skyward, as if to say *you've got to be kidding me!* She began the song, and to everyone's amazement, Tommy chimed in at exactly the right moment. His voice left a lot to be desired but wasn't horrible, and he knew all the words. When the song ended, Miss Francis politely clapped but still looked non-committal. What she had failed to notice was the Teddy had stormed off and disappeared. He was gone for good. Somehow, Tommy Kinder had buffaloed his way into Buffalo Bill.

He had grabbed the role and knew he had better make sure he didn't flop, or instead of being admired by his friends, he'd be jeered off the stage. Once again, he showed an uncanny ability to apply himself so long as he was interested in the endeavor. For the next few days, he spent every waking hour with the script to absorb what he could. He got an eight-track cassette of the play and played it incessantly at home, to the displeasure of his siblings.

His ulterior motive was, of course, to impress and win over Allison Smith. She had initially regarded him as white trash from Apple Town on the wrong side of the river. To her credit, however, she understood how important it was for this late insert to carry off Buffalo Bill's part. It would help no one if she refused at least to be civil to him. In fact, she even worked in some added feminine charm, which he naturally interpreted as her coming on to him, which was anything but the case. Allison proved she had acting talents in more than one arena.

Tommy had never been more exhilarated. He was literally under the spotlight in front of the entire school. No one cared about the D minus he just got on an algebra exam. Also, he was clearly making time with the most popular girl around. And he pulled it off. He became an unspectacular, but acceptable Buffalo Bill for the three performances they had. The play was well-received, and no one hurled tomatoes at him. Even Miss Francis was pleased.

Following the standing tradition, there was a cast party at Papa Juan's a few days later. Tommy was in his glory, reliving the performance. It was about time for him to pursue the other aim of his thespian effort. He saw Allison sitting a few booths over. When one of her girlfriends got up, he scooted right in. She smiled politely but hardly acted eager to see him.

Time to make a move. "Say, Allison, we had so much fun working together on the play, I kind of thought maybe we could continue what we've started. How about a movie Saturday night?" He held his breath and tried to read her expression, but there was no need.

"Drop dead. Loser. Now get up. My friend just came back from the restroom. You took her seat." It was pretty clear she wasn't acting.

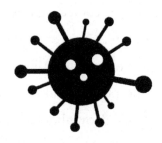

CHAPTER 16

Despite his complete lack of interest in schoolwork, Tommy did enough to scrape by and graduate with his high school class, albeit in the lowest third. At that point, however, he was at a complete loss about what to do next. He wasn't eager to find a regular job where he would have to show up every day and be expected to perform some kind of labor. With their overflowing house, his parents clarified he needed to move out fairly soon. His mediocre grades prohibited him from attending most colleges, but he could sign up at a local junior college, which automatically accepted all high school graduates. With increasing pressure from his parents, he also found a part-time job at Menchies Ice Cream store. He only worked a few hours a week, and the job was hardly taxing. A side benefit was that the place attracted many good-looking girls.

After achieving a marginal grade report of three D's and two C's during his first semester at Cullen Junior College, they placed him on academic probation. While he saw this coming and could have avoided it with a little more effort, there were serious consequences for him. His parents let him know that as long as he was in school and pursuing a degree, he could live at home. If that changed, he'd have to move out. One more bad grade report and they would boot him from school and home, both at the same time. He decided a little more effort would be appropriate.

One of his problems with studying was that he had no place to sit down with some privacy where he could concentrate and not be bothered by his siblings, TV, and all the distractions around his crowded house. He had never been a library nerd but forced himself to spend a few hours each week at the school library, where he could study in peace. Remarkably, his grades picked up, and he started turning in assignments on time. He took no particular pride in this positive turn of events since his choice was to perk up or check out. He wasn't happy at Cullen JC, for another reason. At least in high school, he had a group of friends to hang out with. Cullen was a forty-five-minute drive from Apple Town and a total commuter school. There were no dorms. No one seemed to hang around after class, and he had made no real friends during his first two semesters. The place had turned out to be just another way to put off facing reality and getting on with his life.

One afternoon, Tommy was sitting in the library trying to study. He was having trouble keeping awake and was just about to "bag it" and head home. He was in a writing course, which had been pretty boring so far. He had signed up for it because, after his experience with *Annie Get Your Gun*, he had fantasized a little about writing his own plays. He knew he could be creative. How hard could it be? The other benefits of the class were that it was a large lecture class with over a hundred students, where he could remain anonymous, and it was supposed to be easy. There were no exams and your entire grade depended on a twenty-page paper you turned in.

The professor gave the students wide latitude in choosing a topic for their creative writing paper. Tommy had thought little about it but looked up Annie Oakley in an encyclopedia. Having been a Wild West, shoot-'em-up person, it surprised him to find that she was from Ohio, of all places. He read more about her and got interested in her life. He submitted Annie Oakley to the professor as his term paper topic, and it was approved.

And then a weird thing happened to Tommy Kinder. For the first time in his life, he became interested in a school assignment. He searched every reference in the Cullen library for information about Annie Oakley. He took detailed notes and even went to the enormous City of Houston Library to see what else he could find. He read and re-read the fictionalized book about Annie Oakley by Dorothy Fields and her brother. He titled his paper "If Annie Oakley Lived Today." Unlike any other project he had attempted, he spent hours on this one. It became fun for him. He even attended all the classes and tried to incorporate what he learned into his paper. He reviewed and changed it several times before turning it in. He was pleased with his effort and fully expected to see an 'A' on it. An 'A-plus' was not out of the question.

The semester was almost over, and the writing class was meeting for the last time. Two weeks ago, the deadline had passed for term papers to be submitted. The professor had them in his possession and promised to provide feedback to the class. Tommy was relaxed and light-hearted. He was eager to hear how he had done. There was a cute redhead sitting next to him. Any excuse to start a conversation?

"He is supposed to talk about our term papers today. How do you think you did?" he asked.

"I don't know. There's a rumor going around that there's a problem with the term papers. I'm kind of worried," she replied.

"No! Really. You're kidding me. What kind of problem?"

"Plagiarizing is what I heard."

That surprised and stopped Tommy short. It couldn't affect him. He'd been very careful to footnote and reference anything he used from other texts. Hadn't he?

"Good morning, class," the professor began. He was a young fellow, not too many years out of the classroom as a student himself. His approach had always been down-to-earth and friendly. It wasn't unusual for him to start a session with an amusing anecdote or joke. But not today. There was apprehension in the air.

"I'm afraid I have a matter of great concern to discuss with you." Someone dropped a pen but nobody heard it. "I have reviewed your term papers and am sad to report that there are several instances of plagiarism among them. The act of taking someone else's work and passing it off as your own is perhaps the worst offense any writer can make. It is simply not tolerated in the writing field and will not be tolerated at Cullen Junior College. I know I have discussed this topic at length during the semester."

There was collective shock among the one hundred students. What did he mean? Who did he catch? Would they fail? There were no other grades in this course.

"I have thought long and hard about this very distasteful situation and what to do about it. Let me be clear, not everyone was guilty of this horrible transgression. In fact, there are only a few papers where I have noted problems. If your conscience is clear in your own case, then do not be concerned. Your paper will be graded as normal based on its merit. I thank you for taking the course, wish you a happy summer, and look forward to seeing you back here in the fall."

The transfixed students stirred, and mumblings sounded across the classroom. *What about those who cheated and were caught? Here it comes.*

"So, here's what I have come up with after trying to be as fair as I can without ignoring this grievous situation. If you have plagiarized on your term paper and own up to it to me, I will give you one last chance to submit another fresh paper. In such a case, you will receive a grade of 'D' for the course. That is the bad news. The good news is that you will have passed the course. If you have plagiarized, I caught it, and you do not own up to it, you fail the course. Of course, if I have noticed nothing awry, you are home free to stand on the merits of your work. Review your papers and look into your hearts. You have until noon tomorrow to contact me, after which the chips will fall where they may. Have a pleasant summer." He walked off.

Like everyone else, Tommy was shocked by the professor's comments. He did some immediate soul searching and quickly transitioned to smugness. *I have nothing to worry about. I followed all the rules as he laid them out. Let the chips fall. My paper was great. My A should be assured. I hope. Maybe? I wonder.*

It tormented him all the way home and that night. He had tried to do everything right, but who knows what the goofy teacher may have found? Already on academic probation, if he failed the course, he was toast at the school. He might as well look for an apartment and an actual job. *Gulp!*

There was just one section of his paper that he was really worried about. The Fields' book had some great quotes about Annie's shooting. He just may have borrowed them without footnotes. Maybe the prof caught them? As he drove to Cullen the next morning, he still hadn't decided what to do. He just couldn't afford to fail. He swallowed hard and at 11:45 walked up to the professor's office and was about fourth in line at his door behind some other apparently guilty folks.

When it was his turn, he sauntered glumly into the professor's office. He admitted he probably had failed to footnote and accepted his fate. He would do another complete paper on the history of Texas and accept his inglorious D. The professor shook his head and said he also was sorry. He handed Tommy the Annie Oakley paper he had turned in.

As a morose Tommy walked out into the bright sunshine, he tried to console himself that at least he passed the course and would stay in school by the fuzz on his face. When he got to his car and tossed his original paper on the seat next to him, he noticed some red marks on it. He did double and triple takes. There was 'A' minus 'Great work' noted in red pencil! He flipped through the pages. There was nothing about plagiarism! The prof hadn't caught him! He had turned himself in and didn't have to. He'd sacrificed an 'A' grade for a 'D'. It was too late now. He had admitted to cheating. As if all of that wasn't enough, when all the grades came out, even with the negotiated 'D' in English, they still booted him out of Cullen. Tommy Kinder vowed to never set foot in a classroom again.

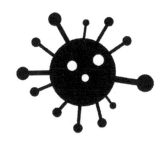

CHAPTER 17

Even though school was out for the summer, Tommy's father quickly figured out his son wasn't going back to the JC in the fall. He let Tommy know in no uncertain terms that he was welcome in their house on Christmas, Thanksgiving, and his birthday. Otherwise, it was time for him to find his own digs. Tommy had no problem with that edict and was eager to be out of that place, except he didn't know where to go or how he would support himself. His gracious father gave him thirty days.

Armed with a less than impressive resume highlighted by scooping goodies at Menchies and failing out of junior college, there weren't bundles of opportunities for him. As he thought things through, there were only two possibilities that excited him even a little. One was acting. His shining high school moment came as Buffalo Bill in the class play. There was no way that would help him, since there wasn't an abundance of high-paying acting gigs around. The other option might be cars. He always liked brand-new flashy cars. Chances of him ever owning one seemed remote, but he fantasized about tooling around Justice in a boss ride with Allison Smith perched in the front seat with him. Another dream that would never come true.

Even realizing there was little chance his job search would be productive, he knew better than to lounge around the house all day. His father might get the idea he wasn't trying, and he could be on the street overnight. While cruising around Justice one afternoon, he noticed the impressive Smith Toyota car dealership. The facility was huge, occupying several acres, and there were hundreds of new cars shimmering in the sunlight. His first instinct was to lament his failure with Allison, but then something else hit him. *Cars! I like new cars. I enjoy talking to people. There are so many of them out there, they must need a boatload of salespeople. I've got to try that.*

He swung into the dealership parking lot but didn't get out of his car when he realized he might be about to walk into a job interview for which he was totally unprepared. He noticed a sales associate in a sports shirt and khaki pants standing just in front of the main door to the showroom. Maybe it would be better if he came back later? No, he'd come this far. He had to go in. He took a deep breath, got out of the car, and walked into the showroom, passing right by the young man who was glued to his cell phone and didn't even look up.

The interior of the showroom sparkled with a fully loaded Lexus and Sierra SUVs prominently displayed. Tommy walked up to a Lexus and marveled at the impeccable workmanship and gleaming finish. He stood there for several minutes, alone, admiring the car. No one bothered him. For a moment, he forgot why he was there. The beautiful cars mesmerized him.

A voice came from the back of the room. "Sir, can I help you?" Tommy looked up to see an older man, perhaps in his forties, walking toward him. "If you can wait just a minute, I'll find our sales associate. He's around here somewhere," the man said as he craned his neck in all directions, looking for the wayward individual.

"Thanks, but I'm not here to buy a car," Tommy stammered. "I guess I am looking for the sales manager."

The man stopped and looked at Tommy. "You found him. Frank Garcia", he said, extending his hand. "What's up?"

Tommy shook the man's hand but didn't know what to say next. He'd never expected to run into the sales manager so quickly. There was no turning back now. Out with it. "Tommy Kinder. Well, I'm home from college for the summer and need a job. I've always loved cars, especially Toyotas, and wondered if you have any sales positions available?"

Frank Garcia gave the kid a once over. "Ever sell cars before?"

"No, sir," he confessed. He sensed his interview was going to end quickly, so he went for it. "But in high school, I used to date Allison Smith. She told me, if I ever needed work, I should try here and mention her name." That, of course, was an outright lie, but he had nothing to lose.

Dropping the name of the owner's daughter didn't seem to register with Garcia. "No, I'm sorry. We're full up at the moment, but check back with us from time to time to see if we have openings." He smiled and pivoted to walk back to his office, leaving a dejected Tommy standing there. And then he stopped and turned around. His long-lost sales agent still had not appeared. "Hold on a minute,

Tommy. I just realized I may have an opening coming up soon. Come back to my office and fill out an application."

Tommy, who had learned not to get his hopes up, was stunned the following Monday when Frank called to hire him. After coming on board at the dealership, he learned that the former totally unaggressive sales agent, who hadn't bothered to approach him, was sent packing. What he did not learn, and what would have amazed him, was that Frank Garcia contacted Allison Smith, who gave him a good recommendation. Perhaps she was trying to make up for treating him so poorly back in high school?

Selling cars isn't for everyone, but for Tommy Kinder, it was a perfect fit. The hours were long, but the work was enjoyable. Without getting his hands dirty, he could use his gab. He loved cars and being around them. He got on well with the customers and quickly became a top producer among the sales staff. There was no mention of his daughter when he finally met the big boss, Mr. Smith.

Tommy learned to handle many types of customers. Often, he dealt with working couples trying to make their way with heavy family obligations, who couldn't truly afford the expensive payments buying a new car demanded. It surprised him the number of such people who cared little about the high payments so long as they could have a fancy new ride to show off to their neighbors. He especially like dealing with young girls whose parents were buying them their first car. He felt important as he explained all the wonderful features of the cars and rode with them on their test drives.

The Smith dealership used a standard method for allocating customers to salespeople. If someone came in and asked for a specific sales associate, of course, that match was made. Otherwise, they used a "next up" system, which was a rotating arrangement where when your turn came, the next walk-in was yours. Tommy was the most aggressive person on the sales staff. Frank Garcia had to warn him several times about cutting in front of the other guys on the next-up system. Tommy listened but didn't stop when he saw a good-looking prospect. He knew his sales manager really cared only about his sales numbers. The heck with the other guys if they were slow. Tommy wouldn't have won the "most popular" sales associate award.

It was a slow midweek afternoon with hardly any customer traffic. Tommy didn't care who was "up" next. He needed two more sales that month to exceed his quota. He would check out the next walk-in. If it turned out to be some young kid or old couple time waster, he'd let one of the other guys take them, but if it looked like a solid sales prospect, he'd grab it. It caught his attention when he saw a super sporty candy apple red one-year-old RCF track edition Lexus pull into the customer spaces outside the showroom. A dapper and fit-looking man in his mid-thirties got out and walked toward the building. He wore a dark blue sport coat with gold buttons, a pink button-down shirt, and khaki pants. His sandy blond hair was neatly trimmed, and he was closely shaven. There was a brief flash of a gold chain bracelet on his right wrist as he walked in. There was a Rolex on the other. The man looked refined, cultured, and rich. Tommy rushed in for the kill.

Tommy leaned against the walkway railing on the steps leading into the showroom, pretending to be checking his phone as the man drew even with him. Unlike his own first experience at Smith Toyota, he wouldn't ignore this fellow. Tommy smiled and gestured at the slick car. "So, how do you like your RCF? Has it met your expectations?"

"Why, yes. It has, as a matter of fact. For years I drove nothing that wasn't fashioned in Europe. Last year, I gave the Japanese a chance and have been quite pleased. Enough so that I am here to buy another Lexus. Is there anyone around that can help me? I'm in a sort of hurry, running late as it is."

I have died and gone to heaven! I sure hope this bloke is for real.

"Of course. Tommy Kinder, at your service. Just how may I help you, sir?" Tommy replied, handing him his embossed business card. "We have the largest on-site inventory in Texas. Where would you like to start? Mr.?"

"Shiner. Randy Shiner. I'm sure you've heard of our family. Actually, I've been reviewing your models online. I've decided on an LC two-door grand tourer with the 354-horsepower hybrid engine. Do you have any?"

Wow! The top of the top of the line. That's a $125,000 car!

Desperately trying to stifle his excitement and act as though he sold several of those babies every day, Tommy replied, "I believe we do, but if not, I know where I can get one in our dealer network on brief notice." It was a complete lie. He'd never even seen an LC.

"Very well. Of course, I want it fully loaded with every option available. My one particular requirement is that the color must be starlight with black glass flake. Is that going to be a problem?"

"Certainly not, Mr. Shiner. That has been a popular selection. Personally, it's my favorite. I commend you on your choice." He wouldn't lose this guy's business under any circumstances. Now he had to figure out if his dealership had any of those super luxury cars on the lot. Mr. Shiner, however, saved him that embarrassment.

"Great, I'm really pressed for time this afternoon. I've got to jet. Here's my card. Just call Linda, my assistant. She can provide all the information for the title work, bill of sale, wiring the funds to pay for it, and such. The sticker price is fine. I have one more favor to ask."

Oh. Oh. Here it comes! "Shoot."

"I must have the new car by this Saturday. I'm giving the car I drove in here to my nephew for his birthday. In fact, we're having a party for him at my beach house in Galveston. Is there a way they could deliver the LS to me down there that afternoon? It would make my life so much simpler."

"Done!" Tommy replied without hesitation. "I'll drive it down myself."

"Excellent. Well, I'll see you then. Thank you. Bye now." Randy Shiner pivoted and walked back to his car without ever entering the showroom.

Tommy stood there in a daze as he watched the sleek sports car glide out of the parking lot. Now all he had to do was find one of those darned things in starlight black glass flake, whatever that was. Heck, to make this sale, he'd paint the car himself, if he had to. As he walked back into the showroom, Frank Garcia, who had apparently been watching his exchange with Randy Shiner, ambushed him.

"Kinder! What in the hell just happened? Do you know who that guy was you were talking to? He's a Shiner—probably the richest family in Texas, if not the country. He didn't even come in. We've been chasing their business for years. You let him get away. You've got a lot to learn about the car business. Why—"

Tommy stood there and took the tongue lashing as long as he could. He finally held up his hand and ordered his irate boss. "Stop. Frank, hold on a minute! Calm down. The customer isn't lost. In fact, I just sold him a fully loaded LC two-door grand tourer at the sticker price. I'm glad that you just assured me he's legit."

Frank glared at him in disbelief. "Are you kidding me? That's terrific, kid. Maybe it's me who's got a lot to learn about the car business."

With Frank Garcia's considerable help, they located an LC that fit Randy Shiner's requirements. It arrived at the Smith dealership in Justice around noon on Saturday, just in time to do a quick dealer prep before Tommy delivered it the twenty-five miles to Galveston for the birthday party. Tommy had several conversations with Linda, Randy's assistant. She had worked with him for many years and was used to his way of doing things—often impulsively and with little forethought. The deal came off exactly as Tommy hoped. Linda handled all the paperwork with Smith Toyota's accounting staff. In fact, a wire transfer in the amount of $130,928.00 in full payment for the car hit the dealership's bank account before the close of business on Friday.

Tommy was a little concerned about missing a busy Saturday afternoon at the dealership, but he was also happy to deliver the new car to Randy Shiner at his beach house. After meeting him and hearing a few side comments from his assistant, he was interested in getting to know the well-heeled little elf a little better. Having grown up in a home with little excess to spare, it fascinated him to think what it must have been like for Randy in one of the richest families. Tommy had to scrimp and scrounge for every break he got. More than once, he'd been slammed down, only to get back up and continue the struggle. He doubted Randy's youth had been much like his. He didn't have time to rub elbows with the wealthy very often. Maybe there could be some longer-term benefit for him here.

Randy's beach house was right on the first row overlooking the Gulf of Mexico in the exclusive Pirates Beach gated community on Galveston Island. He had no trouble finding the address, which was flanked on both sides of the street by dozens of cars. He was about to turn around and look for a parking space further down the street when he noticed a space in the driveway of Randy's house. He quickly concluded that space had been reserved for Randy's new purchase and pulled in. A band was playing, and he could hear their laughter and chatter. He knew he was in the right place.

All the homes at Pirates Beach were built on large wooden pilings pounded into the sand, extending up fifteen feet to the first floor of the living area. The Gulf of Mexico hurricanes on the island weren't a matter of "if." The only question was "when?" With the homes properly constructed, the risk was reduced. Randy's place had two stories above the ground, with a beautiful surrounding deck offering magnificent views of the ocean only a few hundred yards away. There was an enormous kitchen, dining area, and family room with five bedrooms. The ground area under the first floor had a garage, a freshwater shower, tables, benches, barbecues, fire pits, horseshoes, badminton, and various other leisure-time playthings. The walk to the beach was two minutes at most. It impressed Tommy.

He had barely stepped out of Randy's new LS when an attractive, fiftyish, redheaded woman in a two-piece bathing suit came walking up to him. She was holding what appeared to be margaritas in both hands. "Tommy? You must be Tommy. I'm so glad to meet you. You're just a darling to drive all the way down here with the car. Here you go.," she said, handing him one drink. "Oh, I'm Linda, by the way."

"Thanks," he said, quickly slurping from the overflowing glass. "Very nice to meet you. Smith Toyota really appreciates your business."

"I'm not sure where Randy is. He's in there somewhere. Let's go find him." She grabbed his hand. "You can stay for a while, can't you?" The band rocked on in the background.

This might be a fun afternoon!

"Well, I don't want to impose."

"Nonsense! Let's go."

And so, Tommy Kinder let himself be dragged into the party, which was in full swing. It wasn't quite what he had envisioned when Randy mentioned a birthday party for his nephew. He didn't spot any kids or even a birthday cake. This event was strictly for adults, most of which were in their thirties and forties. The alcohol was flowing, and everyone seemed to have a great time. There was an amazing catered food spread and an open bar. Many couples were in beach attire. Some were dancing or just lounging on the wicker patio furniture. Tommy immediately dropped any concern he had that he wouldn't fit in.

Linda spotted Randy across the patio near the bar and started across in that direction. Suddenly, she stopped so quickly Tommy bumped into her. He quickly apologized.

"Hey, that's okay. Let's wait a few minutes. Randy seems to be tied up at the moment."

Tommy looked over and saw a clean-shaven older man with white, neatly trimmed hair in a Hawaiian shirt, deck pants, and sandals, in deep conversation with Randy. The man looked stern, and Randy wasn't pleased. Clearly, they weren't discussing the weather. The topic was serious. Those two seemed totally out of line with everyone else who was having a great time.

Linda saw Tommy watching the two men and felt compelled to offer an explanation. The four previous margaritas had evidently loosened her tongue, and she said more than she would have sobered.

"Over there, Tommy, Randy is talking to his uncle Sanford Shiner, who is Randy's late father's brother. Sanford runs the Shiner oil and gas empire, which he inherited from his father, Randy's grandfather. He's worth billions, and that is with a 'b'."

Tommy nodded. He couldn't conceive of such wealth.

"Anyway," Linda prattled on, sure her voice wouldn't be overheard by the band, "Sanford became the guardian for Randy after his father died. Even though that was several years ago, Sanford still believes he can control Randy's life. He has no legal right to do that, but controls much of the allowance Randy receives. So, if he doesn't like something Randy has done, he can withhold cash from him."

"Why would he do that? Randy must be in his thirties, I would guess. He's no kid,"

"Thirty-six, as a matter of fact. The relationship is complicated. Once you get to know Randy, you'll discover that he's a fine person who never intends to offend anyone. Sadly, Randy had the misfortune of growing up with everything given to him on a silver platter."

Gee, I feel sorry for him already. Just like my childhood.

"He has struggled to find his own way in life. Everyone around him has been so successful. He just doesn't measure up. He's just an average, very rich guy, who tries to follow his own path and often stumbles in ways that cause the esteemed Shiner family embarrassment. It seems like Sanford is always on his butt about something. I wish he'd just leave the poor man alone."

"What is Randy's job, anyway?"

"Technically, he is one of several directors of the Shiner Oil Company, where he owns a bunch of stock, but far less than would be required for any kind of control. His day-in-day-out job is as an investor. He looks for good places to put his money—at least, that is what's supposed to happen. His track record is mighty poor in that regard. A few times, he had invested in alternative energy projects like windmills. Not only were the investments disastrous, but they hardly made his uncle, an oil baron, happy. We love oil, oil, and more oil. My entire job is to steer Randy in directions that don't cause trouble."

That comment made Tommy think. "Does that mean that his buying that car caused a problem in the family?"

"Heck, no. Uncle Sanford would be thrilled if he bought ten cars, so long as he stays away from windmills."

That's a relief.

Uncle Sanford had melted back into the crowd, so Linda and Tommy walked over. Randy lit up when he saw Tommy. "Great to see you! Did you bring it?"

Tommy smiled and nodded.

"You did? Come on. Let's take it for a spin."

Before Linda could object, in view of the amount of alcohol he had consumed, Randy and Tommy hustled out to the sparkling new car. Randy walked around it several times, running his hand over the perfect finish. They jumped in and roared out of the driveway.

The west end of Galveston Island was sparsely populated, consisting mainly of cattle-grazing land. It didn't seem like anyone was around. Randy had his new toy and let it fly. It easily held 120, which was double the posted speed limit. The Galveston County sheriff's deputy had a hard time catching him, but he finally did. They all ended up at the police station for several hours. Tommy had plenty of time that afternoon to get to know Randy well. It was after 9:00 p.m. that night that Uncle Sanford used his influence to spring his nephew. Uncle San was not a happy camper.

CHAPTER 18

Tommy was pumped. He now had a new rich client, whom he could count on for at least one or two new cars every year, a terrific arrangement. Still, Tommy spent a lot of time thinking about Randy Shiner, who basked in the lap of luxury despite himself. He was no mental giant—probably only average. Even at that, he had trouble coping with his wealth. Tommy knew he was much smarter than Randy, and yet he had to scrape and fight for every nickel he got, which wasn't much. As a sales associate at Smith Toyota, he earned an average of $400 per sale that he produced. He was the top sales associate, with an average of fifteen sales per month. With a small salary and everything else all in, he was lucky to earn $75,000 in an entire year. Not bad for Apple Town, but Tommy had moved up from those days.

Even to earn that much, he had to work extremely hard. His hours were long, and he had to deal with all kinds of people—many of whom regarded car sales associates as the bottom rung of the ladder. It forced him to be nice to obnoxious people, even when he knew they were only tire kickers and had no intention of buying. It was a high burnout job, and after a couple of years on the firing line, he was ready to try something else. There must be a better way.

And then he met Mitzi Manzel. Tommy never had much luck with women. His encounter with Allison Smith was more the rule than the exception. He had to be careful about dating customers at the dealership, which was frowned upon by Frank Garcia. Tommy cared little what Frank thought, though. If he met a babe that he wanted to ask out, he just did it. Even so, his dating track record continued to be less than stellar. Tommy knew he was a top producer who Frank would be reluctant to let go.

That all changed one afternoon when a well-developed young woman sashayed into the dealership looking for a Toyota 4Runner. Already a divorcee at age twenty-five, Mitzi Manzel was constantly on the alert for eligible men, whom she openly flirted with upon first contact. She favored tight outfits that accented her plump but shapely legs. She loved black accented leopard-skin outfits with lacey undergarments peeking through here and there to accent her ample chest. Her creamy white skin and sweeping eyelashes were generously dabbed and teased with gobs of makeup. She was a dishwater brunette who loved to bat her chocolate brown eyes. Perhaps the only way she could have been bolder about finding a man would have been to wear a sign around her neck. Mitzi was on the make.

Her advertising efforts weren't lost on Tommy, who was always in the market for attractive women. As he guided her around the showroom, it was impossible not to notice her cleavage as she bent way over to inspect an engine, which she wouldn't know from a sewing machine. He had a hard time concentrating when she sat at his desk with her crossed legs barely covered by a mini skirt. They took an extra-long test drive, during which Tommy wisely decided not to have her pull over in some secluded spot. She didn't buy a car that afternoon, but by the time she left the dealership, they had set a dinner date for next week.

Tommy's few successes with women only came when he flashed cash as an inducement to go out with him. He tried his best to impress his dates by spending. That approach might work with Mitzi, or it would be another "one and done." He took her to an upscale restaurant located directly on Crystal Lake and overlooking a marina. He was just a tad disappointed when he picked her up. She smacked gum for the first ten minutes of their ride. Fortunately, the gum disappeared when they reached the restaurant. Tommy hoped it wasn't stuck under the front seat of his car.

The evening went well for both of them. It turned out they were both sales agents, and each was in the market for what the other was selling. Mitzi was a real estate agent who sold homes in the Justice area. She was fairly new at it, but seemed genuinely pleased with her job. She readily bragged she had made almost 100k in only her second year. Tommy swallowed hard. The floozie across from him made more money than he ever had, despite working himself to death.

"And the best thing, Tommy, is that I enjoy the work. The folks I deal with are pleasant and really interested in buying. My supervising broker is a dream. She pre-qualifies our clients before we ever work for them. I don't have to worry about bad credit or unmotivated, time-wasting tire kickers."

Her comments were not lost on Tommy, who compared them to the car dealership. *Yeah? Sounds like Smith Toyota. We pre-qualify, all right. You're breathing. You're in. We'll try to sell to anyone drawing a breath. We specialize in time-wasters that will never buy.*

"So, tell me. To earn almost a hundred grand, how many sales did you have?"

"Hmm. Let's see. As selling agent, I get half of what my broker gets, which is usually about $4,000 to $5,000 per sale, which would be about twenty for the year. One or two per month."

Holy shit. I'm in the wrong racket. I average 15–20 sales every month and still don't clear what she gets! I am killing myself for nothing.

"I know little about real estate sales. Is it tough to get your license?"

"No, not really. Take a test and work for a while under a licensed broker. Heck, I did it. Anyone can. When Henry jilted me for that tramp, I had to survive." A waiter walking by caught her eye. "Look at that drizzled cheesecake. It looks yummy. Let's get some for dessert." Mitzi wasn't one who could carry on with extended conversations on one subject.

While it might not be correct to say that they made a love connection that night, two kindred souls did crash together. Both were needy, and it marked the start of a relationship. In fact, not only was Mitzi hot in the bedroom, she opened a new professional opportunity for Tommy.

The following week, Mitzi was back to reconsider the 4Runner. This time, however, they took an extended test drive, which ended up on a deserted road and lasted several hours. Frank Garcia noticed

Tommy's absence. Over the next month, Mitzi, who purchased the 4Runner, made several appearances at the showroom to see Tommy. She was hard to miss.

Frank eventually confronted Tommy about the woman. He never demanded that he stop seeing her or resign. He knew how valuable the man was to his sales team. At that point, Tommy was burned out of car sales, anyway. All he needed was a little provoking, which Frank's scolding provided. He handed in his resignation the following week. Frank did nothing to encourage him to stay on. Tommy had no way of knowing that Allison had continued to follow his career at her daddy's dealership. When she heard about Mitzi Manzel, she passed the word that the woman was a low-life floozie. Surely not someone Smith Toyota would want hanging around the business. Strangely, Allison helped Tommy into and out of the car business.

Tommy Kinder never looked back and assumed, for once, he had left a job of his own volition for a better opportunity. He immediately pursued his real estate license. He knew he had to establish a healthy source of income quickly if he wanted to stay in the picture with his new high-maintenance girlfriend.

CHAPTER 19

The new collegians had only been gone for two weeks when they returned home for the Labor Day holiday. Had the pandemic not interceded, it's likely they would have remained in Austin, but suddenly everything had become uncertain. They weren't sure if football practice would resume, and there were rumors they would reschedule the first day of classes. The timing was good for Marshall, who could be home for his mother's birthday. In fact, they arranged a small gathering to celebrate the event. Little did anyone know that tiny party would be the last relaxed social interaction they'd have for some time.

The get-together was held at the Morris residence on Sunday afternoon. Graham, his girlfriend Jennifer, and his parents came by, as did Mallory, Paula, and Barbara Jollen. It turned out to be a pizza and cake affair. Marshall supplied pizzas from the Cow Paddy store and picked up a birthday cake from a local bakery. As happens in such situations, the men clustered out on the rear patio, and the women sat in the kitchen and gabbed away. Freshly squeezed lemonade was the beverage of the day, although had Marshall, Graham, and Mr. Brown had their choice, beer would have been on hand.

Graham's dad was very interested in the football team at CTU. He was eager to hear from the boys about the other players, the coaches, and how it compared to high school. Both boys agreed it was going to be a lot tougher and faster-paced, but they hadn't put on pads or started contact drills. Marshall mentioned that Zack Middleton was on the team, and Mr. Brown remembered how well the boy had played.

A few steps away in the kitchen, the pandemic dominated the conversation. The dreaded disease had now been around for a couple of weeks, and already, the effects were being felt in their day-to-day lives. As a nurse, Sally Morris was particularly concerned. "I just don't see how our schools are going to stay open if this thing becomes as infectious as people are saying. I've heard horror stories from friends back in New York City, where it's spreading like crazy. The hospitals are already worried about having enough space in their Intensive Care Units. It may get that bad here, too."

Paula, of course, who had surfed all over the net, agreed with Marshall's mom. "I think you're right. We're going to be forced to keep from transmitting COVID to each other. And the scary part is that there is no known cure. I read that over 100 people died from it in the country just yesterday."

Mallory's mother smiled and shook her head. "Just our luck. We escape from the end of the earth over in New Orleans, and just when we think we've found the Promised Land, a pestilence shows up from nowhere. My supervisor at Exxon has already talked to us about working from home. They have a contingency plan to close the office, and we would all work from home. That could happen soon."

Mallory sat there and took all of it in. To her, these comments were a surprise. While she was certainly aware of the COVID problem, she hadn't focused on the severity or the impact on their everyday lives. "Wow. I didn't realize things got that bad. Close businesses? Close schools? That just doesn't seem possible. What about all our other activities like going to church, football games, shopping? Surely, you aren't talking about those activities?"

"No one really knows for sure yet, but I can see almost all aspects of our life being affected. If human contact transmits the COVID, how can you go to church with hundreds of other folks and sing safely? The same with football games. Think of the close contact players have," Sally Morris responded.

Mallory jumped back in. "No way. Cancel football in Texas? Never. I just can't believe it could ever happen." The others shook their heads. No football was unthinkable in Texas.

The group looked up as Marshall entered the room. He was staring at his cell phone in his right hand with a perplexed look on his face. "Mom, you will not believe this," he began. Sally Morris was accustomed to hearing such statements from her only child almost every day.

"I'll bite. What, son?"

"I just got a text from Coach Crown. They have canceled football practice until further notice. Can you believe that? At first, I thought Big Daddy Boyd or one of my friends was playing a joke, but it's real. Graham received the same thing. It says that the university regents have put the entire school year on hold. No one is sure what it means, but some delay is now for sure. I can't imagine they would ever cancel football in Texas. Can you?"

The women looked at each other in disbelief.

They spent the rest of the afternoon discussing the ramifications of the regents' decision and how it might set a precedent for other parts of their society. Paula hopped on the web to read the official statement from CTU. She pointed out that the suspension of activities for the semester, which was about to start, was temporary. It remained their full intent to reopen the university as soon as they established proper guidelines and procedures. Although the official statement didn't give a timeline, one commentator suggested a month delay might be most likely.

No one was in much of a partying mood, and after the required birthday serenade for Sally, forty-eight but could have passed for ten years younger, everyone downed their cake and got ready to leave. Marshall presented his mom with a sporty burnt orange CTU sweatshirt. When she tried it on, she guessed it was only about three sizes too big, but she appreciated her son's thoughtfulness.

Mallory had ridden with her mother and sister, so she left with them. Marshall walked her to the car. "I don't know when, or even if, I *will* head back to Austin," he said. "I suppose there could be worse alternatives. At least now, I'll be here at home close to you. We can see each other a lot more. That's not so bad, is it?"

Mallory grinned. The big lug always looked on the bright side. "You bet. Although you may have stated it correctly."

"What do you mean?"

"Look. We can look at each other from an appropriate social distance. That's it, COVID brain."

"Hey, we'll figure a way to work around that issue." He pecked her on the cheek and watched her get into the car.

Marshall was well into his second dish of cereal the next morning, which was the Labor Day Monday holiday. His mother sat across from him reading the Houston Chronicle newspaper.

She looked up from the paper and studied him. "I've been meaning to ask you. Have you heard anything about the results of your COVID test?"

"Nope. Nothing. They said it would be four days to a week. They didn't strike me as too efficient. Who knows when I'll hear? They told us they couldn't email or text the results. We would get a snail mail letter. I guess there's no mail today for the holiday."

"No. Did you check the mailbox on Saturday? I forgot to."

Marshall shoveled in another few scoops of cereal, got up, and wandered out the front door to the mailbox on the street. It never occurred to him he was still in his PJs—not that it would have mattered had he noticed. He opened the box and snatched the contents, which he dropped on the table in front of his mother.

He was about to go for a third round of cereal when he saw an anguished look on his mother's face. She held a letter in her hand.

"Marshall, you're positive for COVID. Here are the test results."

"Oh, no. Mom, what do I do? What do I do?"

CHAPTER 20

E ver the optimist, Marshall suddenly found himself confronted by the unimaginable. He had never dreamed the virus would infect him. That was supposed to happen to other people. He was young, active, and healthy. This stuff hit old people, not teenagers. As was his custom, when confronted with a new dilemma, he immediately panicked.

"Mom, I'm so sorry this has happened. Maybe I'll get well, but even if I don't, you'll get over losing me after a while. I know what a pain I can be to be around. I do nutty things sometimes, which drive you crazy. It'll be quieter around here. Your food bill will go way down. We need to look on the bright side, just in case I don't make it. Maybe you could get a dog?"

She had heard enough, even from him, but couldn't resist teasing him. "Hmm? A dog, huh? That's not a bad idea. I could find a big, bony one with big ears and a droopy face. I might even name him

Mongo. You know, that's kind of close to Marshall. In a week or two, this house can be back to normal, like you never even lived here."

As her son listened to her little jest, he couldn't help but smile. "Mom, we have to take this seriously!"

"Of course we do, and we surely will. Don't forget, I'm a nurse. Everything I read and hear about this virus is not good. It will get much worse before it gets better. No one really knows what's going to happen. There are a few things that seem to be true about it, though. Unfortunately, there's no cure, which is a terrible situation. Also, there is no vaccine for it to prevent infections. The world medical community is already working diligently to develop a vaccine, but no one knows how long that will take. With clinical trials, it usually takes years before the government approves a new vaccine.

"See, I'm doomed. I already have it. There's no way I can wait years for a shot. I'm so sorry, mom."

"Hang on. Hang on. I've told you the worst part. The better news is that, you are correct, the virus seems to strike older and sicker folks harder and more often than kids and young people. The older folks are much more vulnerable. At that, the early reports I have read are that most—and I said 'most'—people who get infected have minor cases or often no symptoms at all. Only about one in ten who becomes infected even has to go to the hospital. Among those that do, about three do not make it. Again, most of those who die are elderly and have other problems. That still means that anyone who gets sick could die, but the odds are very much on the side of young people like you."

Marshall reflected on her statement for a minute and drew his own conclusion, which had rebounded 100% in the opposite direction.

"Whew. That's a relief. I was sure it was time to decide who to give my baseball card collection to. Now I don't have to worry. I'll just carry on as usual."

"No way. Hang on a minute. What I said was the chances of you getting very sick are probably low. You still might. We certainly don't want you infecting other people. You can be a carrier who gives it to others and not be outwardly affected by it yourself. We are going to take this seriously, young man. Do you remember being grounded by me every so often in high school?"

"Yeah. There was the time the police caught us putting a cow in the high school."

Sally rolled her eyes back. "Well, that was nothing compared to what is about to happen to you as of immediately. You are in isolation as of this moment."

"Isolation? What does that mean? I'm heading over to Graham's in a few minutes."

"No, you're not."

"I'm going over to the high school to lift weights this afternoon."

"No, you are not."

"I'm taking Mallory to the movies tonight."

"No, you are not."

"You've got to be kidding me. The next thing you'll be telling me is that I have to stay in my room, just like a seven-year-old."

"Yes, you are. You got it. I know it's going to be tough, but we have no choice. We can't have you out spreading the virus to friends and family."

"You've got to be kidding me. I am a prisoner in my home."

"That's about it."

The impact of her orders hit him hard, but Marshall never lacked a sense of humor. "So, how long is my sentence, warden?"

She smiled. "It all depends on how your sentence works out. If all goes well, you might be out on good behavior in about two weeks."

"Two weeks! I'll never make it."

"Oh, I think you'll survive, but just in case, who do you want to get your baseball card collection?"

"Mom!" he shrieked.

"Okay, Mr. inmate, we need to examine you for any symptoms. I assume that you have been feeling okay for the past several days. I haven't noticed you looking or acting like you don't feel well. Is that right?"

"Right. I feel fine. Better than fine. Say, this whole isolation thing came on such brief notice. Maybe, could we start it tomorrow to give me a day to say goodbye to my friends?"

"Nope. Have you been coughing at all lately?"

"No."

"Do you feel warm, like you have a fever?"

"No."

"Is your throat sore?"

"No."

"Are you extra tired? I mean, do you need to sleep more than your usual twelve hours per night?"

"I need my beauty sleep, but I always have. Nothing unusual."

"Good. So far, it looks like you are anti-symptomatic."

"Please stop the nurse talk. Does that mean I'm okay, cured, can get back out there with my friends?"

"No, it does not. Only that despite your positive test result, you're not showing signs of the sickness yet. That could change. It can take up to two weeks for the virus to incubate in a person after the initial exposure. Hopefully, you'll have a light case, but we can't be sure yet. Have you been around anyone in school who coughed a lot or acted exhausted.?"

Marshall thought for a minute. "Yes. Zack Middleton from Bayside. He's on the team, and we went out with him. He was coughing. We just thought it was allergies."

"Really? He might be the source of your infection. We'll have to see if he tested positive as well." A few days later, they learned that not only had Zack tested positive, but he was also showing obvious symptoms of the virus.

As a nurse, Sally Morris tried to stay on top of the ever-emerging medical procedures concerning the virus. She was certain that she must isolate her son, but wasn't sure whom he had come in contact with should be quarantined. She did immediately call the Grahams and Barbara Jollen to report Marshall's positive test. None of them opted to quarantine, but as a school nurse, she felt compelled to stay away from her job and did so with the full consent of the school staff.

Combining her professional medical opinion with her motherly concerns, she decided that there was no reason at that point to contact a physician about Marshall's case. She did, however, want to test two specific readings on her son. One was his temperature. She waited for a while after his breakfast to ensure she'd get an accurate reading. No problem. He registered slightly low, at 98.3 degrees.

She also wanted to test the oxygen level in his blood, which she could readily do by clipping an oximeter onto his hand. She went into his room, where he was chatting on the phone, reporting far and wide to his friends about his incarceration. He barely glanced at her when she slipped the oximeter clip over a finger.

She ducked out of his room for a moment and returned to check his oxygen blood level. She did a double-take. It registered "seventy-two," a disturbingly low level. Maybe she shouldn't be so confident he was asymptomatic? This virus was tricky and not to be taken lightly. She cleared the reading and re-clipped his finger. He continued to talk on his phone, oblivious to her fussing over him. She folded her arms and glanced around his "boy cave" of a room while she waited.

Oh no. The reading was now seventy—even less than before. This situation had become concerning. She opened her iPhone and scrolled down to their family doctor's number. It would probably be best to at least call him. Before hitting the number, she poked her son and gave him a slashing motion with her hand across her neck. *Hang up, boy, now!*

Marshall looked piqued, but got the message. Reluctantly, he hung up.

"I just ran an oxygen blood test on you, and it didn't look so good. Are you okay?"

"Great, except for my jail, Mom. What's the problem?" As he spoke, he held up both hands where she could see them. She immediately noticed a thick band-aid on one of his fingers. "You put that clippie thing on one of my sore fingers from football practice. It hurt, so I shifted it over."

"To the finger with the Band-Aid on it, I assume."

"Yup. The thing didn't bother me there."

She ran a third test with the inmate having to endure the pain on a bare finger. His reading was in the mid-nineties. She was relieved. Whatever was she going to do with that kid?

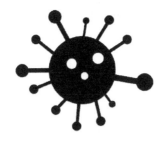

CHAPTER 21

Throughout his brief life, Marshall had prowled and stumbled through many complicated situations and predicaments. He possessed an uncanny knack for getting into them. The kid could never find the simple way out. Luckily, he usually ended up on top. His intentions were admirable. It was his methods that needed some upgrading. He'd always had difficulty remaining in one place for very long.

This quarantine isolation prison sentence was a real challenge for him. It restricted him to his room. He could leave only for the bathroom and brief visits to the backyard for fresh air, once or twice a day. His mom brought his meals and set them on the floor by the door. With Marshall's prodigious appetite, mealtime occurred at least six times each day. His mother had already been exposed, so if she was going to contract the virus from him, it probably would have happened already. The published news and advice about the virus were so confusing. Still, it made sense for her to keep a reasonable distance from him, if possible.

Being sent to "your room" has been the traditional punishment for kids. In recent times, however, the implications of such restriction had transformed immensely. What had once been books and bed now included cell phones, computers, computer games, and television, among many other activities. Like any teenager, he had access to all those things, but limiting him to four walls was still going to be tough. Best guess was two weeks if all went well. They would re-test him with a negative finding needed to grant him parole. What made his incarceration more difficult was that he felt fine, with no symptoms of the disease. That was great, but if he'd felt sick, being cooped up might have been more tolerable.

He had long calls to Mallory, who at first was extremely worried about him. The virus was spreading rapidly around the state and even in Justice, where several cases had been recorded. It seemed to hit older folks more often than younger people, but there were cases in all age groups. Most who caught it didn't have to be hospitalized, but many did, and deaths occurred. There was no cure and no vaccine. National news reported that several pharmaceutical companies were working on a vaccine, but the availability of an effective one was months, if not years, away. Confusion, conflicting reports, and disinformation were rampant.

"Prisoner 911 reporting in," he said into his cell phone. "How's that cake with a saw in it coming, Mal?"

She laughed. "You know, I'd be afraid to bake one for you. With your appetite, you'd likely scoff down the whole thing and never notice the saw."

"That's a good point. The thought of a cake isn't bad, though. Why don't you just bake me one? But not lemon merengue. I hate lemon merengue."

"What! You mean there is a type of food you don't like? Impossible. Maybe you *are* sick."

"I'm going crazy in this cell all by myself. Maybe you could come over just for a little while? My mother isn't working, but she goes out shopping now and then. I feel like I've been locked up in here forever."

"Sorry, big boy. Not a chance. This stuff is too scary. No one's really sure how it gets passed around. Oh, and by my calculations, as of this moment, you have been in solitary for about four hours."

"It seems like much longer," he whined.

"My mom needs me. Got to go. Talk to you later. I miss you," she said as she clicked off.

A text rang through on Marshall's phone. It was from Graham. It read:

Badman of Allthetrash, (aka Birdman of Alcatraz),

Your gang is planning a secret gastronomic delivery to your lockup. Can you say CowPaddy Supreme all the way? Advise best time to rendezvous.

Lefty.

Marshall's spirits leaped. They were going to sneak him a pizza all the way. He didn't think his mom would mind, but she would surely get all prissy about his friends getting near him. She was going to a meeting about school that evening. It might be best if the pizza arrived around 8:00 when she wasn't home. He could grab it through his bedroom window, and he could also talk to the guys for a little while. That's a plan. He fired a text back to "Lefty". He only hoped he could survive until the pizza got there.

Marshall counted down the minutes and seconds until the agreed time. At 8:00 p.m., no one appeared. Marshall became irritated. He knew darn well Graham would show but didn't put it past his friend to be late just to aggravate him. It was almost 8:30 when the pungent smell of roasted garlic and tomatoes wafted through his open window. He saw both Graham and Big Daddy Boyd scrambling through the bushes.

"Let me have it. Come on, you guys. I'm starved," Marshall pleaded.

Graham looked up at him and spread his hands apart. "What? Oh, yeah, we were supposed to bring a pizza, I forgot. Did you get one, Big Daddy?"

Marshall had enough of them. He was famished and could smell the pie. They chuckled and then handed it up to him. In doing so, the pizza almost slid right out of the box into the dirt of the flowerbed under Marshall's window. Now, *that* would have made him ill.

Marshall had worked his way through about half of the pie when he finally looked up and between bites asked, "So what's new around town? I've been out of circulation for a while."

"Less than a day, by my count. Do you feel sick at all?" Graham asked.

"Other than my hunger pains every few hours. I feel fine. I assume your COVID test came back negative? You were around Zack too."

"It didn't show any infection. I don't know why you got it and I didn't. Maybe it was the babe you were with that night?"

"Shut it!" Marshall screamed. If looks could kill, Graham could not have purchased life insurance at that moment.

Big Daddy perked up. "Babe? What babe?"

Silence. Time for a subject change.

"We're shut down at CTU for at least a month. What about the schools here?"

"The Justice superintendent of schools announced the same for here. Lock them until October 1 at the earliest, the high school included. They're studying the situation. Apparently, when they reopen, it's likely much of the classes will be virtual online."

"That doesn't seem workable to me. Goodbye football?"

"Afraid so," Big Daddy chimed in. "What a bummer that would be. From what I hear, working at Cow Paddy's, there are a lot more controls and changes in the works. They're talking about shutting down businesses—especially bars and restaurants. I could be out of a job. Our store might never re-open. It could get bad."

"Boy, I hope not. I couldn't survive on Papa Juan's wet cardboard excuse for pizza. Well, maybe I could struggle through if that was all that was left." Marshall added.

"This is Texas," Big Daddy continued. "We have a lot of pride and an independent spirit. You know. 'Remember the Alamo. Come and take it.' And stuff like that. We love our freedom and don't take kindly to being told what to do. My boss said he'll be damned if he'll shut down and risk losing his business just because some bureaucrat in Austin, or worse yet, Washington, tells him to do it. A few people are getting sick. True, but 95% are just fine. And some of the sick ones, just like the Badman of Allthetrash here, aren't really sick at all. The ones that are getting it the most are the old, old folks, who are already sick anyway. We just can't stop living."

"I see your point, but we've got to control this pandemic somehow. If it's passed between people, bars and restaurants are probably great places to get it. I can understand the need to control them somewhat," Graham commented in his typically conservative way.

"Masks." Big Daddy added. "What about them? Washington first said they aren't needed and don't protect you. Now they aren't so sure. They could make them mandatory. Can you imagine me working in front of that sizzling oven wearing a mask?"

Marshall couldn't resist. "I, for one, believe it would improve your appearance."

Graham guffawed.

"Hilarious. There's already a lot of opposition to the government taking our rights. I know there's one group of students that's waiting to see what restrictions they will place on high school students. They could band together and protest."

"I'll bet I know who they are. The long-haired jerks and gangs who get poor grades and do drugs. None of them ever take part in school activities," Graham said.

"I'm not sure about that, but they may see this as their chance to rock the boat."

"You guys are just a bundle of cheerfulness. Maybe I'll just stay cooped up here for a while. Say, could we make this a daily meeting? I rather enjoyed saving the world with you young men today. It was invigorating. Only one thing: tomorrow, would you ask them to hold the anchovies?"

Marshall looked down, but both of his friends had disappeared into the night.

CHAPTER 22

As if he thought he could fool his mother, Marshall tried to cover up the contraband pizza delivery. Lacking a better place to hide the smelly box, he slipped it under his mattress. The obvious evidence was out of sight, but his room still reeked of garlic, cheese, and all the other toppings. He spied a can of Old Spice aftershave sitting unused on his dresser since Christmas and splashed it all over this face and neck. The theory was the smell of that stuff would hide the pizza smell. It was a little after 9:00 p.m. when his mother looked in to tell him she was home and say good night. He was lying in his bed playing a video game.

"I'm home. It was a quick meeting. Everyone was nervous about being around each other. The virus seems to spread rapidly. I don't see the schools reopening soon. Everyone is trying to figure out how to work from home."

"That's a bummer. I sure hope CTU doesn't stay closed for long."

"No idea about that. So, how are you feeling? Any signs or symptoms? Fever, cough, fatigue? I want to take your temperature and oxygen before I go to bed."

"No. I feel fine, except for climbing these four walls. You said a week max, right, Mom?"

"Nice try, Marshall. Plan for two weeks unless any symptoms appear. Phew!" She wrinkled her nose. "What is that awful smell in here? Did you knock over a can of deodorant?"

Marshall knew she had nabbed him, but tried one weak attempt to scramble out of it. "You know this room is pretty small, and it gets stuffy in here. I haven't had my shower yet. I just thought a puff or two of that stuff I got as a gift and never used might make it a little more livable here in my cell."

She smiled, but was having none of that. "I see. So, what did you do with the box here in your 'cell'?"

He feigned a puzzled look. She answered her own question.

"I see part of it sticking out from under your mattress. Maybe you're onto something here. The fishy smell of anchovies from the stained, smelly pizza box could make you feel you are sitting on the beach by the water. It could help you with your incarceration," she joked, but then changed her tone. "I know this is tough for you, but we need to be careful. I don't mind your friends bringing pizza. I just hope you didn't get too close to them."

"No, they stayed outside." He pointed to the window.

"I guess that was good, but you don't have to be so sneaky next time. They could bring it to me, and I could give it to you." She felt bad for him, but he'd just have to curb his activities and let this thing run its course. Little did she know what else he had planned.

The Badman of Allthetrash, unlike his namesake on the rock in San Francisco Bay, didn't have little feathered friends to amuse him while in captivity. By the middle of the first week, he was climbing the walls. He didn't feel the least bit sick and was convinced he either had a very light case or didn't have the virus at all. His mother kept reminding him that even though he might be correct in his assessment of his condition, he still could be a carrier of the disease and give it to other people.

He chatted with Mallory several times a day and was getting more and more desperate to see her. They were just a few blocks apart. She steadfastly refused to come to his house without her mother's consent, which hadn't been given. How many times did she tell Prisoner 911 that two weeks weren't forever? Of course, Marshall wouldn't give up, and as only he could do, he concocted a plan for them to meet.

After a while, she tired of his incessant badgering. In a weak moment, she finally relented to meet him in the late evening at the Justice High football field. He solemnly agreed there'd be no hanky-panky, and they'd stay at least six feet apart. They wouldn't do more than look at each other and talk. She immediately regretted agreeing to the clandestine meeting, but there was no deterring Marshall Morris now. They would meet at 11:00 p.m. long after everyone else in Mallory's and Marshall's house had turned in.

Mallory lay in bed with her clothes on. She heard her mother brush her teeth and close her bedroom door just before 10:00 p.m. The house was dark, and she assumed Paula was also fast asleep, dreaming about ways she could torment her big sister. She pulled back the covers, silently got out of bed, and grabbed her shoes. Luckily, she lived only a few blocks from the football field. She could easily walk and didn't have to drive. She stood at her bedroom door and listened. The house was quiet. She slowly opened the door and peeked out. The coast was clear, so she tiptoed to the kitchen and carefully opened the back door. She wouldn't lock it, expecting to be back within the hour. Standing in the backyard, she eased the door closed. The final click seemed loud enough to wake up the entire neighborhood, but nothing stirred.

After slipping on her shoes, she took a deep breath in the dark and walked around the house toward the street. As she rounded the corner, a dark figure suddenly jumped out of the shadows in front of her. She stifled her first inclination to scream when she recognized the shape.

"What are you doing here?" she hissed.

"Me? I was watering Mom's flowers. You? Where are you going, Mal-o-ree?" her little sister asked. "You really shouldn't talk so loud in your room."

Mallory knew she had been caught and had to think fast. There was no point in arguing with the little antagonist. They couldn't stand there in the dark and debate the matter. Mom would hear them eventually if she hadn't already. As incensed as Mallory was, she had only one choice. "Come on! Just keep your big mouth shut!" she said, walking toward the street.

Paula broke out with a big smile and, of course, could not keep a lid on it. "Gee, thanks, Sis. It's so nice to do things together," she said as she skipped along behind.

The night was moonless and particularly dark and spooky. Actually, she wouldn't have minded company from anyone other than her bratty sibling. There were few cars on the streets, and there were no lights on in most of the houses they passed. To get to the football stadium, they had to walk on a long sidewalk under a line of old oak trees that bordered the high school's intramural fields. The dark maze of thick trunks and twisted branches cast eerie shadows along their path, where there were no lamp posts.

Brave Paula took a couple of quick steps to be closer to Mallory, who trudged on in silence. It didn't help the spirits of either of them when Paula remarked, "You know anybody could hide behind these scary trees."

Mallory didn't respond but quickened her pace. She was regretting her foolish agreement to meet Marshall. They entered the vast parking lot, which during the day teemed with cars and kids. Late at night, it was almost empty, although she saw one dark pickup truck sitting off against the fence in the right corner. She couldn't see anyone around. "Whose truck is that?" she wondered loud enough for Paula to hear.

"I don't know, and I don't want to find out. Maybe this whole thing is a bad idea. What do you say we turn around and go home, Mallory? Why did you make me come with you? It's creepy here. Come on, let's go."

Mallory wasn't brimming with self-confidence at the moment. It was scary, but her little sister's moaning only reinforced her determination to find Marshall. Served the little pain right if she was scared. Maybe next time, she'd think twice about interfering with her life.

They approached the white cement block ticket office under the back of the network of metal girders and seats that extended out over head. To enter the field, they had to walk through an open chain-link gate, which led to a walkway through the stands out to the field. Mallory stopped and looked around. There was no sign of Marshall. She expected to see his OC car parked right by the gate, but there was nothing and no one other than the ominous black truck off to the side. Surely, he hadn't changed his mind. No, that hadn't happened. He was probably just running a little late. Of course, that was his style.

What were they worried about? Justice always appeared on the lists of the safest towns in Texas. Crime was just about non-existent. She decided they would just go in and sit in the stands where they could see the entire field. She'd give him ten minutes. If he didn't show, they would boogie, and he'd be due a major ear burning from her in the morning.

She started for the gate. "Wait. Wait. Are you sure we should go in there?" her sister pleaded.

Mallory didn't answer or break stride. Not wanting to be left alone, her young, frightened companion scurried after her. Mallory reached for the gate, which was closed but not locked. It screeched as she pulled it open for the two of them to enter and proceed under the stands toward the walkway out to the field. It was even darker inside.

Mallory was determined to get out to the field as quickly as possible and became irritated when she felt her sister's frantic fingernails dig into her left arm.

"Ouch!" she yelled.

"What was that?" Paula asked. Mallory stopped to listen. She heard it too.

KLOP. KLOP. KLOP. It seemed to come from the other side of the ticket office.

"Mal! Mal! Look over there!"

"KLOP. KLOP. KLOP."

Mallory turned her head. She squinted, not believing what she saw. Her heart leaped into her mouth. A massive, black, menacing figure was limping toward them. It had emerged from around a corner and was only twenty feet away, cutting off their way back to the parking lot.

"Eeek! Eeek! Oh, no! We're going to die!" Paula screamed at the top of her lungs. She broke away from her sister and bolted up the ramp toward the field.

Mallory stood frozen, unbelieving for a few seconds. Finally, she took after her sister, yelling, "Run! Run!" Both girls came out of the tunnel and down the steps of a section of seats to the fence that separated the stands from the running track that surrounded the football field. Paula was over it in a flash and was hot-footing it for all she was worth across the fifty-yard line. Mallory had more trouble with the fence than her sister. She landed on the running track and was about to chase after her when she heard a voice calling her name. Could it be? She dared to look back and stopped. Yes, the monster was standing there, but suddenly he looked familiar.

"Mallory, it's me, Marshall. Where are you going? It is me. I know we haven't seen each other for a couple of weeks, but have I changed that much?"

She looked at him, looked away, and then looked again, trying to make sure her eyes weren't playing tricks on her. "It is you." Her relief was immense, but it immediately flipped over to anger. "What the heck is that getup? You scared the living heck out of us."

Marshall gave himself a quick once over as if he hadn't remembered what he was wearing. "Oh, yeah. This, this. Well, I was so concerned not to transmit the virus to you, if I am contagious, which I may or may not be, and this suit was the best I could think of to protect you. I don't have any special hazmat gear. I think it should be safe."

"So, you felt a skin-diving wet suit complete with flippers and mask would do the trick?"

"Sure, it was the best I could do. I left my snorkel home. Well, it is working, isn't it? Do you feel sick?"

Despite her impulse to be extremely upset, staring at the large black rubber man, Mallory was unsuccessful in stifling her chuckle. "How did you get here? We didn't see your car."

"That was a problem. I just couldn't drive with these flippers on. I rode my bike. It was still tough, but I made it." He looked over Mallory's head and saw Paula, who had finally stopped running and apparently identified Marshall, and was now standing at about the ten-yard line.

Terrified? Frightened? Scared? Not anymore. "Say, Marshall, when are you going to fix me up with Big Daddy again?"

CHAPTER 23

As he expected, his two-week sentence ended without further incident or onset of virus symptoms. Marshall exhibited no outward indications that he'd been infected. It had become very clear that no one, including the government and medical community, had been prepared for a pandemic of this sort. There was no cure for the disease or vaccination against it. The indications were that it originated in Asia and had been transmitted around the world. Just getting a test to see if you had it could take days or even weeks before the results were known. They limited testing to people who were showing possible symptoms or were recovering, such as Marshall. After having tested positive, his mom could get him re-tested at Crystal River Hospital. It took a full week to get his results, which were negative, as expected.

"See, Mom, all that jail time was for nothing. I never had the stuff. I must have had a false positive test at CTU. If you had seen the geek that tested me, you wouldn't be surprised."

"Really? They need to get with that guy right away. Someone who can control the virus on demand, as he apparently can, would be invaluable to the medical community."

"He was a strange dude. Graham said he heard we'll start classes for the semester in a couple of weeks. Most of it will probably be virtual. There will be all kinds of rules, procedures, and social distancing. He also told me that several of the big college football conferences, including the Big 10 and Pac 12, have already canceled their football seasons. Ours hasn't decided yet. I sure never expected this to happen. What a way to start a college career. I guess this thing is getting pretty bad."

"It sure is. I keep up with the latest through my nurses' association website. The virus has struck almost every country. Europe and Italy, in particular, have been very hard hit. I have talked to some of my friends back in New York, where the virus is going wild. You remember how close people live together up there? It can spread more easily than here, where things are more spread out. Even with most infections not being too serious like yours, the hospital beds in the city are getting filled almost to capacity. What's worse is that the most serious cases require breathing respirators in Intensive Care Units, and that space is already full. They are setting up temporary hospitals in athletic stadiums, and they have brought in a military hospital ship to the Brooklyn Navy yard. Things are not good."

"That's a shame. I hope my friends up there are all okay. I'm sure glad we live here where it isn't so bad. My case was no big deal, and I don't even know anyone else who is sick, other than Zack Middleton.

He definitely had the stuff, but he has recovered and is fine now. I hope it stays away from here."

"Me too, but it's already here and getting worse every day. It's mainly striking older people who already have other health problems. Your age group has been spared so far. I need to emphasize to you that, even though you tested positive once, you still need to be careful. You may not have had it and could catch it for real this time. It's also possible you could be a carrier who gives it to other people. I know you wouldn't want that on your conscience."

"Of course not. I would feel terrible if I thought I had given it to someone else. "

"Just make sure you observe social distancing, wash your hands a lot, and wear a face mask. Will you promise me that?"

"I suppose so, although I'm not happy about the mask. Didn't the director of the Centers for Disease Control in Atlanta say that masks don't protect you, although they may help a little in keeping you from spreading it? My friends and I have been talking about that a lot. We hate the darn things. It's hard to breathe or talk. They get itchy, hot, and smelly. It's an infringement of our personal freedom. And they don't work."

Sally became agitated. "Listen to me, son. I have been a licensed nurse for over twenty years. The talking heads say something on the boob tube, but I don't give a flying flip. I also have zero pity for the slight inconvenience wearing masks might cause to your group's social life. You will wear one. Period. End of discussion. Have I made myself clear, young man?"

She certainly had. Whether Marshall agreed, he was smart enough to know his only response was to shake his head and not argue further. While he would never openly defy his mom, he still wasn't convinced the pandemic was as bad as she had made it out to be. After all, they weren't in New York, where everyone lived on top of everyone else. He had seen how many poor families there crowded several generations into small apartments. It wasn't surprising the infections ran wild. But this was Texas, with wide-open spaces and plenty of air to breathe. Their lifestyle was much different. He'd had the virus, and there was nothing to it. Marshall knew that many of his friends didn't see the pandemic as a big deal and were balking at the idea of having to wear face coverings everywhere. He wouldn't blindly go with the flow, but it was absolutely clear that the kids were wrong about things.

The virus aside and the start of college classes uncertain, Marshall had some time to fill at home. Already, most activities that involved groups of folks had been stopped. No movies. Libraries and even restaurants had shut down table service, rendering takeout the rule of the day. Mallory's server job was put on hold, although she got a few hours each week in the food preparation area. It bummed Marshall out when he passed Bigaburger's empty parking lot. With cash always an issue, he tried to resume his pizza delivery career at Cow Paddy's. Surely, the demand for takeout would have increased their business. He had performed well there and been a top worker who had left on good terms to go off to college. It didn't surprise him when the owner politely turned him down. In view of Marshall's positive test, despite his excellent past performance, the man was reluctant to hire him to deliver food. For the first time, Marshall felt the impact of the pandemic on people's everyday lives.

It had been a while since he had talked to his group of old vets at Falling Oaks old folks' home. They had banded together to rescue the Sam Jacinto monument in Winston Park. He had become friendly with ex-Marine major Bob Lindsay. The major's group of old vets enjoyed their interaction with youthful Marshall. Correspondingly, Marshall was in awe of their never-ending series of war stories, especially since most of them were based on fact, with only slight modifications.

Marshall piloted the OC into the Falling Oaks parking lot, which was almost empty. He had a standing Tuesday noon delivery there in the past to provide lunch for the major and his pal's poker game. He didn't need to call ahead. They would certainly be there. It surprised him when the main door to the property office was locked. He then noticed a big sign on the door: "NO VISITORS. NO EXCEPTIONS. FAMILIES INCLUDED." At first, he wasn't sure what to make of that situation. He'd walked in dozens of times.

He went back to his car and called the major on his cell phone. As usual, the man answered after only one ring. "Major Lindsay, here."

"Hey, major. How the heck are you? Marshall, excuse me, PFC Marshall Morris here. Reporting for duty, sir!"

There was an uncharacteristic pause on the other end. Finally, a decidedly subdued response. "Marshall. Nice to hear from you, son. How are things at college?"

His friend's tone surprised Marshall. "Okay, sir. I'm home for a couple of weeks until they get this virus thing figured out. I expect to go back in a week. I just thought I'd pop in and see how you and the crew are doing. In fact, I actually came to Falling Oaks, but the door was locked, and a sign said there were no visitors allowed. What's up with that?"

"If you have a minute, let me explain."

CHAPTER 24

ajor Robert V. Lindsay was a decorated war hero who served in the Vietnam. A Texan by birth, the US Marine career officer had survived multiple combat engagements as an infantry rifle platoon commander. He lived in the Veterans Administration rent-supplemented apartment project of Falling Oaks in Justice. Physically spent but still mentally vigorous, the major, along with three other resident veterans, had a standing poker game in the recreation center's card room. Wheelchair-bound Rodney Wexford was ex-Air Force. Sarah Moran was a Navy Lieutenant Commander who had captained PT boats. Top Warren Cook had been a master sergeant with the US Army Special Forces.

When a local real estate developer attempted to buy the land under a memorial to a local medal of honor winner, the major led the resistance to preserve the sacred place. At one point, after recruiting Marshall and Graham, they fought a physical battle against hired thugs bent on stealing old Sam Jacinto's statue. In the end, they preserved the memorial. Each of the old veterans was in their eighties and suffered from a variety of maladies. The Battle for Sam Jacinto was heralded locally, and for a moment, a spotlight shined on those old vets.

"Life is a funny thing, Marshall," the major began. "The four of us in here have probably dodged more angry hot metal than everyone else who lives in Justice combined. As you know, but for the heroics of Sam Jacinto, my life would have ended in the jungles of Vietnam when we were surrounded by Vietcong. In fact, I was pretty sure I was a goner, but it didn't happen. Lieutenant Commander Moran had two PT patrol boats shot out from under her on the Mekong River. She came home in one piece. Even Rodney, who sat in the rear of a B-52 bomber and dropped bombs on Hanoi, was lucky enough to choose a plane that made it through the missiles and anti-aircraft fire. As a member of the Army Special Forces, Top Cook often operated behind enemy lines. In fact, the North Vietnamese captured him. He spent over two years in a tiger cage cell. But for the grace of God, none of us would have ever set foot in this great country again. Some awful mean folks wanted us dead pretty badly, but we just wouldn't give in."

"Of course, we all knew we were closer to taps than reveille, which wasn't really a problem. The four of us were proud of our accomplishments. It is the nature of the military that casualties and loss of life in battle are inevitable and to be expected. Still, that doesn't make them any easier. We must soldier on."

He stopped talking. Marshall's mood had tumbled from bright and cheerful to uncertain and worried. He'd never heard the major talk like this in the past. He was almost certain he'd heard a sniffle, but he couldn't imagine the man he idolized would display such emotion, even if he felt it. His mood was ominous, and Marshall could sense as much through the phone.

The old man began again. "And so, my young friend, I must report some rather bad news to you. A hot round in combat weighs a few ounces. When you hold one in your hand, it's easy to imagine what it would do to your insides. Then, there are bacteria that are microscopic but can also rapidly do you in. Finally, there is this virus that is virtually undetectable and somehow worms its way into your lungs. The irony? Chances are the infection comes from a friend or loved ones without your knowledge. You can fight, but sadly, there is nothing known to cure it."

Again, a pause.

"While our accommodations in here are comfortable and much more than adequate, there is no way we can avoid each other. It's simply not possible. If those damn viruses are around, no amount of scrubbing will keep them away from us old folks who aren't in the best of shape, anyway. First, it was Top, a hell of a fighter if there ever was one. He developed a cough and fever. They soon moved him to the hospital, where he was put on a ventilator. He battled hard, as usual, but there was no hope. A week later, he was gone. Sarah was next. She seemed fine one day, but very sick the next. She actually passed on here in her room before they could get her to the hospital. To look at him, you would have thought Rodney would have been easy pickings for the damn disease. He's skinny, wheelchair bound, and always looks pallid to me. They took him to the hospital for a week. He was tough enough to recover—enough so to come back here. Finally, he went back and has been on life support for weeks. He just won't give in and may be the toughest one of all of us. Imagine that from an Air Force punk?" he tried a weak joke.

Marshall said nothing, as they both were lost in their thoughts.

"It all happened so quickly. As I mentioned, we were all old codgers, whose better days are far behind us. For any or all of us to move on to the next life is inevitable and expected sooner than later. Do you know, though, what is the saddest thing about losing my comrades?" He did not wait for Marshall to answer. "It is this; they all died alone. No one was with them. Because of this confounded virus, they had to be completely isolated from any human contact. There were only nurses and attendants around them. There was no one who really cared. No family, friends, loved ones, pastors, priests, or rabbis. No one to say goodbye. We can't even have a proper military burial for them. I'm lost without them but seeing them go without the honor and ceremony they richly earned is tearing me up."

"So, PFC Morris, for now, Rodney and I are it. Not sure for how long, but as of the moment, I'm physically doing okay. That could change."

Marshall was speechless, but he knew he had to say something. "Major, I'm so sorry. I just don't know what to say."

"Then don't, son. There is nothing that can be said. They were wonderful people who lived terrific lives. They're at peace now. Just promise me one thing."

"What, sir?"

"Only that you take this pandemic seriously. It can do what an enemy's bombs and bullets cannot do. Please keep in touch. And that's an order."

"Yes, sir. I will."

Click. He was gone.

Marshall couldn't keep it together driving home. The tears flowed freely. Two—maybe three—of the four wiped out. Sure, they were old, but they were the toughest group of people he had ever known.

It was after 6:00 p.m. when Marshall arrived at his house. He needed to share this horrible news with his mom. She'd help him feel better. She always did. He walked in and didn't see her right away, although he could smell his dinner in the oven. He walked back and found her lying on her bed.

"Mom?"

"Oh, hi, Marshall. Your dinner is in the oven. I needed to lie down for a few minutes. It was a long day. I don't feel that great."

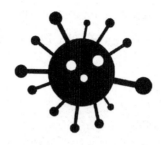

CHAPTER 25

The gaunt man in scrubs stood aside as the attendant pushed the gurney loaded with a sheet-covered figure down the corridor of what had become the virus ward of Crystal Lake Hospital. There were dozens of masked and sheathed health care workers milling around the central nurse's station. Some were reading patient charts. Others were preparing medications. Still others moved in and out of the patients' rooms along the two corridors that radiated out from the center core. There was a perceptible mood of immediacy bordering on frenzy.

"Another one. That makes two today, doesn't it?" he asked the senior nurse, who was standing next to him.

"No, Dr. Clark. That's the third one today. That old gal was a fighter. She had been here a few weeks ago and recovered enough to think about sending her home. It looked at the time like she was going to make it. She was going to be one of our rare victories. Sadly, at her age and with other issues, the virus struck back. This time, we couldn't save her. She was one of the most pleasant and cheery people I have ever met, which makes losing her even tougher," she explained in a matter-of-fact monotone that belied the deep emotion she was feeling.

"That's tough, but they're all tough. How are we doing for beds, ICU space, and ventilators?"

"We're okay for the moment on all three counts. We're running about 80% full and have some unused ventilators available. At the rate of new infections, though, if something doesn't change, we'll reach capacity soon. I don't know what we'll do then?"

"I keep reading in the news that Washington has several big drug companies going all out to develop a vaccine. There are supposed to be a few that are promising."

"Maybe, Doctor, but I won't hold my breath. You mentioned the magic word, *Washington*. When did anything good ever happen there fast? New drugs take years to get approved. Our needs are now. Plus, a vaccine may be the answer to stopping this virus, but here in the hospital, even if we had a vaccine, it wouldn't help us. When we get patients, they're already infected and very sick. What we need is a cure to get them well. So far, we haven't been able to find anything that attacks the virus and cures the patient. Have you heard anything about that?"

The doctor rubbed the stubble on his chin and yawned. Like most of the staff, he was tired and weary from his eighteen-hour shifts. "No, I haven't, Carmella. I've heard some rumors about drugs that might help, but nothing's been confirmed."

"I pray for something soon. Your shift is over. Go home and get some rest. I see some of my people are still here helping out, even after their shifts are over. Please excuse me while I go round them up. See you tomorrow." He watched the lady wade into the fray and tap on shoulders. He marveled at the dedication in this crisis of these frontline workers.

Clarence Clark, MD, was exhausted from his long shift at the hospital. He changed out of his scrubs, cleaned up thoroughly, and walked out to the parking lot where his ten-year-old yellow BMW was waiting for him. As he drove away from the hospital toward his apartment in Justice, a few miles down the freeway, he realized it was early afternoon. The sun was shining, and the humidity was through the roof, as usual. His next shift wasn't until 6:00 a.m. the next morning. Sleep could wait.

He stopped by a local watering hole for a drink or two. He needed to relax and unwind. The intense atmosphere of the COVID ward got to anyone after a while. His job wasn't as tough as some. Even though he was an MD, he wasn't specifically assigned to patient care. His job was to supervise the administration, care, and handling of all drugs and medications used in the virus ward. He worked closely with the hospital pharmacy. The hospital supervisors recognized that the pace and volume of activity in the designated virus ward necessitated special precaution, especially in the handing of drugs.

Normally, a full-fledged licensed doctor would not have been assigned such a job, but Dr. Clark knew he was lucky to be employed there at all. It was only thanks to the pandemic that they had hired him. There just simply were not enough health care professionals available to meet the critical needs. He had a grievance pending, and his case was being considered before the Texas State Medical Review Board. They had granted him a special waiver to practice medicine until the board could review his situation and issue a ruling. When they did, his license might be revoked altogether.

He pulled into the Mucky Duck parking lot, where there were just a few cars in the middle of the day. Rather than sit at the bar, he took a four-seater off in the corner. Experience had taught him that the type of people who frequented bars in the middle of the day were alcoholics down on their luck. They loved to chat about their problems. He'd much rather sit by himself and stew about his own situation all alone. He had enough on his plate without having to hear the woes of other losers.

The server set a Jack Daniels and Coke in front of him. He took a big sip and then another. The alcohol burned some as it slid down his throat. Within a minute, he had emptied the glass and was shaking the ice cubes to drain every drop of the drink. He felt the beginning of a buzz coming on and relaxed for the first time in several hours. As he motioned to the server for a refill, he reflected on his conversation with the nurse supervisor, Carmella.

Though he had read about epidemics and pandemics during his medical training, he had never ever experienced anything like what was happening in Texas, the United States, and the world. No one and nowhere was exempt. The incestuous reach of the virus was incredible. It was multiplying unchecked. No one, least of all the government, had any idea how bad it would get. There was lots of lip service about vaccines, which seemed to be the ultimate answer. The question, of course, was: when would one be produced that could be given to millions of people? The size of the problem worsened with every day that passed. Hopefully, an effective vaccine would become available soon.

That said, Carmella had put her finger on a unique twist to the matter. In the long run, a good vaccine might eventually solve the problem, but in the meantime, hospitals had to deal with patients who were already infected and very ill. Vaccines wouldn't help them. They needed a cure. So far, nothing much had proved safe and effective against the virus. There had been a few miracle drugs mentioned in the media, but none had survived the scrutiny of medical testing.

He supposed that if a wonder drug appeared that cured the disease, it could eventually solve the entire problem. The statistics showed that only a tiny percentage of people who became infected had to be hospitalized, and of those, an even smaller percentage died. The fear and tragedy of the virus, of course, was the possibility you could die from it. If there was a drug that would prevent that possibility, the ominous nature of the pandemic would be lessened. Getting sick was one thing. Possibly dying was quite another.

Clarence Clark had suffered mightily during his medical career at the hands of the medical community bureaucracy. He had no confidence, even now, that prejudice, favoritism, and kickbacks would not impede the path to approval of a new drug. It was entirely possible that a truly effective wonder drug might be forthcoming, only to be quashed by the staid and unbending US medical power brokers. A major billion-dollar pharmaceutical giant with inexhaustible resources and money at its disposal would have a far greater chance of getting a drug approved than a small research company. It was possible, in his view, that a very effective, potentially life-saving drug might never be tested.

Sure, he was bitter. He felt he had a right to be. "Waitress, hurry with my refill!"

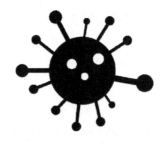

CHAPTER 26

Anyone who looks back at their high school yearbook, twenty or thirty years later, will inevitably notice a few classmates who were so anonymous and unexceptional that it's hard to remember much about them. They were the quiet ones who never acted up or said much of anything. They didn't sit way in the back or even up front. They just sort of blended into plain sight. Strangely enough, even though they were virtually unnoticed back then, many of those kids were late bloomers. They secured fine careers as lawyers, teachers, successful business executives, and even doctors. Clarence Clark was one of those kids.

His parents came to the Crystal Lake area of Texas during the space boom. Both were engineers for NASA contractors. Those had been exciting days in south Texas when the first space shots began and culminated with a man walking on the moon. They married and had a pleasant life until, at one of the many splash-down parties, after too much booze, Clarence's father fell for another woman. Their son was only ten years old when his parents divorced. It devastated him. As an only child, the already introverted youngster withdrew even further into his shell. Clarence's parents had shared custody, which turned out to be a constant shuffling back and forth, as if neither really wanted him.

As a result, he retreated into a world of computers and video games, with hardly any friends or social life. Clarence Clark, however, possessed a brilliant intellect and graduated third in his high school class. Though it was a painful experience, he gave a brief speech at graduation, which both parents were too busy to attend. At the urging of guidance counselors, he applied and was immediately accepted to the University of Houston.

One day during his first semester at UH, he was sitting on campus under an oak tree near the student union. He was between classes during the lunch break and was nibbling on a micro green sandwich with his nose in a computer theory textbook. He looked up for a moment and noticed a young lady sitting on the other end of his bench. He was about to go back to his reading when he saw she was crying. No big deal, but when he tried to open his book, her sniffles continued to distract him.

Judging by her backpack, she was obviously a student. Her legs were crossed under a flowered print dress that exposed the very top of her knee. She wore white running shoes and barely visible tennis socks. For reasons he couldn't explain, her suntanned bare leg, from her knee to socks, grabbed his attention. She was anything but trim and lithe, although most of her body was hidden by the red button-down sweater she was wearing. In fact, she was a chunky young lady.

Her long straight brown hair extended down on either side of her face and was punctuated by glasses with thick black frames. He noticed her full cheeks and flushed complexion as she dabbed her hazel eyes with an overused Kleenex. Her current state of anguish notwithstanding, she had a wholesome look about her, although she wasn't the type to catch much attention from male students.

Clarence was reserved and introverted, but an untapped pool of empathy lurked within him. "Hey, are you okay? Whatever it is, it couldn't be all that bad. Maybe you got a C in English?"

She looked over at him. "Sorry. I didn't mean to ruin your lunch. I'll move," she said, already gathering her things and standing up.

An odd feeling washed over Clarence. For some strange reason, he didn't want her to leave. "Oh. No. No. You're no bother. I just noticed that you are upset, and I feel bad for you. Please stay."

She eased back down. "Okay. I just got some bad news, and I'm trying to deal with it. I'm not normally like this. Honest." She really needed a soft shoulder at that very moment. Maybe this skinny geek, who also wore glasses with thick black frames, could provide one.

Clarence sensed she wanted to talk, so he asked straightaway. "Well, why are you so sad?"

He was a complete stranger who she'd likely never see again. There was little downside to letting it all come tumbling out. "It's my mom. She has cancer. I just found out it's inoperable. I'm so upset. My dad is gone. I'm an only child, and Mama is all I have."

"That's terrible. I am so sorry, but you probably don't have all the facts yet. I'll bet there is much more to her story. You can't give up now. Surely, your mom hasn't."

She looked at him with pleading eyes. "Thanks. You're right, I'm sure about that. She needs me to be strong now more than ever," she said, reaching out to take his hand. Little did she know, he'd never held a girl's hand before.

And so began his relationship with Carol Jenkins. It would be the only romance Clarence Clark ever had. Soon, they were dating, which continued through their junior year when they got married. Both were unabashedly convinced they were in love and shared many common interests. From all appearances, it was the perfect match. Clarence had been correct about Carol's mother. She lived another two full years, although her life was a never-ending stream of tests, doctors' visits, and treatments. It was her plight that got him interested in medicine, and with the firm support of Carol, he applied for and was accepted at the Central Texas University Medical School branch in Galveston. For the first time in his life, Clarence Clark had a purpose and direction, along with a partner, to share it all. What could ever go wrong?

The first few years of their marriage were filled with stress and difficulties. Clarence was a full-time student, and they had to rely on Carol's modest salary as an elementary school teacher. They had a tiny one-bedroom apartment near the island's Strand district. Somehow, they never took those romantic moonlit walks on the beach that they envisioned back in undergraduate school. Money was always tight. Also, it was the first time those two only children had to share space with another person. The change was especially hard for Clarence, but as newlyweds, they both expected there would be bumps along the road.

Always brilliant in academics, Clarence had little trouble with the rigorous curriculum at the medical school and was consistently ranked at the top of his class. Unfortunately, he continued to rail against authority and being told what to do by the administrative systems and procedures. He just didn't work well with others. He had many petty run-ins with fellow students and instructors. In one case, the dean reprimanded him in a dispute over lab time. He breezed through the state licensing examination but couldn't find an acceptable hospital for his residency. Apparently, word of his social problems had gotten around.

His best (and only alternative) turned out to be the military, which, in retrospect, was a very unlikely place for him. He entered the Army and was given the rank of captain. His first and only duty station was the giant base at Fort Hood in central Texas. They promptly assigned him to the new induction unit, where he supervised enlistment physicals for new recruits by the hundreds. He hated his job and the Army, but understood he had to stick it out for three years to meet his residency requirements. The couple found Army life more appealing than medical school. They had free quarters on the base, and after just a few months at Fort Hood, Carol became pregnant. Clarence accepted the news with grim resignation. He acted thrilled when daughter Amy was born, but privately wondered if they could afford a family.

The methods of doing things in the Army were based upon rote, repetition, and patterns, which was precisely the type of situation he detested, but Captain Clark stayed out of trouble and pulled through, receiving marginal fitness reports from his senior officers. As soon as his residency was complete and his obligated time was up, he immediately left the Army and headed back to Houston.

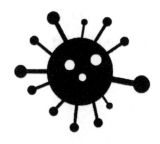

CHAPTER 27

Dr. Clarence Clark wasn't naïve but was disappointed when the expected fruits of being a physician failed to accumulate before him. He was fully licensed to practice medicine in the state of Texas but had no specialty or experience other than general medicine. Many inquiries to small doctor practices and local hospitals produced no employment opportunities. He had no wherewithal or desire to set up his own practice. The cost of malpractice insurance alone was very high. He ended up joining a non-profit group, which provided care to the less fortunate and poor in a clinic in the barrio on the east side of the city. After a few months, it surprised him he rather enjoyed the work, which exposed him to a wide variety of diseases and health issues. There was little structure to the job and no one in particular to stand over him and criticize. He also felt satisfied to be doing well for the first time. He was actually needed by someone.

Ten years had passed since Carol Jenkins and Clarence Clark were married. The mutual discomfort they'd attributed to early marriage adjustment never disappeared, as they had hoped it would. Carol and Amy were very close, but Clarence, much like his parents before him, seemed to have little interest in his daughter. He noticed her only when she threw a childish tantrum, usually by ordering Carol to shut her up. He spent most of his free time at home on the Internet or reading. While their home life wasn't one of constant fights and bickering, it had become two individuals living under the same roof but having little else in common.

When he left the Army, Clarence had been optimistic that eventually he would reap the high-paying benefits of being a doctor. In anticipation of that situation, he purchased a gracious home in a toney Houston subdivision for a price they couldn't afford. It was one of the few aggressive personal moves he had ever dared make. Sadly, his salary at the clinic was closer to a greeter at Walmart than a flashy doctor. They struggled to keep up the payments and were soon behind. Carol loved the place and had become friendly with their neighbors. The bank eventually posted the home for foreclosure, and they had to move back into a two-bedroom apartment. Carol was crushed. Clarence seethed about the hit to his credit report and the unfairness of banking bureaucracy. As had been the case most of his life, the government and big bureaucracy were out to get him.

If a loveless home and money problems weren't enough to crater their marriage, one last event occurred to send it careening into the ditch. At the clinic, Dr. Clark saw a never-ending stream of patients who couldn't afford to seek treatment elsewhere. He encountered maladies ranging from very trivial skinned knees to life-threatening heart problems. The clinic followed sound medical systems and procedures but lacked the equipment or resources to perform much other than basic tests. His caseload was extremely high. There simply wasn't enough time to devote to patients, as would have been the case in a wealthier practice.

Mostly, he did his job competently, yet he was typically abrupt and businesslike. He didn't have the time or inclination to chat with the folks that came in. On a scale of one to ten, his bedside manner might have earned a two. In his view, the job was to give out accurate medical treatment advice and not entertainment. He saw most of his patients once or twice. They were cured, or he referred them to practices that could accommodate their specific needs. It was almost as if he worked on an assembly line in an auto plant. The arrangement was fine with him.

After about a year at the clinic, one exceptionally busy day, a heavy-set woman in her mid-thirties came into his examining room. She didn't appear to be in obvious discomfort, although she had a slightly elevated temperature. She clearly wasn't pleased to be there and complained about everything, including Dr. Clark's appearance. He was prematurely balding, with the only hair left on his shiny head was around his ears and the back, giving him. something of a Clarabelle Clown look. He and the woman immediately disliked each other. He couldn't wait to get her out of his office, and she couldn't wait to see a real doctor. The reason for her visit was she had been vomiting heavily for several days. She was grossly overweight, and he was eager to be rid of her. He prescribed antacids and sent her on her way.

In many practices that aren't short-staffed like his clinic, the normal procedure is for a nurse or assistant to take a patient's vital signs before he or she sees the doctor. Sometimes that was the case at the clinic, but in most cases, he actually took them himself. With this obnoxious woman, for whatever reason, he failed to take her blood pressure, which was extremely high that day. Perhaps in his haste to get rid of her, he simply forgot to take it. The very next day, she had a stroke and was left completely disabled. Of course, to make matters worse, she was the sister-in-law of the mayor of Houston. When it came to light that the woman had seen Dr. Clark just one day before her stroke and he hadn't taken her blood pressure, they immediately filed a malpractice lawsuit against the clinic and Dr. Clark. While there was malpractice insurance in place to protect against financial ruin, Dr. Clark's license wasn't automatically covered. He had made a grave error, and he was certain that miserable woman, who knew people in the right places, would do everything she could to take away his right to practice. They reported him to the State Medical Review Board. Serious sanctions or even license revocation were genuine possibilities.

He was immediately suspended, pending resolution of his case, which meant he couldn't work at the clinic. Carol was distraught when she heard the news. They could hardly scrape together enough to get by when he was working. He'd been laid off with no income and would be around the house all day long. She recognized that their marriage had been a joke for some time. This problem was the final straw. Clarence accepted the decision that she and Amy leave, as if he'd been expecting it. They moved out within a week. He expected a divorce petition almost any day. With no family and no means to support himself, there was tremendous irony that when the pandemic exploded to the detriment of the entire world, he benefited. He actually found work because of it.

He jiggled the ice cubes around in his glass as he thought about his consistently bad luck. Clearly, a good part of it was because of the suffocating governmental system, which repeatedly did him in. He knew he couldn't beat it, but there must be a way around it. So many other doctors were doing well. Heck, he had scored better grades than most of them in med school. What was the problem?

Then it hit him. It was simple. He was a pauper. Rich people held everything worthwhile in the United States. He needed a big hit to set him right. It wouldn't happen by looking at little brats' tonsils in an indigent clinic. He needed a big hit. How could he get one and soon?

CHAPTER 28

Marshall had a long talk with his mom the next morning about the horrible situation at the Falling Oaks old folks' home. She tried her best to console him with little success. She explained that nursing homes were being hit especially hard by the virus. People who lived in them were elderly and often had other major illnesses to contend with. They ate and lived in very confined spaces. All of which made elderly homes prime targets for the virus. A large percentage of the deaths because of COVID were in nursing homes. It was very sad the community where his veteran friends lived had been so severely affected.

His mother sipped her morning tea as they sat at their kitchen table. Marshall was loading up on pancakes. Sally could tell he was upset because he limited his consumption to only two helpings. She had no appetite herself and barely nibbled at the piece of toast she'd fixed for herself.

Marshall looked over at her. She looked unusually haggard that morning. Sally was a morning person who was used to rising early and being off to work before 8:00 a.m. Of course, now with the pandemic, she was working from home with no reason to dress up or even put her makeup on. It was unusual that it was almost 9:00 a.m., and she was still in her nightclothes and bathrobe.

"Mom, are you all right? You don't look so good. Are you feeling okay?"

She brushed him off. "Sure. I feel fine. I didn't sleep well last night. I never do this time of year without air conditioning, but it's still humid. I'm fine."

"Are you sure?"

"Marshall, for heaven's sake. I happen to be a nurse. I even took my temperature when I woke up. 98.4, for your information. It's low. I'm tired, but otherwise fine."

"I hope so. Last night, I could hear you coughing in your room."

"Maybe once or twice, and I certainly know why. Every year, the fires in the forests of central America create smoke, which drifts up here and pollutes our air. I saw it on the news last night. That's happening right now."

She's just like a little kid with an excuse for everything. Where does she get it from?

"I hope you're right. I brought that stuff home with me and exposed you to it. I would feel horrible if I gave it to you.

"Hey, son. That's enough. I'm not sick, and even if I were, there is zero chance I caught it from you." Quick subject change. "As bad as things are with the vets, maybe it's a blessing of sorts if it convinces you to take this disease seriously."

"That it does. I promised the major about that. I wired your orders and his advice into my brain."

"I hope so. Now, just to help you in that regard, I spent a little time sewing and have come up with three masks for you to wear at all times outside of the house." She went into the other room and returned, holding three pieces of cloth in her hands. "Here you are," she said, handing them to him.

He held up the first one, which was fuzzy and blue. It had a big dark half-pie-shaped mouth, bulging white eyes and black pupils floating in different directions. "Cookie Monster, of course?" She nodded. The second one. "Bozo, the clown." She smiled. And the third. "I'm not sure? Some teacher? Oh, I know, Fred Rogers. Mr. Rogers. Thanks." She giggled. "There you are. Wear whichever one suits your mood, but wear them!"

"Yes, ma'am." He said, getting up, grabbing them, and giving her a peck on the cheek. He stopped and fumbled with Cookie Monster, eventually getting it on his face. He issued a fake hunger growl. Cookie it would be. "I'm off, Mom. See you later." He was out the door.

Marshall had planned to spend the morning looking for anything he might do to earn a few bucks before he went back to CTU. The rumor was that classes would start in about a week. About the only place that needed help just then was the drive-through COVID testing facility that was set up in the high school parking lot. Anyone, after making an appointment, who thought they might have the virus, could drive over there and get their car in line. There were healthcare workers who would administer the test right from your car. Volunteers were needed. But there was no pay. He'd do that as a last resort.

Mallory told him there was a planned kids' rally in Winston Park at noon. She was going, so he agreed to meet her there. The national and local news had passed the word to avoid large gatherings, which were prime places to transmit the virus. Unfortunately, in a country founded on personal freedom, there were certain folks who viewed common sense virus restrictions as an unfair infringement of their freedom.

Masks were a prime example, which these people simply refused to wear. Most of the scientific evidence showed that masks offered little protection from the virus. When these statistics were coupled with the fact that the virus was in its worst and most virulent form almost only affected old people, there seemed little reason for young people to wear the stuffy, smelly things. A few Justice High students assumed that when the schools reopened, masks would be mandatory. The rally in the park was to drive up sentiment against such a mandate.

With school out and not much else to do, there were several hundred kids milling around in the park. Many wore masks, but most of them did not. This gathering was typical of what in the future they would call a "super-spreading" event. A "super spreader" was a gathering where there are many attendees who ignore social distancing and certain people who have the virus infect many of the attendees. Marshall spotted Mallory, who loved his Cookie Monster mask. He wanted to grab her hand, but was strong enough to resist. He knew she'd probably slap it away, anyway. The organizers of the rally set up on the small amphitheater, which was used to put on plays and small summer concerts. A couple of band members had shown up with their instruments.

Marshall recognized Mitchell Matz, who had been a year behind him at Justice High. Mitchell had a reputation as a non-conformist and druggie. He'd never been seen anywhere without his jeans, leather jacket, and boots. His unkempt hair was as long as he could get away with and stay in school. He rode his Harley everywhere. Having been made to conform against his will, Mitchell saw this situation as a chance to rise against the school administration, which he hated. He stood on the stage with a bullhorn in his hand.

"My brothers! My sisters! Students!" he screamed. "It's time to stand up for yourselves. It's time to quash the rumors they are spreading about this so-called disease. It only affects the old and already sick. Not us young people. The experts and scientists have proven beyond a doubt that masks do not protect you. I repeat. Masks do not protect you. Proven by scientists. When our schools reopen, everyone will have to wear them. Can you believe that? How many eighty-year-olds are in the tenth grade? We must band together against this abuse of our sacred personal liberties."

Marshall watched this display with increasing agitation. This guy was an idiot. He was lying to the kids standing there, many of whom probably didn't know the facts. The crowd seemed to watch Matz's display with interest, but it was impossible to tell if any were buying what he was selling.

"Are you with me?" he screamed to the apathetic audience. Ignoring their lack of response, he tried another tactic. He reached into his pocket and took out a paper mask, which he held out in front of him. "Here, kids. Watch this," he said as he took his cigarette lighter and torched the mask in front of everyone. "There. That's what we need to do to this symbol of communism being thrust upon us. Are you all with me?"

There were scattered cheers from the crowd. And then a few masks were tossed on the stage next to him as he clapped his hands and beat time to the music.

Mallory was so entranced by Matz's antics, she didn't even notice that Marshall was no longer standing next to her. And then her mouth dropped open as she saw Cookie Monster up there on stage, walking toward the greasy biker. The crowd also noticed. There were a few cheers and some clapping. Some may have recognized Marshall or maybe thought it was just a part of the planned show.

Matz turned as Marshall reached him. He executed a perfect fake flinch, as if he were afraid of him. He seized the moment before Marshall could speak. "What do we have here?" he screamed. "Cookie? Cookie? I forgot to mention something else folks, but my Sesame simpleton here makes the point better than I ever could. See just how stupid anyone looks wearing that piece of cloth? Do you all want to look dorky like this guy?" A huge laugh came up from the crowd.

Now Marshall wasn't just irritated; he was blistering mad. After his promises to his mom and the major, and what had happened at Falling Oaks, he couldn't stand by and let that ass carry on any longer. He ripped the bull horn away from Matz and tossed it off the stage.

"Look, kids, he began. This jerk is full of crap. He doesn't know what he's talking about. This virus is dangerous for everyone. We have to work together to defeat it." Then, with his voice cracking, he said,

"I just lost three of my best friends in the world. They died alone and couldn't even have decent funerals." He looked down, unable to continue.

In his anguish and concern to deliver his message, Marshall failed to notice that Mitchell Matz and his band members had disappeared from the stage when he started talking. As the crowd was rapidly thinning, he also didn't notice the two blue-uniformed Justice police officers who came up behind him on the stage. When Matz planned the rally, he never bothered to get a permit from the town.

One officer looked at Marshall and said, "Okay, pal. That's enough. Come with us. I think we have a cookie for you down at the station."

CHAPTER 29

The Shiner oil and gas empire included considerable business activity in Venezuela, which had some of the richest oil and gas deposits in the Western Hemisphere. In recent years, political relations between the United States and that country had declined significantly. President Hugo Chavez and his successor were authoritarian dictators who chose not to live with the business agreements already in place with US energy companies. Until the recent problems, Shiner Oil had been active in Venezuela for many years. In fact, just after graduation from Southern Methodist University in Dallas, Randy Shiner had been sent by his uncle to Caracas, Venezuela, to learn about the oil business. It also got the young, lazy nephew out from underfoot.

Randy spent five years there and learned very little about the oil business. Despite their authoritarian government, however, the Venezuelans were a happy and fun-loving people. He rented a gorgeous penthouse in an exclusive neighborhood, very close to the entertainment district. He frequented the bars and restaurants and almost never made it out to the rugged mountains where Shiner Oil drilled for oil. He had several local girlfriends and soon gained the reputation of a rich American party boy with plenty of money to spend.

One of his closest friends during that period was Yordan Valdez, who was a graduate student at a local university. Yordan loved to party with Randy, but was also very interested in the country's political activity. He felt that the leaders of his country were being taken advantage of by greedy Americans, just like his good friend Randolph Shiner. As the years passed by, Yordan's position in Venezuela politics rose to where he was appointed the head of the country's administration of culture. His primary job was to erase the perception of his country in the world as a glorified dictatorship that oppressed the population and recast it as one of education and understanding. It was an impossible job, but Yordan worked hard to elevate his country's image despite the constant tyrannical actions of the leaders in power.

The COVID pandemic hit Venezuela especially hard. Corruption, mismanagement, and the failure of programs of the dictatorship led to widespread poverty and severe economic crises for what had at one time been a prosperous country. They were completely unprepared to deal with the disease. There was almost no testing available. Food production was low and malnutrition rampant. Hourly wage rates were pitiful, and inflation was extremely high.

Among the hardest-hit groups were the healthcare workers. Doctors and nurses were leaving the country in droves, even before the pandemic hit. Those that were left had to work in unsanitary conditions without proper protection. Huge numbers of those critical workers came down with the virus. Gloves, face masks, and even disinfectants were in short supply. Few hospitals even had safe potable water.

The country needed help—and soon. Unfortunately, the regime in power failed to recognize the gravity of the situation. They resisted and pushed away international groups that wanted to help. They blatantly seized the assets of former partners like Shiner Oil and deported the executives that had run them. As a result, the United States put economic sanctions in place against the country, which only worsened conditions. Things were getting desperate.

Though it had been several years since Randy had left Caracas and returned to Texas, Yordan made it a point to keep in touch with his former running mate. With the relations between Washington and Venezuelan leaders at an all-time low, finding wealthy American friends was difficult. Yordan had been savvy enough to keep his connection open to Randy. They had even met a few times for brief holidays and a bit of fun on Saint Kitts and Nevis in the Western Bahamas.

It didn't surprise Randy one morning when he received an email from his old friend suggesting that they meet again soon. Randy was delighted with the idea and promptly replied that he would check his schedule in the weeks ahead to find a convenient block of days. It surprised him when Yordan came right back to him with dates and reservations made at the Saint Kitts Marriott Resort for the very next week. He checked his schedule and decided he could rearrange his haircut appointment, and his mother would have to make her annual presentation to her garden club without his presence. He knew better than to contact Uncle Stanford, who was still seething over

Venezuela's, robbing them of their oil and gas assets and booting them out of their country. He wouldn't have looked fondly on his nephew's drunken playboy holiday with a senior official from that rotten country.

CHAPTER 30

Randy Shiner eased back and let the warm after-dinner cognac slide slowly down his throat. He returned the smile of the gracious flight attendant in the first-class cabin of United Airlines Flight 202. It was a six-hour trip from Houston to Basseterre, the capital of Saint Kitts and Nevis. After debating the matter for a day or two, he decided to rough it a bit and fly commercially to the island beach paradise. Normally, he would have used one of Shiner Oil's several planes, but Uncle San might get wind of that. He didn't want to have to explain things to the old boy.

The email from Yordan suggesting they get together had come at an excellent time, although the short notice was a little surprising. He had been seeing a pole dancer from a local club. The conniving woman realized what she potentially had in him and was coming on strong. He was glad to get away for a while to relax in the sun and the surf without another care in the world. He deserved a break from any serious business. He was in for a surprise.

After taking a cab to the Marriott, he checked into his suite and found that his pal, Yordan, had already arrived and left a voicemail to meet him at the bar. After changing into shorts, a T-shirt, and sandals, he headed out to join his friend. He hadn't felt more relaxed in weeks. When he saw Yordan waving to him from the far corner of the room, he did a double take. He hadn't seen the Venezuelan since he had taken an official position with the current ruling administration, which must have been about seven or eight years ago. Yordan always seemed to be serious and focused, but he had a fun side that quickly emerged after a few drinks. He was almost unrecognizable with a full bushy black Fidel Castro-like beard.

"Mi Amigo!" Randy said as he walked up and gave the man a Texas-style hug.

"Greetings, Randy. You look well and prosperous." He ogled Randy's arm. "That isn't a wedding ring I saw there on your hand, was it?"

"Are you kidding me? No way," he said as his eyes swept the sun-drenched swimming pool where dozens of bikini-clad women lay.

Yordan smiled. You had to love Americans. Here, his stupid country had stolen billions of dollars from Shiner Oil and thrown them out of the country. Actions you'd think would incense the man. Instead, all he wanted to do was drink and chase women. They spent the next hour catching up. Randy did almost all the boasting and talking. After a while, he realized Yordan had been listening, but not adding much. He knew things were tough in his country, but beyond that obvious backdrop, he sensed that something else had his friend preoccupied. Finally, he stopped bragging. "So, how bad is it down there, Yordan?"

"Not good. Not good at all, my friend. Even before the pandemic, our country was hurting from a very weak economy. Inflation was skyrocketing. Wages were low, and there was a shortage of everything. Even basic food stocks were unavailable. Our people were suffering, and then the virus hit."

Randy was sad to hear this news. He enjoyed his time in Caracas and felt warmly toward the Venezuelan people. He knew, of course, that a major reason for the problems was the attitude and actions of the regime in power. They had kicked out all westerners and seized their assets. Beyond that, they continued to badmouth the United States at every opportunity. They even refused to accept international humanitarian aid. They brought much of those horrible conditions upon themselves. Yordan was very much aware of these things, and it would do no good to point them out to him.

"And on top of all this," Yordan continued, "a worldwide pandemic blows in. Our country was completely unprepared for it. We have virtually no ability to test for it. Our hospitals are marginal, to begin with. Equipment shortages are everywhere. To make matters even worse, our best doctors and nurses fled the country when things started getting bad a few years ago. The infection rates and cases are mushrooming. No one believes that the virus figures issued by the government are anywhere near accurate. They are way understated for political purposes. I just don't see a solution to all these problems for many years to come."

Randy reached out and gently patted his friend's shoulder to console him. "I'm so sorry to hear all this. Despite the politics and what happened to my uncle's company, I love Venezuela and the people. Can you appeal to the international community for help?"

A half-smile flashed on Yordan's face. "Of course, that's the obvious answer. Unfortunately, our wise leaders have done their best to alienate most of the free world. They rejected the US in favor of Cuba and China. Both countries have their own problems, and, although they make promises, very little has been forthcoming from them. We're the big neighborhood bully who's been hit by a car and is now lying in the street bleeding. Everyone remembers what we did, and no one is eager to help."

"Yes, I get it and am truly sorry, but look, here we are in a wonderful playground. A few days away from it all is just what you need. You need to kick back and relax. You've been working too hard. Recharge your batteries, and you'll be more effective when you go back." He stopped for a second as a shapely lady in a tiny leopard-skin bikini walked past them, obviously to catch their attention. Her tactic worked, as both men followed her every step. "See, there you are." Randy continued. "We're here to have some fun. Let's do it. And one more thing. There'll be no argument from you. This trip is on me, Shiner Oil. You pay for nothing. I can't imagine your salary from the government leaves you much left over for hell raising. Okay?"

Yordan remained expressionless throughout Randy's pep talk and monologue. There were clearly other things on his mind besides fun in the sun. Finally, he replied, "Yeah, sure, but there *is* someone I want you to meet. Please join us for dinner at the restaurant in an hour." Without another word, he got up and left.

Randy sat back on his barstool, ordered another drink, and scratched his head. *What's up with that guy? He always wanted to be an outspoken revolutionary leader of the people, but that stuff usually disappeared after a couple of tequilas. I suppose he's just depressed by the enormity of what he deals with daily. I can't imagine what it would be like to live in those conditions. He will be chasing senoritas by tomorrow morning. I hope.*

I have to admit, it surprised me when I heard he took the job as head of the ministry of culture with the regime in power. I didn't think he wanted anything to do with that group and was opposed to many of their ridiculous and shortsighted policies. Maybe he's put together a group to overthrow them? Wouldn't that be something? I might even get Uncle Stan to kick in on that one.

Oh! I think I figured it out. He's obviously brought a lady with him using a holiday with me as an excuse. It has to be that. That rascal. That shouldn't be a problem. Those Venezuelans. They think they have to be so prim and proper around us Yankees with such high morals. That devil. I wonder if she's a blond or brunette? I'll find out shortly.

Rarely had Randy Shiner been so wrong.

CHAPTER 31

At first, Randy couldn't find Yordan and his secret lady as he looked around the resort's restaurant. He had played mind games trying to guess what his friend's babe would look like. He had settled on a dark, slinky, and mysterious woman with a firebrand personality. There was no one there who looked anything like that. Then he spied Yordan tucked away in a corner. He had chosen that table for privacy, which Randy thought was going a little too far. What was the chance anyone he knew would catch them in a remote resort in the West Indies?

He headed across the room. When he almost reached the table, he could see Yordan's friend more clearly. There was a man sitting next to him. Unless Yordan had really changed, his call on a secret paramour was way off. Well, maybe he wasn't wrong after all? As Randy approached the table, both men rose to greet him. They shook hands and sat down with Randy to Yordan's left, across from the man.

"Randy," Yordan began, "I would like you to meet Dr. Nacho Vita. Dr. Vita is the head of the Venezuelan Institute for Scientific Research. His background is in medical research, particularly regarding viruses and bacterial infections. He's studied all over the world and has authored numerous articles in prestigious medical journals."

The doctor blinked twice and smiled at this introduction.

During the first few minutes he sat there, Randy couldn't help being fascinated by Yordan's companion. Who the heck was this joker? He didn't give off the vibe of being a fun addition to their planned good times. The doctor was rail-thin, with a gaunt face and powdery white skin. Randy guessed the man spent many more hours peering through a microscope than basking on the beach. Both his tiny pointed goatee and the thin line of his mustache were dark gray. He wore rimless wire frames that seemed to defy gravity perched upon a prominent but narrow nose. Deep drooping brown eyes peered through the lenses. Waves of bushy gray hair covered his head and hung down his back in unkempt strands. He wore a maroon dress shirt with a flat floppy collar. He displayed no personal jewelry of any kind, except for a gold imitation Rolex watch he felt compelled to check constantly. Randy looked at Yordan for an explanation.

"As we have discussed for a variety of reasons, our country is facing an economic and health crisis of huge proportions. That said, Venezuela has always been resourceful and able to substitute hard work, creativity, and determination for what we lack in capital and an abundance of resources as compared with other countries. A prime example of this situation is the very pandemic that we have been discussing. While we desperately need health care professionals, equipment, ICU space, and many other items, our research group under Dr. Vita has achieved some very noteworthy results."

Yordan stopped, and Dr. Nacho smiled.

Randy was finding this entire episode more and more bizarre. He tried hard not to roll his eyes. *I suppose he's going to tell me this Dr. Strangelove has found a cure for COVID!*

Yordan continued. "In fact, Randy, Dr. Vita and his team working feverishly at their facility in the Andes mountains have developed a serum, which limited tests have confirmed cures the virus in an overwhelming majority of cases."

Randy's mouth dropped open. All he could say was, "Come on."

Yordan looked to his left. "Dr. Vita."

"It is so," the bushy-haired man began in heavily accented English. "Despite the problems we have in our country, we have always believed in medical research, which is the primary function of my organization, the Venezuelan Institute for Scientific Research. It may interest you to know that when the virus hit, our team had already spent years studying similar diseases such as the bird flu, for example. We had a head start. So, when El Presidente ordered us to find a cure and vaccine, we were already hard at work."

Randy listened attentively. It was interesting, but he still wasn't sure where the conversation was headed. *So, El Presidente ordered them to find a cure. Hmm? I wonder what would have happened to them if they had failed?*

"*Vennizator*, Senior Shiner. Vennizator is the name of the drug we have developed with care and exactitude to combat this horrible virus. It is based upon an extract from jalapeno peppers, which, combined in certain ratios with other medical components, aggressively attacks the virus particles that attach to an infected patient's lungs. The results we have received to date are astounding from a medical and scientific perspective. They are, of course, quite limited compared to the long and arduous testing procedure that any new drug must pass in the United States to be approved by the Centers for Disease Control. Your procedures are admirable and thorough, but I'm afraid we just don't have the luxury of time. Our people are dying in increasing numbers daily."

Randy played along. "You say this miracle drug Venna-something is effective. Just how effective, doctor?"

"Let me correct one thing right away. I did not refer to Vennizator as a miracle drug. It is a highly effective drug that can save millions of lives worldwide. So far, in our country, we have administrated it to over 200 patients infected with the virus. In that group, many were elderly and otherwise ill, but people from every age group have benefited. In over 160 of those 200 cases, substantial improvement was recorded, with most completely recovering. That is over 80%, a truly astonishing number. El Presidente was extremely pleased, as we knew he would be."

Randy didn't know if the numbers they were flinging at him were good or not. Jalapenos? He *was* sure that, whatever the initial results, they were preliminary and would never meet US standards. In fact, Dr. Nacho had admitted that. "I am pleased to hear about your success after all the bad news that surrounds Venezuela these days. I'm surprised that El Presidente isn't out bragging about Vennizator to the world. You could use the favorable publicity."

Yordan, who had been watching Randy's reaction closely during Dr. Vita's presentation, broke in. "In fact, he has. He has publicly announced the drug to our people and internationally. He announced it as a miracle medication that neutralizes the effects of the virus with no side effects. Unfortunately, his remarks were immediately rebuffed by the biased international medical community, who said there was no substantiation for the ridiculous claim. Our country has established such an evil reputation in some parts of the world that such a reaction was not unexpected. It really is too bad. The potential for this drug is unlimited."

"Well, honestly, I can understand some folks being upset with the current regime. Heck, they only stole a couple of billion from my uncle's company. Why would anyone believe him?"

The doctor looked like he had checked out of things, but Yordan nodded in agreement.

"I am happy to hear there is some hope to combat the virus, but why are you telling me this? I'm here for fun and sun and to get *away* from solving the world's problems."

"Of course, Randy, but that can wait a bit. We have a favor to ask of you. A big one."

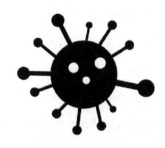

CHAPTER 32

The Justice police officers who broke up the unauthorized gathering in the park recognized Marshall right away. He had gained notoriety during the Battle for Sam Jacinto in the park a few months ago. A motley band of old vets and high school kids had fought off a group of thugs who tried to steal the statue of that war hero. Once the crowd had dispersed, they tapped elbows with Marshall's and headed off. They had no intent to bring him to the police station.

Mallory, of course, was relieved. For a few minutes, she was sure her boyfriend was destined for the JPD to be fingerprinted and booked. Marshall had calmed down considerably but still was concerned about Matz and his rallying the kids to ignore the serious implications of the pandemic.

"While you were standing there in the crowd, Mal, did you get the impression most of the kids were agreeing with the crap he was dishing out?", he asked.

"I don't think so. I'm guessing that most of them showed up here because school is out and there is nothing else to do. Music, too, will always attract a crowd—especially kids. Everyone knows Michell Matz is a pothead. I can't believe many would take him seriously."

"That's comforting, and I agree with you. The problem is that when you're young, you assume you're bulletproof. Also, people are being asked to do things that can be uncomfortable and inconvenient. Wearing a mask is a pain, although I've gotten attached to my Cookie Monster mask." Mallory chuckled. "I wonder if the kids will adhere to six-foot gaps for social distancing and not partying. Somehow, I just don't see those fun night beach parties in Galveston ending just because some goofy-looking doctor on TV says it's a good idea. Unless these kids get hit hard by the virus, I'm afraid they won't change much of their behavior at all."

"You're probably right. What they fail to realize or maybe even care about is that by not wearing masks or taking precautions, they still can transmit the disease to others and not even know it," she said.

"That would really tear me up. It's one thing to catch the stuff because you're not careful. It's ten times worse to give it to a family member, friend, or loved one. Just look at how it spread like wildfire through Falling Oaks. My good friends were wiped out in a few weeks. I pray that the major stays healthy," he said.

They had been walking together through residential neighborhoods toward Mallory's house. It was an unusually pleasant September day, with low humidity and temperatures in the mid-seventies. In that part of Texas, September unquestionably belonged to summer, but there was a definite hint of fall in the air. They stopped in front of Mallory's house. They looked into each other's eyes through their masks. As much as Marshall wanted to hug his tiny friend and hold her tight, he simply forced himself not to do so. He'd had the virus. Who knows? He might still be a carrier.

"I've gotten to know you well over this summer, Mr. Cookie," she began. "I know you sometimes operate in ways that no one, even yourself, can understand. But please realize that this pandemic mess is bigger than all of us. Don't try to control other kids' attitudes and actions all by yourself. They'll do what they want to do. If you see someone in a store without a mask, please don't go up to them and read the riot act. You're a good person, but you're not the community moral police officer. As concerned as you are about everything, people will do what they want. Please tell me you will try to behave."

He stared down at her and realized why she was so special to him. She understood him better than anyone. He swallowed. "Sure. I know you're right. I will do my best. I realize I can't impose my values on everyone, which is too ad because I'm always right." They both chuckled, but their eyes remained locked and hearts intertwined. There was no telling what might have happened, even right there in front of Mallory's house in broad daylight, if not for the pandemic.

A voice. "Hey, Marshall, I know something you don't."

Oh, no. Could it be? Of course. Never one to miss a chance to wiggle in on her big sister's privacy. Paula stood on the front steps where she had a front-row seat for their intimate exchange. Talk about a mood breaker.

Marshall turned. "Okay, I'll bite. What do you know this time?"

"Only that on the news they just announced that CTU would begin classes in two weeks. There will be all kinds of social distancing guidelines in place that they haven't even worked out yet. Also, despite the cancellation of football in other big conferences, the Elite 11 will play at least a partial schedule this fall. So, ta-ta, Marshall. I guess it's back to Austin for you."

Of course, this was big news. He would immediately call Graham to see what he had heard. He squeezed Mallory's hand, waved to the little urchin, and started hoofing toward home. As he walked, he talked to Graham and confirmed the news. The coaches wanted the team back on campus by next Monday. They agreed to drive back to school together on Sunday, which was only two days away.

He walked into the kitchen and found his mom sitting at the table, stirring a cup of hot tea. He immediately told her about college reopening and the resumption of football practice. She smiled and said that was a good thing. She also mentioned that there was some mail for him on the dining room table. He then launched into a ten-minute monologue about Mitchell Matz and the rally. He conveniently forgot to mention the cops breaking it up. She listened attentively, sipping her tea. When he finally unwound from the day's events, he stopped for a second. This moment was always when his mother would say, "I'll bet you're hungry," before proceeding to get up, grab a pick and shovel and fix his lunch, but this time she didn't move.

"Son, I'm sure, as always, you're famished, but today I just don't have the energy to get up. Would you mind finding something for yourself just this once?"

Marshall was shocked. Never, ever, had his mom refused to feed him. Something must be wrong. He looked more closely at her and immediately saw it. She looked terrible. Her skin was pale. Her eyes were swollen and red. She wore no makeup and was still dressed in her housecoat at 1:00 p.m. His mother never acted like that, even when she planned to work at home all day.

"Mom, what's wrong?" he pleaded. He touched her brow. She was warm. As a nurse, she should have been the first to recognize the onset of the COVID symptoms. Perhaps she just assumed that as a medical professional, something would somehow spare her. Now, though, she knew she had the virus.

"I'm sorry, Marshall, but it looks like I have the darn stuff. I've been suspicious for the past few days but wasn't sure. It shouldn't be any big deal. As we know, in most cases, the symptoms are light. With a few days' rest, I should be fine."

Marshall was beside himself. His mom. His precious mom was now sick. "No way, mom. Let's call your doctor and see what he recommends."

Sally called their general practitioner and did her best to play down her situation. As a nurse, though, she had recorded her oxygen readings. When she related them, the doctor immediately ordered her to go to the hospital—with zero additional debate. End of discussion. Do it. He was about to send an EMS, but she assured him her son could get her there just as quickly. As soon as she hung up, Marshall had her out the door and into her car. He was as nervous as he had ever been during the fifteen-minute drive to the hospital.

On the hospital grounds, he followed the signs to the Emergency Room, but when he drove up, a uniformed man asked if he had a COVID case. He was directed to another entrance around the corner. As he approached, several people completely protected in hazmat scrubs came out with a gurney. They helped his mom out of the car and onto the gurney. He got out to help, but an orderly stopped him and told him to leave the area. He didn't even have time to say goodbye or tell her how much he loved her. She disappeared inside without him knowing if he'd ever see her again.

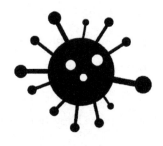

CHAPTER 33

Marshall was devastated. He pulled into the first available parking space and dashed back to the Emergency Room reception area. The person on duty there was of little help. COVID patients were subject to procedures that varied from the norm. She suggested he contact his mother's doctor. The answering service politely took his message, but the doctor was unavailable. Marshall didn't know what to do, but he definitely wasn't going to just sit in a waiting room. He headed for Mallory's house.

The tears were streaming down his face when she let him in. Her mother and guess who came into their living room where he sat holding Mallory's hand and struggling to control his emotions. None of them could ever remember seeing him really upset—never mind crying his eyes out.

"I just don't know what to do. My mom. We have always been so close. I've never had a father, brother, or sister. I don't even know who my father was. It was always just Mom and me. We took a big chance moving to Texas from New York City, but we made it. When I first went to school, I felt so out of place and different. *You all speak a language different from up there.* Mom told me not to worry. I even talked to her about dating you, Mal. She told me to go for it. We're so close; I can't even think about losing her. What would I do?"

"Hold on there, Marshall," Barbara Jollen said. "You're getting way ahead of yourself. Just because her doctor wanted to be extra careful and put her in the hospital doesn't mean the end of the world. Likely, he is just being cautious, which is a good thing. In the hospital, they can watch her carefully and make sure she doesn't get worse. Most folks who are hospitalized make it just fine and are back home in a few days. Have you heard from her doctor?"

"No, my call went to voicemail."

"I'm sure he's very busy at this moment."

"Maybe, but not knowing anything makes it ten times worse. I drove her to the hospital and was directed to a special entrance. They took her away and just about shoved me back in my car. I couldn't even say goodbye. There's no one to talk to. No one seems to know anything."

"The virus is so contagious; they have to be very careful to isolate infected people soon and completely. The hospital staff must be overwhelmed. As unfortunate as it might be, it's most important that they care for the patients first. Advising loved ones becomes secondary."

"I suppose, but I feel so bad." He said, barely able to control his whimpering. "I'm sure she caught the virus from me. I gave it to my mom. I brought it back from Austin. She was around me, taking care of me. That has to be what happened. I wasn't even sick, and now she's in the hospital. It's not fair. I'm to blame. If only I could trade places with her."

"Stop blaming yourself." Mrs. Jollen said. "It's not your fault. She could have caught it anywhere, especially working as a nurse. You can't look at it that way."

Marshall wasn't convinced, but before he could react, his cell phone buzzed, and he fumbled to dig it out of his pocket. His eyes bulged as he read the screen. "Mom!"

He pressed the button to answer. "Mom! Are you okay? Where are you? Please tell me you're okay. Please?"

Though she was surely quite ill, Sally Morris knew her first job was to settle her son down. She expected he'd be distraught and upset, so she summoned all of her strength. "Yes. Yes. I'm doing okay. Sorry they had to rush me away as they did, but they just have to do it that way right now. I'm lying in a bed in a two-person room. It's not the ICU—just a regular room. They're giving me fluids with an IV. I'm as comfortable as I can be at the moment. The doctor just left. He wants to watch me closely for the next few days to make sure my case doesn't worsen; then, maybe I can come home."

"I guess that's good, Mom. Now that I think about it, I'm happy you are where they can care for you if you need it. When I dropped you off, it was so abrupt, it scared me to death. When can I come to see you? How about right now?"

"No, that's a problem. COVID patients can't have visitors. There's just too much risk of spreading the disease. The best we can do is talk on the phone. Where are you right now?"

"At Mallory's with her, her mother, and sister."

"Please give them my regards."

"They told me to tell you they are praying for you, Mom."

Her voice cracked. "Please thank them for me. It would probably be a good thing if you didn't stay there too long. No sense taking chances."

"Okay, I'll leave right away. I love you, mom."

"And I love you, Marshall."

Now there wasn't a dry eye among the four of them. Marshall thanked them all and left.

As soon as he got back in the car, his phone rang again. It was Graham.

"I heard about your mom. That's tough. I'm sure she'll be fine in a few days."

"I hope you're right. There's no way I am going back to school with my mom in the hospital. So, I won't be with you on Sunday."

"I would have been surprised otherwise. I don't know all the rules and stuff about football, but I read something about opting out. Even if the team players and individual players can opt out for this season. You might look into that."

Marshall thanked his friend for the information, but football was the last thing on his mind at that moment.

CHAPTER 34

The perpetually buoyant Marshall Morris plunged into a funk unlike he had ever experienced. He was totally lost without his mother and couldn't get over the fact that he was probably responsible for her illness. The ultimate sign of his concern was his enormous appetite declining to where he only needed food four or five times a day instead of seven or eight. Since no one from the outside was permitted anywhere near the COVID ward at the hospital, he couldn't even visit her. He did, however, talk to her several times a day on the phone. She sounded okay, but he knew she would put up a good front even if she felt terrible. Her doctor was so busy, he was of little use. All three Jollens understood his predicament and did their best to assist and comfort him.

Marshall talked to coach Crown at CTU, who was sympathetic to his situation. The coach suggested Marshall opt out of playing for the current season, which already looked like it would be shortened and restricted. Even under normal circumstances without a pandemic, he might have been red-shirted, anyway. If that happened, he wouldn't have played either. The coach said he would pray for his mother and advised him not to worry about football. There were more important things in life. Marshall also postponed his enrollment in classes to at least the next semester.

Having settled those issues, Marshall found himself with time on his hands. He wasn't someone who could just sit around and stare into a video screen. He needed to find a job, not only to keep himself busy, but also to earn some money. On the first morning, his mom was in the hospital; after a bowl of cereal (or two), he fired up the OC and drove around town with no particular destination in mind. He was still totally preoccupied, worried, and missing his mom. He turned down a residential street in one of the nicer parts of Justice and noticed an SUV pulled over in front of a home that had a Welcome Home Realty "For Sale" sign in front of it. As he drove by, he saw that the grass in front of the house was very high and hadn't been cut for weeks. In fact, the SUV had a "Welcome Home" sign on the side, and there was a man inside talking on his phone.

Marshall abruptly pulled over. There's a job right there. Surely that real estate agent couldn't expect to sell that property with grass a foot high. Marshall had spent many hours behind a power mower. He jumped out and walked over to the SUV.

He heard the loud voice of the man inside. "I don't care about having to go to Mexico! You were supposed to take care of this place. It's a mess. How am I going to sell a house that looks so bad? Hello? Jose? Jose?" The other party had hung up, and it startled him when he saw Cookie Monster staring him in the face.

"Good morning, sir," Marshall began. "Do you know who owns this house?"

"Why? Do you want to buy it?"

"No, but the yard sure is a mess. I'd be interested in cutting the grass and cleaning it up."

"You would? Maybe this will be my lucky day after all. My name is Tommy Kinder. I own Welcome Home Realty. I have the listing of this house. With the pandemic, I can't find buyers or anyone who will work."

"Well, I'm Marshall Morris. I've already had the virus, so I'm supposed to be bulletproof. I need to work."

Tommy looked over at the tall Cookie Monster character standing before him. There wasn't much he could tell about the kid, but he was in a spot. "Fine. Fifty bucks, if you'll do it today. There is a mower over at my office on Main St. Meet me there in a half-hour." Marshall flashed a thumbs up and so began a relationship that would take several strange twists and turns before it was over.

It took Marshall most of the morning to cut, edge, and clean up the grass in front of the house, which looked 100% better when he was through. He drove back to Welcome Home Realty's office to return the mower and collect his money. At first, he thought the place was closed. The lights weren't on, and the place was dark, although the SUV was parked out front. As he walked in, he heard Mr. Kinder on the phone.

"Yes, yes, I know, baby. That table will go just perfectly with the other furniture, and you got it on sale at a hundred dollars off. That's great, but I'm sitting here looking at your Macy's bill for over two thousand dollars. The pandemic has killed my business. How am I supposed to pay for that?"

Marshall walked further into the office so that Mr. Kinder could see him through a glass partition. He was holding his phone several inches from his ear. Occasionally he would say "Uh, huh" or "I understand, Mitzi" to someone chatting a blue streak on the other end. He saw Marshall standing there and signaled for him to wait. After another five minutes, he finally hung up and motioned Marshall to come in and have a seat in front of his desk.

"You're young. I hope you've never been married. Plenty of girlfriends, though, I expect?"

Marshall had come there to collect fifty bucks, not seek advice from the lovelorn. That was hardly the question he'd expected. "Yes, a few. I've had a few girlfriends," he replied.

"A word of advice, son. Be very careful. All the romance and stuff can be great, but there's a lot more to it." He held up his phone. "That woman can blow through money like an alligator after a water rat. My business is down, and she expects me to cover all her charge card bills. Here I am at the office, and she's on the way to get her hair done for the third time this week. Sorry, you didn't come here to hear about my problems. Did you cut the grass out there?"

"Yes, sir, and I edged and pulled a few weeds. It looks much better."

"Well, thanks. I appreciate your effort. As you can see," he said, pointing to his dark office, "I'm very short-staffed at the moment. Say, I just had a thought. What's your background, Matthew?"

"Marshall. It's Marshall, Mr. Kinder. I just graduated from Justice High and was about to start at CTU when the pandemic hit. They delayed everything, and I put off my studies until after the holidays." He saw no reason to go into his mom's situation with this man.

"And you say you already had the virus?"

"Yes, sir. I think I caught it in Austin at CTU, where I tested positive. I came home and quarantined. My symptoms were non-existent. I was tested a week ago, and everything was negative, so I guess I'm okay."

"You know anything about real estate?"

"Honestly, sir. Not much, but I'll learn. I have lived in Justice most of my life and feel like I know the town pretty well. I delivered pizzas for a while. You get to know your way around in that business."

Kinder sat there staring at Marshall, who had removed his mask when he entered the building and saw no one else was around. Finally, he spoke. "Okay, here's what I'm thinking. As you saw this morning, we hadn't cut the grass at that house for some time. Business is hard enough without offering an inferior product to the buying public. My regular maintenance crews have disappeared, and my office staff is gone. When you list a house for sale, you need to present it the best way possible. I need to keep the grass cut, make sure we keep the insides looking sharp, and unlock the properties before each showing. Nothing that takes a lot of experience—just the ability to follow instructions and common sense. How does that sound to you?"

"I can surely do all of those things, Mr. Kinder."

"Here's the other thing. I hate having my office here dark. Even in the pandemic, I need to let my customers know I'm open for business. I need someone to come in here every day and open up. Then sit here and answer phones. Greet anyone who stops in."

Marshall looked a lot more uncertain. "Well, I could do all that, but I really couldn't help much on selling the homes."

"Look. you're obviously a bright kid, but I don't want you selling homes, which is illegal until you have a real estate license. I'll be here most of the time and instantly available by phone. You just refer everything to me. I think you could do it." The super salesperson was obviously turning into his closing pitch.

"Well, I guess so. I've never had an office job before."

"No problem. Then we have a deal. Great. Fifteen bucks per hour. 10:00 a.m. to 6:00 p.m. Start tomorrow morning."

Marshall felt somehow railroaded, but the deal seemed perfect for him. He smiled and said, "Sure," although he was careful not to shake Tommy's hand. Tommy glanced down at his phone and was about to dial when he noticed Marshall hadn't left yet and was still sitting there. He was about to ask him to leave when he realized why the kid hadn't moved. "Oh, yeah. Sorry, it almost slipped my mind. Here you go," he said, digging into his wallet and handing Marshall two twenties, which was all the cash he had on him. Marshall took the cash but did not move. "That's right, it was fifty, wasn't it? Hang on a sec." Tommy got up and walked out of his office into the open bull pen. He walked toward the back to the coffeepot, next to which he found a jar of loose change put there by his salespeople when they took a cup. He dug into it and scrounged ten more dollars with nine ones and four quarters. He handed the crumpled wad to Marshall and with a big smile said "See you tomorrow."

Marshall was pleased about the morning. He'd worked, earned fifty dollars, been paid, and found a new job. That Mr. Kinder was a strange dude, though.

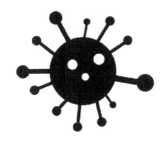

CHAPTER 35

Marshall was thinking he'd heard Mr. Kinder wrong when he showed up the next morning at 9:45 and by 10:30, no one else had arrived. He was about to leave when the Welcome Home Realty SUV whizzed into the parking lot. Mr. Kinder got out and apologized to Marshall—something about taking Mitzi's chihuahua to the vet. They went inside and spent the next hour going over the office and how to use the phone. After he'd oriented Marshall, he gave him a key and made sure he had his personal cell number.

"Okay, Matthew. Oops. Sorry, I mean Marshall. It'll take a few days to get comfortable, but that should give you an idea about our office setup. Now, here's the thing, and don't take this the wrong way, but all I want from you is basic caretaking help. I don't expect you to understand or *try* to understand this business. I want you to open the office in the morning and close it in the evening. You will answer the phone and you will tell the caller I'm not here and jot down a message. Listen to me. Unless I tell you otherwise, you will tell the callers I'm unavailable, even if I'm sitting in my office. I will check with you every so often to see who has called, and I'll decide who to call back. When I'm not here, I will call in every so often for messages. Your job is to play dumb. Got it?"

This man was full of surprises, but in the past, Marshall had often successfully played dumb. "Yes, sir. I can handle that."

"Good. Now, there will also be times when I need you to go out to a house we have listed for some specific reason. Maybe to check on something. All of our listings have lock boxes which contain house keys attached to the front door. Other brokers have master keys that access those boxes. It lets them in for showings without bothering us. Sometimes, though, we need to meet someone on the property. When we do, we don't walk through with them. We stay outside. Remember, all questions are referred to me. I'm only a cell call away. Okay? Questions?"

"No. I don't think so." Tommy nodded and disappeared into his office, where he immediately got on his phone.

Marshall took a seat behind what had been the receptionist's desk. He was a little nervous being right up front in a business on Main St. He was the first thing you saw when you walked into the office. Almost immediately, the phone rang. Marshall panicked. *Should I answer it? Oh, yeah, that's what I'm supposed to do.* He grabbed the handset and put it to his ear. He froze for a second, but then "Cow Paddy Pizza" came tumbling out of his mouth.

"Cow what? Sorry, I dialed the wrong number." *Click.*

Marshall's face was redder than the pies he used to deliver. The phone rang again. The caller obviously had redialed. This time, he got it right. "Welcome Home Realty" he correctly announced.

"Well, that's better. Give me Tommy Kinder," the caller demanded.

"One moment, please. I'll put him on," Marshall replied with a smile on his face. *This job won't be difficult at all.* He tried to remember how to transfer the call to Mr. Kinder's office when he stopped short. Whoops. He was supposed to tell everyone that he was unavailable, even if he was sitting right there. Now he had a choice, bother the boss with his screw-up or go back to the caller and lie to him. He chose the second.

"I'm sorry, sir, but Mr. Kinder is unavailable."

"Is that so? He's obviously right there in his office, not taking calls. You tell that bozo he needs to contact Anna Snodgrass at Kinkos Office Supply immediately about his bill, which is sixty days past due. He has the number. And bozo junior, it's Ms. Snodgrass not sir!" *Click.* Mercifully, she was gone. And so, Marshall's first office job was off to a rousing start.

At 11:30, Tommy got up from his office and stopped by Marshall's desk on his way out the door. He picked up the pink telephone note Marshall had prepared for Kinko's and tossed it into the trash with barely a glance. "Oh, Matt, Marshall. See that 'For Sale' sign leaning against the wall over there?"

Marshall nodded.

"We just signed a listing agreement on 202 Seamist Lane. I need you to take it over there and plant it in the front yard where it's best visible from the street. You can do it on your half-hour lunch break. I'm off to lunch myself. See you this afternoon." And with that, he disappeared out the door.

That man was something else, but Marshall was seeing how hard it would be to run a business alone. He waited until noon and fielded a few more phone calls, most of which were ads and robocalls. Then, he grabbed the metal sign and tossed it into the OC. He knew exactly where Seamist was. He found the house. No one seemed to be home. He had a little trouble pounding it into the ground, but found a chunk of concrete to use as a hammer. He didn't bend the sign too much. He stepped back and admired his work. Not too bad. *It was 302 Seamist, right?*

Although he suspected Mr. Kinder's lunch would last a while, it was his first day. He didn't want to be late getting back. He had just enough time to run by Mallory's house, where there were three sandwiches waiting for him to gobble down. When he called his mom, she wanted to hear about his new job. She mentioned she was feeling better and was going to ask the doctor when she could come home. Marshall was encouraged, but she still didn't sound like her old self. He was back at the Welcome Home Realty front desk slightly after 1:00 p.m.

He was still new on the job, but he could already see that there were going to be long periods of boredom. The phone rang little, and when it did, it was folks trying to sell something. There were a few more creditors looking for Tommy Kinder. They would back off when they realized Marshall was truly a temp who didn't know where the boss was. In fact, although Tommy had promised to return that afternoon, he never did.

Marshall was getting itchy around 5:00 p.m. He still had an hour to go and was famished. He figured he might make it to 6:00 p.m. He answered the phone and heard a man's voice. He was sure this time. "Is this Welcome Home Realty?" the voice asked.

"Yes, sir. It is."

"I am the owner of 302 Seamist."

Aha. Marshall recognized the address. He hoped the man didn't have technical questions about the listing agreement.

"What in the hell is that for sale sign doing in my front yard? Is that supposed to be some kind of joke? We have lived here for thirty years and expect to be here for another thirty. All the neighbors are calling us. My kids are crying. They think we're moving. What kind of business are you running there? I pulled the sign out of the ground and wrenched my back. You get that thing off my property within the hour, or I'm calling the cops. Am I clear?"

"Very clear, sir. I'm sorry for the confusion. The sign will be gone shortly. This sort of—" Marshall tried to make an excuse for the mistake, but the guy had hung up.

As he locked up the office and headed out to the OC, he thought, *You know, I think Tommy said 202 Seamist.*

CHAPTER 36

If Tommy heard anything about Marshall's sign gaffe, he never mentioned it the next morning. He seemed pleased to see Marshall sitting there with the office open and the lights on when he arrived. He took the six messages Marshall had written the day before and walked toward his office. He stopped and turned to Marshall.

"Make a note. I still want you to tell everyone who calls that I'm not available and will call them back—except for one person. Randy Shiner. Chances are Mr. Shiner will always call me on my cell, but he might try the business number. If he calls, immediately interrupt me, and I will take his call."

"Randy Shiner, as in Shiner Oil and Gas?"

"Yes, that Randy Shiner."

Marshall went about his business fielding maybe three or four calls an hour. He was tired of being just another pretty face and was about to ask Tommy for something else to do when a man called and said he was very interested in one of their listed homes but couldn't get in. Marshall broke the "not available" rule and put the man on hold. He got up and went into Tommy's office. Tommy looked up from a travel brochure he was studying and asked what he wanted.

"There is a man on the phone who says he is very interested in 106 Mayberry but can't get in to see it."

"106 Mayberry. I know it's on lockbox. There should be a key in the box?"

Marshall shrugged his shoulders.

"I suppose it could be an independent broker who isn't on multi-list and doesn't have the lockbox master. Or, better yet, a real buyer without a broker, which means we could get a full commission. That house has been on the market too long, anyway. Why don't you get out there and let him in?"

"Okay, Mr. Kinder. I'm on it."

Marshall was happy to get out of the office and made it out to Mayberry Place in less than a half-hour. 106 Mayberry was in one of the nicer subdivisions in Justice with big lots and plentiful greenery featuring many mature trees. Although the house wasn't occupied, the owners hadn't yet moved out and all their furniture and belongings were still inside. A seasoned real estate professional would have found it unusual that the two "buyers" were casually dressed young men in their thirties who drove a ten-year-old pickup truck.

Marshall noticed nothing unusual about them. He had a master key to the lockbox on the front door. He opened the box and used the key inside to open the front door. He smiled as he held the door open for the two gentlemen, who promptly filed in. As instructed, he waited patiently outside for them to make their inspection. They took only a few minutes.

He was eager to get their impressions of the place, but had been coached to keep quiet. For once, he did. He asked them for business cards, which they didn't have. He wrote the names and phone numbers they gave him, but it didn't seem like there had been a love connection with the property. Everyone's time had been wasted. After they left, he made a brief walk through the house and turned off any lights that had been left on. He replaced the house key in the lockbox and snapped it shut. He never noticed that a first-floor window in the master bedroom had been unlocked. By the time he got back to the office, Tommy had disappeared.

***

Hiring the college kid to run interference for him was definitively a good move, but the pressure on Tommy Kinder was reaching the point of becoming unbearable. His business was in the ditch, he was deep in debt, and the hellcat he had hooked up with was making everything even worse. The woman had no appreciation for his problems. All she knew how to do was spend and spend and spend and spend. He found more and more that he had to unwind with a few drinks before he headed home.

After sending the kid out to let the buyers in, he left his office and drove to the Mucky Duck, one of his usual watering holes. It was on the Crystal River side of the freeway, and the likelihood of one of his clients seeing him getting buzzed was less than if he stayed in Justice. The bar was fairly crowded for a weekday afternoon, and as he looked around, he noticed Dr. Clarence Clark drowning his sorrows at a table near the back of the room. He had done a little business with the man in the past and considered him to be a bit of a whacko. With not a lot of other choices, he walked over and sat down next to the doctor, who brightened when he saw him.

"Mr. Kinder, long time no see. What have you been up to lately? Have you been social distancing like a good boy? I'll bet it's fun selling houses over the phone."

"It's a bitch. No one is doing anything right now until they see how bad it's going to get. What do you think? You're still a doctor, aren't you?"

Clarence Walker took a big swig of his drink before he answered. "Yes, I am, for the moment. In fact, COVID has actually been good for me. I run the drug program at the hospital in the COVID ward. I get a regular paycheck. It doesn't come near covering my child support and other expenses, but it's better than nothing. Say, how did the boob job turn out?"

Tommy scowled, "Freaking horrible."

"No kidding. Did they screw it up?"

"No, in fact, she loves them. She thinks they're perfect and can't wait to show them off to whoever is around. And they are pretty impressive."

"So, what's the problem?"

"The cost. Fifty grand didn't seem too bad when I was closing twenty houses a month. But now it's dropped to three, and I can't afford to feed her dog, let alone pay for new knockers."

"I hope you don't blame me. I hooked you up with a guy I knew from med school. I had nothing to do with the price. The surgery went well, and I am happy about it.

"No, I don't blame you. It's my own stupid fault for thinking the good times would never end. How long do you think this COVID thing will last?"

"No idea. With this screwed-up government, we may never get out of it. I've busted my butt for a long time and have zip to show for it. At least you've climbed the mountains, so to speak." They both laughed.

"You asked what I think. I think they're looking at this virus from the wrong angle. Yes, we desperately need a vaccine, but what we really need is a cure. If we had a cure, no one would be that worried about catching it. If a pill or medicine cured you, all the fear of dying would go away. When a vaccine is developed, we then have to inoculate some three hundred million people. How's that for a goal? Show me a cure. That's the way to go."

"So, how do we make some money in the meantime?" Tommy asked? "Doctors are broke. Brokers are broke. What does that leave?"

"I don't know, but if I could manage one big payday from somewhere, I'd be out of here for good."

"I'm with you, doc. Hey, waitress, how about a double?"

CHAPTER 37

Marshall found it hard to stay home very much. Without his mom around, the place was cold and empty. He also missed Graham, who had gone back to CTU. They did chat on the phone almost every day. The practices now included full pads and thumping heads. Unlike Graham, who liked that part of football, Marshall was happy to miss it. Graham hadn't seen Zack Middleton since he returned and didn't know what his status was. And no, he hadn't been back to that Austin bar.

After he got off work, he had a standing invitation to have dinner with Mrs. Jollen and her two daughters. They sympathized with his situation and prayed that Sally's hospital stay would be a short one. Paula was especially pleased with the arrangement, which enabled her to keep close tabs on her sister's love life. In actuality, Marshall was so concerned about his mom that he had little interest in anything else.

The virus was continuing to rage with scant direction from the government on how to avoid it. Staying at home and avoiding interaction in group gatherings is the best advice for everyone. The Jollens tried to follow that basic rule, except with Paula constantly hovering, Mallory and Marshall just had to get away now and then. The evening following the morning he'd opened the house on Mayberry, he and Mallory escaped the little urchin by going for a ride in the OC. They had no special place to go and certainly did not want to stop anywhere where there were groups of people. As they drove around their pleasant little town, Mallory made an accurate but surprising observation. Even though the microscopic virus bug had radically changed everyone's lives, by driving around aimlessly, they were doing exactly what they would have been doing on a normal night. They both chuckled at the thought. Some things never change.

It had gotten dark, and they'd finished the cones they purchased at the Dairy Queen drive-through. No sit-down restaurants were open, but many were trying to keep alive by offering takeout and window service. Marshall knew he had to take Mallory home before it got too late, but he just hated going home to an empty house. He noticed they were just a few streets over from Mayberry, so he drove over that way to show her their listed house. It was getting late to take her in. He also wasn't sure that would have been appropriate real estate practice.

As they cruised slowly by the attractive, upscale home, Marshall described the inside to her. The owners obviously took great pride in their residence, which was beautifully furnished and decorated. Marshall thought the owner was a NASA engineer who was getting transferred. They had just passed the dark house when Marshall noticed a flash of light in an upper bedroom window. It seemed to disappear, and then there it was again.

"Oh, no." he lamented to Mallory. "You know me. I can't get anything right the first time." She had a good chuckle when he told her about offering the wrong house for sale. That was her boyfriend through and through. "Mr. Kinder was adamant that after opening a house, I go back and check it out to make sure nothing was messed up or lights left on."

"You didn't check this one out after the people left?"

"Yes, I did, but it was during the day. I probably missed the upstairs bedroom. Darn it. It'll just take a second to switch off that light. I'll be right back." he said as he pulled over in front of the adjacent house, got out, and jogged back towards 106 Mayberry.

"Marshall, are you sure?" Mallory yelled after him, but he never heard her.

Marshall rapidly reached the front door and had the lockbox master key ready. In a few seconds, he had the front door key out and was turning it in the lock. As the door swung open, he got the surprise of his life. There in the dark, just a few feet from him, stood two shadowy figures with ski masks covering their heads. One held a white pillowcase, and the other held a crystal vase. From their dark silhouettes, Marshall recognized the pair from that afternoon. They weren't buyers. They were burglars casing the joint. And he'd helped them!

All the emotions of the past several days gushed to the surface. Marshall should have turned and called the police, but he wasn't thinking like a rational person at that very moment. These crooks incensed him. The man saw red. He took the matter personally. He had worked out long and hard getting ready to play football that fall. He might as well use his muscles for something.

In fact, he never heard the closer man say, "We have a gun!" as he barreled forward and knocked him backward into his pal, so they all went down in a heap. He grabbed the man's ski mask and ripped it off. That accomplished, he pummeled him with his fists. The guy's nose exploded, and a fountain of blood shot upward. The man, who was hardly a weakling, grabbed Marshall's flailing wrists and tried to roll him off of his body. On any other day, they probably would have been a suitable match for each other, but Marshall's delirium and surprise move had given him the advantage. He was winning the battle but had failed to consider what might happen next. He had no way to hold the robbers other than by battling them.

When the second man saw the fury of Marshalls' attack and the spray of blood, he worked himself out from under the other two and started running for the door. He was ready to leave his partner to deal with the madman. Then, when he realized Marshall was alone and didn't have a weapon, however, he had a quick change of heart. He snagged a decorative wooden Indian figure on a table in the entryway where they were fighting. Marshall continued to get the better of the first thug but hadn't even considered the second man, when he felt a great pain on the top of his head, and the world went black. He crumbled to the stone-paved floor next to his bloodied opponent. The second man had bashed Marshall with the wooden Indian. He then reached down and helped up his woozy, fallen friend. They both turned to rush out the front door and hadn't taken a half-dozen steps before they ran smack into six black gun barrels pointing at them from inches away—weapons wielded by uniformed Justice police officers. They immediately fell to their knees and pleaded, "We're not armed! Please don't shoot!" The police had them restrained in seconds.

Marshall couldn't focus. His head hurt like crazy, but he kept hearing a familiar voice calling his name. Mallory was kneeling next to him, cradling his head in her lap. Gradually, his head cleared. Her face was the most wonderful sight he had ever seen. "Where did you come from?" he asked.

"I've gotten to know you too well, my friend. A flashing light in a darkened empty room in a vacant house was a lot more suspicious to me than you. I followed you to the door and immediately called the police. There have been several robberies in town lately and they think these jokers may be responsible. There's a good chance you broke up a burglary ring."

"Really? I saw those guys in the house and just lost it. I suppose charging them was pretty dumb of me, but I reacted without thinking. So much for social distancing."

An EMT unit showed up at the scene. They examined Marshall, who was up and about. He seemed fine, except for a big knot in his head. When Mallory assured them he would stay at her house overnight and not be alone, they felt it was okay not to take him to the hospital.

The next morning, when Tommy Kinder heard about the incident, he would reprimand Marshall for leaving the house unlocked. Before he could do that, a reporter from the local newspaper walked in. At first, it was Tommy's plan to use Marshall as a scapegoat, but he quickly recognized that his temporary receptionist was hardly the one to blame. In fact, the kid was being regarded as a hero for breaking up a burglary ring. Tommy called the reporter into his office and quickly reversed gears. He extolled the virtues of Marshall Morris and highlighted the swift decisive action taken by Welcome Home Realty. Favorable press for the company or not, the transferred NASA engineer called that morning and revoked the listing agreement on the house.

CHAPTER 38

Randy Shiner was already into his second scotch and water in the first-class cabin of American Airlines Flight 103, which had left St. Kitts-Nevis bound for Houston less than thirty minutes ago. The weekend fun junket with his buddy from Venezuela hadn't turned out as he'd expected. He was planning on a few days on the beach, drinking, and chasing women. Instead, he had been dragged into one of the weirdest business proposals of his life. It was nutty and bizarre. There was no way he should have agreed to it. He should have laughed it off before Yordan really got into it. Had he really agreed to the wild scheme? Yes, he had, or at least to give it his best effort to try.

While he was sorry for the terrible conditions, the pandemic had caused in Venezuela, one of his favorite countries, he was getting bored hearing about it from the two men sitting in the bar. He'd come to play, not to solve the world's problems. When Yordan had suddenly turned to him and told him point-blank that they needed a big favor, he'd blinked, but instantly restored his undivided attention to the man. He thought about the conversation.

"It is unnecessary for me to rehash world politics to point out that on the international stage, despite all its faults and problems, the United States is still regarded as the most stable and reputable nation in the world. Our small, beleaguered country's credibility is much, much less. I'm not interested in debating the reasons behind this situation. I'm merely accepting this state of affairs as fact. The world is inclined to follow America and reject Venezuela. Do you agree?" Yordan asked.

"I suppose so," Randy agreed.

"My esteemed colleague here, Dr. Vita, has described to you the astounding success of his wonder drug, Vennizator, which could save millions of lives. Our test results have been astoundingly encouraging. In a perfect world, we would offer it to the global medical community, and before long, Vennizator would be in mass production by all the largest pharmaceutical companies. In fact, El Presidente has offered it, only to be ridiculed, and the merits of our accomplishment obscured by the unfortunate reputation that we have. Had your president done the same, I'm certain all would quickly embrace the drug. Basically, Mr. Shiner, it's a simple question of the messenger, not the message."

"So, you want our president to go on TV and tell the world how wonderful your drug is? Never going to happen. Come on. Get serious." Randy responded.

"Of course not! Please hear me out. That would be absurd. Based on the relations our two countries have had lately, no one would believe your guy either. But, if we could show Vennizator works and actually saves lives in the United States, the entire world would have to consider seriously the virtues of it. If deathly ill COVID patients in the United States are dramatically saved by our drug, everything will change. Do you agree?"

Randy hesitated. He now had some idea where this ridiculous discussion was headed. "Maybe, but they'd never approve your drug for the US. It takes years of study, testing, reviews, approvals, etc. Forget it."

"Of course, but we must face the facts. We don't have years to wait. Even in your country, the virus is out of control. They're talking about a vaccine. The world needs a cure. We have one! A good one. How can we sit by and let politics kill millions of people?"

"Look, I'm no doctor and honestly have no clue about this stuff. If we assume for a moment that Venizzz—whatever is a miracle cure, and no one believes you guys for whatever reason, how could it ever be used in the US? The approval process—"

"Stop! Hold it right there," Yordan shouted. "That is where you come in, Randy,"

"Huh? Me? How? I'm not in medicine. I don't have contacts in Washington."

"Maybe not, but you have the one magic ingredient that makes America tick: Cash. Money. Dinero. With enough of it, you can do anything in your country. You know I am correct about that."

Randy knew he had a point and didn't respond.

"We believe that using your connections and substantial resources, you can arrange for our miracle drug, Vennizator, to be administered to terminally ill COVID patients in US hospitals. Of course, no one would know beforehand about the drug. We would only disclose it when the miracles happen and patients recover. There would be actual demonstrated proof that our drug works on the globe's biggest stage. The world would take notice. The reputation of our medical researchers would be elevated. They would see us in a new light. Grants and funds for further research would flow back into our country. All because we have shown our drug to work in the United States of America."

"Fine, but what if it fails, and the patient dies?"

"That surely won't happen, but if it did, the patient was going to die anyway without our drug. We only give it to terminally ill patients. There's only the wonderful upside of saving a life. There is no worse alternative."

"So, how would I get this miracle stuff into a hospital?"

"That part is up to you. We can package it and deliver it, so it looks very generic in labeling. As we understand it, drugs are closely monitored by hospitals, although the COVID crisis has made things a lot more crowded, confused, and open for mistakes. It shouldn't be that difficult to get Vennizator ordered and into the inventory of a hospital. Getting it prescribed and administered to a patient is probably going to be the toughest part."

"Okay, Yordan, tell me, why would I ever even consider this wild scheme? As you point out, money is hardly a motivator to me, and I'm hardly a fan of your crooked government."

"True enough, although I am sure you would like to help the Venezuelan people, who are especially suffering under the pandemic. I know it doesn't thrill you with your own government's mass of regulations and red tape. You, Randolph Shiner, can make a difference and save lives—probably millions of them. Frankly, you had the disadvantage of being born rich, which I know can be a difficult thing. You have never been challenged to do something really great."

For the first time, Yordan had struck a sensitive area. For much of his privileged life, Randy had felt useless. He was right. It *would* be wonderful to do something significant.

"Oh, and one more thing," Yordan added.

"What's that?

"As we both know only too well, when El Presidente took over, he nationalized all of our oil and gas. Shiner Oil and Gas was removed from the country."

"Cost us over two billion! Can't believe you would bring that up."

"Silencio! Listen to me closely. El Presidente told me specifically. If you and I can work a deal, he will immediately begin negotiations with your company for reparations or perhaps the recast of a partnership of our oil and gas with Shiner."

Randy just stared at the man. "Are you serious?"

"Absolutely. We need your help in more ways than one, even if we refuse to admit it publicly."

Holy shit!

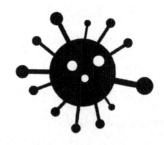

CHAPTER 39

Randy had agreed to Yordan's bizarre proposal but knew that holding up his end was going to be difficult, if not impossible. If he failed, he wasn't all that worried about it. There was little the Venezuelans could do to affect him. If by some strange coincidence he could pull it off, the implications could be enormous. He fantasized about walking into Uncle Sanford's office and telling the old fart that he might recover a few billion his company had lost in South America. He made a list of people he knew in medicine, but it wasn't long or promising. His contacts were all reputable and unlikely to go for a wild deal. To pull it off, he also needed a middleman. He certainly couldn't expose his involvement. The scheme had dire implications if it went off the rails, which was likely.

The arrangement was that a case of the medicine suitable for intravenous injection would be delivered to an address indicated by Shiner. They could store it at room temperature, and it didn't have to stay frozen. The packaging would feature innocuous and irrelevant serial numbers. Rather than dealing with the inevitable hullabaloo that would ensue after they gave the Vennizator to a patient without authority, they decided that Dr. Nacho Vita would call the matter to the attention of the public from Venezuela. He could brag about the drug and its lifesaving qualities. Hopefully, the amazing success of the drug would minimize the potentially severe ramifications of its use within a US hospital without authorization. Those directly involved would have covered their tracks by then. The plan was for two injections: a man and a woman.

***

After Tommy left the car business, he'd had little occasion to run into Randy Shiner. When life got good for Tommy and the houses were selling, he joined the exclusive country club across the freeway in Crystal River, where Randy also had a membership. Tommy was months behind in his dues and on the cusp of being kicked out for non-payment. He was sitting in the men's grill one afternoon when in walks Randy Shiner, who had just played several sets of tennis. Tommy was pleased to see his old, wealthy friend and invited him to have a drink.

"So, how've you been, Tommy?" Randy asked. "I'm getting ready to trade my ride in, but I guess that doesn't involve you anymore?"

Tommy grinned. "Nope, I'm now in the real estate business. Sometimes I wish I'd stayed selling cars. Nobody's buying homes right now, but I guess it's tough all over with this virus. I was just talking to a doctor friend of mine who's on the staff at the hospital. He's down and out, too. Everybody's affected. How about you? Still solving the world's problems?"

"I suppose things are about the same for me. Where I sit, not much changes. An up or down economy worries my uncle, but as long as my allowance hits the bank, I care little. Actually, you mentioned solving the world's problems. I'm not about to do that, but I'm working on a pretty big deal. It's a real longshot, though. Did I hear you say you have a friend who's a doctor at Crystal River Regional?"

"Yeah. I guess he's a friend—more of a business associate. Kind of loser, but friendly enough."

"Is he a GP or surgeon? What's his specialty?"

"I don't even know. He has something to do with monitoring the drugs in the COIVID ward."

Randy couldn't believe what he'd just heard. "Really? I need a doctor. Have you got a half-hour? Let's take a ride."

"I'm not sure you want this guy, but sure. Let's go."

Within five minutes, the two of them were flying down the Gulf Freeway toward Galveston.

"Okay, Tom, before I say anything more, I have to get your assurance that none of this ever leaves this car. There is only a slight chance what I am going to tell you about will ever happen. Still, I need your confidence. There's an excellent opportunity here for you to pocket a good chunk of change."

Tommy raised his eyes. "I hope it doesn't involve robbing a bank. I'd have to think about that. Otherwise, I'm in. Sure, my lips are sealed."

"Good, and that includes my involvement. Nothing can ever lead back to me. The doctor, if he gets involved, must never hear my name. Am I very clear about that?"

"Randy, I sold cars for a living. I can keep my mouth shut."

"Here it is. The pandemic is running wild. The number of new cases is exploding. I don't see Washington doing much about it. They are talking about a vaccine, but we need a cure. It will take years to vaccinate 300 million people."

"Funny you should say that. The doctor told me exactly the same thing."

"Really? I like this guy already. I've run across a drug that's been tested and is almost 100% effective against the virus. Studies have shown that it works for all age groups. It's a true miracle drug."

"No kidding. Then why doesn't the government have it and use it?"

"Politics, red tape, and time. Approval of a new drug takes years, especially if it's a foreign drug, which this one is. I won't tell you where it comes from, but we need a drug now to save lives, and this one can do it."

"So, why do you need me?"

"The maker of the drug wants to get it introduced in the US. He wants to see it actually save lives. When that happens, the powers that be will have to accept it. Our country represents the brightest stage in the world, so it will be secretly given to terminal COVID patients here, who will hopefully recover. Then, the source can be identified."

"Sounds okay, but what if the patients die after taking it?"

"Think about that. It's only given to patients that are going to die, anyway. We'll probably save them, but even if we don't, their fate was already sealed. We're their only chance to beat sure death from the virus."

"I guess that makes sense. So, we have to get a contraband drug into the hospital and into a terminal COVID patient. That's about it. Do you think your friend can help us? Oh, and we need at least two injections—a man and a woman."

"Whew. That's a lot to ask. I don't know. What is his or our incentive?" He held his breath.

Randy didn't hesitate. "$2,000,000 deposited in an offshore account of your choosing. You decide how to split it with the doctor. Half the payment is made when the first drops of the drug enter the first patient's system. The rest when the second injection is made. I need to be quietly be kept in the loop until we make the injection. There must be two injections—one to a man and the other a woman."

Tommy was speechless. He really didn't know what to say.

"Well?"

"It all depends on the doctor, but if he's in, we've got a deal. And we just might save the world along the way."

Randy smiled. He looked in his rearview mirror. He could hear the siren and see the flashing lights. The speedometer only read 105. *Won't those guys ever leave me alone? After all, I'm saving the world here.*

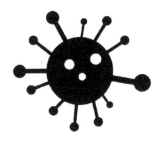

CHAPTER 40

Tommy Kinder didn't believe in miracles. He'd certainly never experienced one in his life. Suddenly, a potential double miracle had appeared out of thin air. The virus could be cured, and all of his financial woes would be eliminated. As he ran over Shiner's proposal in his head, he kept coming back to the same conclusion; it was preposterous and could never work. That poor little rich boy was distracted from reality. He should just forget it and move on. And then he thought of the stack of unpaid bills on his desk—and the credit card monster at home. Two mil! That would solve all of his problems. He'd probably head to the Bahamas, or maybe Costa Rica, and start all over. That thought thrilled him.

Of course, although he was only the middleman who took the stuff from A and gave it to B, his neck would be on the line if the deal imploded. Dr. Strangelove would do the actual work. Maybe the whole idea was ridiculous to even think about. Still, he would never forgive himself if he just let this opportunity pass. What would it hurt to talk to Clarence Clark? At least then, if he blew it off, it would be knowing that the idea was crazy.

Marshall was hard at work with the SUDOKU in the morning newspaper. He brightened when Tommy walked in around 10:00 a.m. "All quiet, Mr. Kinder. No calls. No drop-ins so far."

"Good. I'm expecting a Dr. Clark here at 10:30. When he arrives, get him a cup of coffee, and show him right into my office."

"Will do."

Less than a half-hour later, a gaunt man with thick glasses appeared at the reception desk. He announced he was Clarence Clark and had a 10:30 meeting with Tommy Kinder. He declined Marshall's offer for coffee and followed him into Mr. Kinder's office. Marshall left, shutting the door behind him. Tommy debated bringing the man here, but his office was so dead these days, there was almost no possibility someone would overhear them. Certainly, the kid out front wasn't sharp enough to worry about.

Clarence Clark looked tired and was definitely feeling the effects of an eighteen-hour shift in the COVID ward. He was eager to get home and to bed. Never blessed with the gift of gab, he jumped right into it. "So, Tommy, what is it you have that needs me to lose my beauty sleep after hours of hell at that hospital? At least, if we could have found an open bar, I could be self-medicating while we talk."

Tom looked at the dreadful-looking wretch. Maybe he should forget the whole thing. No, he needed to feel this man out, at least.

"So, Clarence, tell me a little about the COVID ward, ICU, and all. I get the impression it gets a little hectic."

"Not 'at times.' *All* the time. Constantly. It's a madhouse. Fresh cases are arriving more rapidly than we can accept them. We're still guessing about treatment and aren't sure what to do with the critical patients. There aren't enough ventilators. We horribly overwork the staff, but they're doing their best. Still, we're losing patients almost every day. A few months ago, I would have assumed such conditions could never exist in a modern American hospital."

"So, I suppose someone makes a mistake now and then?"

"They can't be avoided. You just hope and pray you aren't the one. Say, what are you getting at? I'm about to collapse from fatigue, mental and physical. I'm in no mood to run down the medical profession. The government? Well, that's a different story."

"Sorry, I respect how hard you all are working and by no means intend to demean you or your cohorts. In fact, maybe I've come across something that could be beneficial to everyone."

"What, like a miracle cure? There are plenty of them out there. We hear about them every day. Come on, Tommy. I'm exhausted. Why don't we resume this thrilling conversation at the Mucky Duck in a few days?" he said and got up.

"Okay, go home and take your nap. In the meantime. I'll find someone else. I thought a big payday might interest you. I guess I was wrong. Bye, now."

The doctor hesitated and then dropped back into his seat. "Payday? What are you talking about? Nobody needs a boatload of cash more than I do."

"First. Before I say anything else, I must have your word. All this is in strict confidence between us. No one else. Your dog included. Can I trust you?"

"Yes, but I don't see what choice you have otherwise. All I can tell you is that I'm extremely motivated by cash. The prospect of it will seal my lips."

The quack was right. He really had no choice. If this guy didn't come through, the deal was dead. If it *lived*, he was a big part of it and would keep his mouth shut. "Okay, here it is. I'm in contact with the source that has developed what is believed to be a cure for the virus. It would serve no purpose for me to disclose details about this source other than to say it is foreign and very substantial. You are better off not knowing details."

Dr. Clark looked like he wanted to interrupt, but held his tongue for the moment.

"I have been told that this group is concerned about their credibility internationally. If success could be shown in the United States, their credibility would be enhanced. I'm in no position to agree or disagree with that judgment."

The doctor jumped in. "So, you want me to inject our patients with this voodoo medicine? That's the most ridiculous thing I have ever heard. I am close to losing my license to practice as it is. That could send me to prison."

"I only know what they have asked me to arrange. I don't know whether it could be done, irrespective of whether someone would do it. That is strictly up to you. Remember, the drug would only be administered to a patient that has no other alternatives and will die, anyway. This drug would truly be a person's last hope. Not giving it to him would mean certain death."

"That sounds weirdly reasonable, but I can tell you that no one ever feels a patient is doomed to die. There is always hope right up to the end. That said, could what you propose actually be done? I'm not sure, but based upon the chaos that exists in our COVID ward? Perhaps. It would take some inside knowledge and proper timing. Still, it would be very difficult and the repercussions, the patient's immediate status before he got the drug notwithstanding, could be severe. That's not something I would want to try. So, forget it."

"I understand completely. I admire your adherence to your principles, considering what the system has done to you. Does it matter at all that this drug just might provide the elusive cure for the virus and ultimately save millions of lives?"

"Come on, Tommy. Get serious. Hardly."

"Well, we both could have used a healthy shot in the arm, so to speak," Tommy said.

"You never mentioned how much this mysterious source will pay?"

"No, I didn't and won't. You just told me it wasn't for you."

There was a silence in the room. Finally, the doctor spoke. "Just suppose I might consider it. Give me a number."

"How about $500,000 wired to an offshore account of your choosing?"

The doctor blinked. That got his attention. Tommy had considered long and hard how much to offer him. Clearly, his own greed had taken over. By acting as the middleman, he would collect three times the amount the man doing all the work would get. But the doctor would never know.

"I know how tired you are, Clarence, and I have lunch plans. Thanks for coming by," Tommy said.

"Cut the crap, Kinder," a brand-new voice responded. "If I were to consider this wacky deal, let me tell you how it would have to work. First, I would have to research this miracle drug on my own. I'm not going to intentionally poison our patients."

"We expected you'd say that. I'll put you in touch with the creator of the drug, who's an esteemed research biologist. You won't get his identity, but you'll be free to ask him anything you want about the drug. It will be an anonymous conversation on the dark web. You can reach your own conclusions."

"If I'm not happy with that, then it's a no-go."

Tommy nodded.

"The drug will have to look as if it was ordered from our hospital from a vendor here in the United States. The packaging must all be in English, and the label shouldn't be conspicuous or colorful. It will be labeled as a muscle relaxer. A supply of the drug will be handed to me outside the hospital. I'll put it into our inventory in our pharmacy, along with thousands of other medications."

"No problem. A company in New Mexico distributes the drug. I'll hand it to you at your call." Tommy said.

"It will then be up to me to have it prescribed and given to two gravely ill virus patients without being able to trace it back to me. My name will be nowhere near it. And then, I'm done. Period. End of story. Right?"

"Except that you will have likely saved two lives and are incredibly better off and wealthier than before. There's one more thing. I need the names of the patients and the dates they get the drug. Verbally. Nothing written."

"Okay. Let me be very clear. I can back out of this deal. I may not like the drug after I study it. Or I might have other reasons. This part is non-negotiable."

"Then you're in?" Tommy asked.

The man across from him looked him straight in the eyes. He never said another word and disappeared from the office.

CHAPTER 41

Marshall watched the peculiar, disheveled man bolt out of Tommy's office. He never said a word as he blew through the reception area and out of the building. Since the man had identified himself as a doctor, Marshall was hoping to speak to him after his meeting with Tommy. Just maybe he worked at the hospital and might know something about his mom. No such luck. The guy was in a rush. A few minutes later, Tommy emerged on his way to lunch. He wore a big smile on his face, and—as if it were necessary—told Marshall not to expect him back until the next morning. Marshall asked him about Dr. Clark, but Tommy had nothing to offer other than that he worked at the hospital.

Although his mother talked a good game, Marshall was increasingly worried about her. She just didn't seem to get any better. In fact, it may have been his imagination, but over the last few days, she seemed more tired and less forthcoming. She'd been there almost a week. In normal times, when someone was ill, you could visit them in their room at the hospital. He couldn't even do that. A blurry, jittery cell phone on Skype was the best he could do. After Tommy left, when he called her cell, it went to voicemail, which was unusual because she was just lying there with nothing else to do. Maybe she was napping or with a doctor? He tried her again later in the afternoon with the same results.

Sitting at dinner that evening at the Jollens' house, he offered little to the conversation. Mrs. Jollen had fixed a few dozen tacos, most of which went untouched. No one had ever seen Marshall Morris without an appetite. He was preoccupied and not his normal self. Paula tried her usual "bugging" to help fix him up. It had become a comedy routine between them. She pestered him, and he ignored her. Both laughed when it was done. Tonight, when she stated, Marshall immediately replied he would think about it and clammed up. No jokes, no fun. Of course, everyone knew why he was so down. All three of them were resolute in their attempts to cheer him up, but as the days dragged on with no change in Sally's condition, their collective worries mounted.

Mallory was clearing the table just before dessert when Marshall's phone buzzed. He glanced at the caller ID and excused himself to take the call. The others were absently stirring their bowls of ice cream when he returned to the room. They'd never seen him look as he did at that moment. His face was ashen, and his lips were quivering. He stood there and spoke. "It was my mom's doctor," he said, swallowing hard. "My mom's not doing well. She's gotten worse. She's now in the ICU. She is on a ventilator and has a tube in her throat. They're doing all they can for her. She is stable for now, but her prospects aren't good. They just don't have a cure yet and are trying anything that might work. I feel so helpless. If only I'd been more careful when I brought the virus home from CTU. Why isn't it me lying there? My mom is so wonderful. I'm just a jerk most of the time. What am I going to do?"

Once again, there wasn't a dry eye among the four of them. If Marshall hadn't been right there with them, Mallory and Paula would have been outright wailing. Mrs. Jollen spoke. "Marshall, that's bad news, but certainly not the end. The virus ebbs and flows in intensity. Ventilators are often used to help folks breathe. It is standard procedure. You need to keep the faith. And stop blaming yourself. You do not know if she caught it from you. She's a nurse who saw sick kids every day. Get the whole notion of guilt out of your head. Let's all just continue to pray for Sally."

Being around the Jollens helped. Marshall's spirits eased a bit, and he felt a little better. He chatted daily with Graham, who was so stiff he could hardly walk from football scrimmaging. The days at Welcome Home Realty were the worst because he had little to do except dwell on his mom's situation. The doctor promised to call him if there was any change in his mother's condition. It was literally in God's hands. Marshall knew there was nothing he could do, but that didn't help his frustration.

Strangely enough, as Marshall's karma took a nosedive, Tommy Kinder was decidedly upbeat. He joked with Marshall every time he passed by, which was something he'd never done before. In fairness, he was oblivious to Marshall's depression, since he never was told about Mrs. Morris' illness. A few days later, a FedEx delivery arrived at the Welcome Home Realty Office, just before Tommy arrived.

Marshall noticed it was addressed to Tommy and came from some company in New Mexico. He set it on Tommy's desk. A half-hour after Tommy arrived, he called Marshall into his office.

"Marshall, do you remember that squirrely doctor who came in here last week?"

Marshall did.

"Good. I want you to take this bag and hand it to him. You are to meet him in the park at the Sam Jacinto monument. I know you can find that." He grinned. "He should be there at 11:00 sharp. Make sure it's him; hand this bag to him; then, get out of there. Got it?"

Marshall's boss sometimes acted in strange ways. He knew better than to ask about this task, which was curious, but no big deal. He took the bag, which was a woven cloth shopping bag with handles from one of the local grocery stores, and walked out. Once he got outside, he glanced down, but could only see that there were several flimsy plastic bags inside the outer bag. He couldn't see what was in them.

He pulled up to the Sam Jacinto monument a few minutes early. No one else was there yet. As he reached across the seat of the OC and grasped the woven bag, it twisted in his hand and a white bottle tumbled out onto his seat. He snatched it quickly before it could roll off, pass through the hole in the floor of the OC, and smash on the pavement below. As he put the bottle back in the plastic bag it had fallen out of, he read the label on the small bottle that looked very much like medicine. It said 'Vennizator: Muscle Relaxer.' It made no sense to him.

Once he had his package back together, he looked up, and there was a car parked right next to him. It was a scowling Doctor Clark, who looked as if he were mad at the world. Marshall got out of his car and ambled over. He hoped to ask him about his mom, but again, the opportunity never presented itself. The doctor rolled down his window, reached out, and wrestled the bag out of Marshall's hands. With a slight nod and no change in his stoic expression, the man backed out and disappeared into traffic. Driving back, Marshall was perplexed. *I thought Tommy was in real estate. Was that a real estate deal? I hope I didn't just do a* drug *deal! Maybe it's time to look for another job?*

When Tommy saw the FedEx package from New Mexico on his desk, he knew immediately it was the Venezuelan miracle drug. The first thing he wanted to do was destroy the FedEx labeling that had his name on it. He threw away the envelope and took the vials out of their packing box. Lacking a better option, he wrapped each of the six doses of Vennizator in a plastic bag and put them all in a woven grocery bag. He felt like no one would suspect anything suspicious about that packaging. He then decided it would be best to have his kid out front meet the doctor instead of doing it himself, where someone just might recognize them together. Everything worked as he planned, except he failed to factor in Marshall's clumsiness.

CHAPTER 42

Clarence's skepticism regarding the scheme to inject Crystal River Hospital COVID patients had dissipated. The man was obsessed with executing the plan to perfection. Although he was motivated by the half-mil to right his financial ship, which was fast taking on water, he was also driven to beat the system that had treated him so poorly. His common sense and objectivity clouded over when he thought about being clever enough to pull this off.

He had spent two hours in a dark web internet chat with the so-called developer of this magical Vennizator. After logging off, he wasn't at all convinced that this concoction, derived from a jalapeno of all things, could cure the virus. If it contained the ingredients, the mystery man described, he didn't see how it would affect COVID patients negatively. It was certainly unlikely to kill them. That thought reassured him somewhat.

Since it was likely that he was going to lose his license to practice medicine anyway, he had little to lose. The financial windfall would open up a new life for him. His actions wouldn't kill anyone, and there was the infinitesimal but possible chance, this stuff just might work. It had become a game to him. He was determined to come out on top for once in his miserable life.

Well aware of the schedules of the pharmacy staff, he had no trouble entering the hospital with the shopping bag during a time when most of the staff were off. After changing into his scrubs and protective gear, he placed the vials of Vennizator all the way back on a rear shelf among dozens of other pain killers where it might not be noticed for months. He kept two vials in his pocket. His next step was to identify the two very sick COVID patients to receive the medication. Although there could be fifteen candidates at any one time, this group was constantly changing as patients improved and others worsened. He also wanted to add that medication to the charts of the two he'd selected so that Vennizator would appear as a prescribed approved medication for that patient, even if not specifically ordered by their doctor. As a practical matter, these poor souls had dozens of medications on their charts, all of which were supposed to be approved by their attending doctors. From his unique position as a pharmacy go-between, he could access those charts. With a minimum of preparation, he was ready for the ultimate step: simply snapping the Vennizator vial into the patient's IV line and hoping for the best.

Under normal conditions, none of what he planned would have been remotely possible, but the enormous volume of patients and resulting confusion lent itself to mistakes, intentional or otherwise. Dr. Clark felt strangely like an executioner as he walked among the dozens of COVID-infected folks scattered about the ward. He decided that if he was going to stick to the very sick and likely terminal criteria, he would select only someone struggling on a ventilator. As a practical matter, most patients who needed a ventilator didn't make it. That was a statement of fact. There were six men and four women to choose from.

After reading their charts, looking them over, and enduring a considerable internal debate, he chose Rodney Wexford, the Air Force veteran and close comrade of Major Lindsay at the Falling Oaks home for the elderly. That poor fellow had been in, out, and then back in the hospital, proving himself a battler. The man was rail thin and in his 80s. He looked as if he might pass at any moment. In fact, even though he continued to receive required attention from the ICU staff, most everyone seemed to have conceded that Mr. Wexford's condition was dire and irreversible. Out of necessity, the short staff's greatest concern was diverted to other cases whose prospects were brighter. Dr. Clark noted that there was less activity around him and the opportunity to slip the Vennizator into his system would be easier.

Dr. Clark had to keep reminding himself that, although he was breaking major practical and ethical guidelines with this unapproved medication, he wasn't euthanizing the people he selected. In fact, the medication should have no noticeable reaction to their health. It might even save their lives.

Still, as the flurry of activity moved away from poor Rodney's bed, the doctor felt a cold sweat break out on his brow. He positioned himself so that any monitoring cameras wouldn't catch his actions. His hand trembled as he reached into his pocket and withdrew the vial, which he almost dropped. He glanced over at Rodney's face. The poor man was struggling mightily to breathe, coughing and wheezing, despite the ventilator's pulsations. He seemed to be in a deep sleep. The doctor, who had performed the insertion of medication into an IV line dozens of times, fumbled with this one. What should have taken a few seconds seemed to take forever. Finally, however, he did. *Snap!* The vial was in line, and the Vennizator streamed into Rodney Wexford's system. The doctor removed the empty vial and was about to step away when he looked over at the patient's face. A chill ran through him when he noticed two big pleading brown eyes staring up at him.

What have you done to me?

The deed done, he stifled his impulse to run from the room and tried to walk slowly away, much as the bank robber didn't want to exceed the speed limit in the getaway car. He noted that with incredible relief that none of the dozens of readouts from the array of monitors around Rodney showed any immediate reaction to the medication. No buzzes, bells, whistles, or sirens. He took a deep breath, put his head down, and headed for the exit. He hadn't taken more than a step or two when he almost bowled over head nurse Carmella.

"Dr. Clark. Slow down. Where are you headed in such a rush? It's already so congested in here already. Please be more careful." Carmella said.

The head nurse. Of all the people he didn't want to meet right now. "Sorry. I just got a message on my phone, and I need to get right on it" He was thankful his mask and plastic face shield hid the red glow on his face.

"Yeah. I know we're all rushing around. Maybe it will slow down soon. Say, I saw you over there by Mr. Wexford, the old vet. I'm sure rooting for him. How do you think he looks?"

"Okay, I guess, but it would be tough to be too optimistic in his case. Now, please excuse me. Got to run,"

He stepped around her. *She watched me with Wexford. I wonder what she saw? That woman misses nothing.*

CHAPTER 43

One down and one to go. As he suspected, it hadn't been that difficult at all. There was so much activity in the COVID ward, it was unavoidable that some of the routine vigilance would become lax. Hopefully, his discrete injection into patient Wexford would go entirely unnoticed, unless the man made a miraculous recovery. In that case, he planned to be long gone from the hospital when the mysterious foreign source crowed about it. Still, he was haunted by the pathetic, pleading look in the man's eyes when he administered the drug.

As a doctor, he was sworn to do everything possible to help a patient. He didn't think he'd done anything to kill the man, but he had certainly taken a selfish action with a critically ill person. He wasn't sure he would ever get over the personal disappointment he felt with himself for his actions. It was probably a good thing that his days as a doctor were soon to end. He simply wasn't fit to care for people. His initial inclination was to head straight to the Mucky Duck to drown himself in alcohol. He decided he didn't want to chance having to talk to anyone that evening, especially Tommy Kinder. After a brief detour to the liquor store, he spent the night alone in his apartment, nursing his woes with a quart of gin.

Clarence Ward dreaded going back to the hospital for his next shift two days later. His guilt hung over him like a cloud and must have been obvious to anyone around him. He entered the pharmacy and tried to busy himself with paperwork to avoid any interaction with staff members. He had no desire to go up to the COVID ward, although he checked the daily list of fatalities and didn't see Rodney Wexford's name. He would have to go up there eventually to administer the second dose. The first eight hours of his shift passed without incident. There was just so much he could do to hide. Everything seemed quiet, so he hesitantly went up to the ward.

As usual, there was frenetic activity everywhere. No one paid any attention to him. He moved hesitantly toward the ICU. A morbid curiosity urged him toward Rodney Wexford's station. He didn't get too close, but could see that the man was still breathing and seemed to look so peaceful. He turned away and then glanced back at him. Was he seeing things correctly? The patient who seemed near death two days ago was now off his ventilator! Could that possibly be? Yes, it was. The dose of Vennizator?

The doctor couldn't believe his eyes but was aware that this confounding disease had peculiar ways of ebbing and flowing within the human body. Could his apparent rally and the secret injection be related? He was standing there contemplating that possibility when nurse Carmella walked up to him. She was the last person he wanted to meet, but he had no choice.

"Hello, Dr. Clark. Did you notice the improvement in our favorite veteran this morning?"

"He's off his ventilator, isn't he?"

"Yes, and we're monitoring him closely. If all goes well and he continues to gain strength, we'll take him out of the ICU tomorrow. He has made a miraculous improvement from two days ago. Was that the last time you saw him? I believe we spoke briefly about him then."

"Yes. I've been off," he replied.

Their conversation was interrupted by an alarm sounding two stations over. An unfortunate man had gone into cardiac arrest.

"Excuse me, doctor. Pray for Mr. Wexford." Carmella said as she ran towards the emergency. It thrilled Clarence to end their conversation. He wanted very much to leave the ward, but he had some unfinished business. There were only two women on ventilators at that moment. Both of their charts showed they were in dire shape and sinking fast. He spent little time trying to decide. The woman he chose was in her forties. He knew nothing about her and decided he much preferred it that way. The helpless, pathetic look Rodney Wexford gave him as their eyes met would live with him forever. He would try to complete the second injection on his next shift two days later.

It was after midnight when he got off and left the hospital. Rodney Wexford had totally consumed his mind. The man had rebounded when it appeared he was about to pass on. Had the injection helped him? In his heart, Clarence was still convinced there was no way a jalapeno-based concoction could be effective against the virus. But maybe, just maybe, it was. At least it relieved him that his action hadn't killed the man. That alone should have eased his guilt, but it did not. His actions embarrassed and disappointed him. They would haunt him for the rest of his life.

He should stop things right now, while no damage seemed to have been done to a patient. Any pent-up cynicism he had for the system had ceased. He was surprised at his reaction when he accessed his offshore bank account and found it had been increased by $250,000 above the twenty-five bucks he'd scraped up to open it. He should have been thrilled and excited. That first half wasn't enough to solve all of his problems and recast his life, but it was a big step in that direction. Receiving the rest after the second injection could truly set him free. He should have been elated, but he remained consumed by his wanton disregard for basic principles of his doctoral oath.

Maybe he should just disappear? No, that would accomplish nothing, only prolonging his already rotten life. Being perfectly rational, shooting up old Rodney hadn't been very difficult. There was no reason the woman would be any different. Rodney seemed to have been unharmed by the shot, or maybe he'd been saved by it. He couldn't clear his conscience by taking back what he'd done to Rodney. After the woman, he would at least have enough cash to be financially independent, so long as they didn't catch him, of course. That was always a possibility, but it was too late now to stew over it. After injecting the woman, he would exit the practice of medicine for the rest of his life.

He remained cloistered in his apartment for the eighteen hours between his shifts, during which he consumed another bottle of gin to strengthen his resolve. He hoped the telltale smell of alcohol wasn't on his breath as he dressed in the staff area for his shift. He placed the vial in his pocket and walked to the pharmacy. He sat at his desk and began some routine busy work to consume a few hours before he went up to the COVID ward at the end of his shift.

He had been there about an hour when he checked the latest list of admissions and fatalities. His targeted woman was still there in the ICU. Then he saw it. Oh, no! Rodney Wexford had passed! Horrible news. The man had been an incredible battler, but the virus had finally won and claimed another victim. It shook Clarence to his very core. The man he had injected died four days later. He tried to rationalize and convince himself that the man was doomed before he ever approached him and his action did nothing to change that, but somehow, he couldn't accept that now. He wanted so much to believe the Vennizator really worked. By doing so, he could almost justify his deceitful action. Clearly, that wasn't an option now. He may have knowingly contributed to the patient's death. That was hard to swallow.

Fortunately, Clarence Ward could avoid close contact with any other staff members until the very end of his shift at midnight. He experienced severe mental agony during that time as he struggled to decide what to do. Several times, he started for the exit but returned to his desk. He was so close to being done. He couldn't erase Rodney Wexford from his mind. It was too late for that. By not doing the woman, it wouldn't alter his guilt over Rodney, who would never go away. His torment was extreme, but he finally decided that he couldn't go on with this madness. There was only one escape. Inject the woman and inject her right now on this shift. If he left the building, he would never come back. Get it over with. Get it over with before she died, anyway.

He patted the vial. It was still there in his pants pocket. He got up to leave, but something nagged at him. Of course, he was supposed to alert Kinder about what was happening. He wasn't sure what his mental state would be after the woman, so he did it right then. No texts, no emails, nothing in writing. Kinder had given him a burner phone to call. He had tossed it into his doctor's bag and forgotten about it. He reached under his desk and dug it out. He knew he was supposed to call another number Kinder had given him, but he didn't know what it was. In his stressed mental state, he just called the first number he came across, which was the Welcome Home Realty line. He would only say a few brief words. The call might be traceable to Welcome Home Realty, but only back to his burner, which would have been destroyed by that point. It would be Kinder's problem, not his.

He dialed the number and listened to the ring.

CHAPTER 44

There was now no denying that a pandemic had seized the world, the likes of which had not been seen in modern times. New virus cases were spreading rapidly throughout the United States, with hospitalizations and fatalities approaching alarming levels. Justice, Texas, was no exception. The politicians in Washington were prattling on about producing a vaccine, but no timetable for a realistic prospect was on the horizon. Cases of the virus had been recorded in all age groups, although the highest concentration of severe cases and resulting deaths occurred among the elderly, especially among the infirm.

The Falling Oaks home for the elderly was hit especially hard. Marine retired major Robert Lindsay witnessed the passing of several close friends, who had proudly served in the US armed forces with him. The major was a tough old bird by any definition, but losing his friends was devastating. Valiant heroes who had escaped enemy bombs and bullets succumbed to a microscopic microbe.

"I regret to report, Sergeant Morris, the passing last night of Airman First Class Rodney Wexford at Crystal River Hospital."

Marshall gripped his cell phone extra tight, sitting at the reception desk at Welcome Home Realty, as the major spoke those distressing words. Marshall had become close to the group of old vets when they saved the Sam Jacinto statue from being destroyed. There had been four of them just a few months ago, and now, with Rodney gone, only the major remained. "Major, I'm so sorry to hear that news. I prayed there was hope for him. You told me he rallied enough to come home, only to return to the hospital."

"To look at him, you'd think a stiff breeze would blow him over, but he was probably the toughest human being I have ever met, even though he wasn't a marine. The hospital told me he even rallied again the day before we lost him. I will always admire his spirit." the major replied.

"Will there be any honors at his burial?"

"Not permitted. Damn it! This disease has forced everything to lockdown. I couldn't even be with him at the hospital. We will definitely have services and honors for all of them when this thing disappears. Say, how is your mom?"

"I'm not sure, sir, but not good. I can tell you that. She's now on a ventilator. She's fairly young to be so sick and was healthy otherwise. She talks a good game on the phone, but I'm plenty worried. You just said it. I can't even go see her. They've set up the COVID ward like a fortress."

"That's too bad, son, but I'm sure she'll pull through. You know, if we had a mind to, we could penetrate that fortress just like standing up for old Sam."

Marshall half-grinned despite himself. "Let's stay in touch."

"Absolutely! That's an order, Morris. Semper Fi." *Click.* He was gone.

Marshall was very sad about Rodney, who seemed like the weakest of that group but may have been the strongest. He hadn't seen Tommy Kinder for a couple of days. He said something about going to the Bahamas to look at a property. For the past week, he was upbeat. He wondered if it had anything to do with those vials he delivered to the oddball doctor? What could they be up to? Were they selling drugs? It didn't seem like any kind of drug deal he'd ever heard about. That doctor worked at the hospital near his mom. He wished he could have befriended him a bit to get some information, but the man was curt and standoffish. He and Tommy must be up to something. Marshall's gut instincts were running on overdrive with that man.

The phone on his desk rang just as Marshall was looking up a crossword puzzle word on his cell phone. As usual, he didn't have enough hands or fingers to do both at once. He finally fumbled around and grabbed the phone after about five rings. There was silence. No one spoke. And then, a whisper, "Kinder?"

Marshall impulsively replied, "Yes." Another silence followed by a barely audible voice.

"Wexford, two days ago. Passed. Sally Morris gets it today." *Click.* Dial tone.

Marshall held out the receiver and stared at it.

What the heck was that? His heart jumped. The voice had mentioned his mother. *Huh? Why? Who? The voice sounded familiar. He also mentioned Rodney, who just died. Whoever called thought I was Tommy. The call was for him. Oh, my gosh! I recognize that voice. It was Doctor Clark. I'd bet on it. Those two are up to something with that medicine. Rodney just died. They must have given it to him! He said my mom is next. Oh, no! Oh, no! I can't let that happen. Mom! Mom!* he wailed as he ran out of the office to his car.

Marshall was frenzied and gave no thought to who he might call—if there was anyone at all. Crystal River hospital was across the Gulf Freeway about five miles away through heavy traffic. Fifteen minutes would have been fast. Marshall screeched into a parking lot at the hospital in seven. He never looked at a stoplight barreling through traffic. Many horns blew, and more than one obscene gesture popped up at him. The lot he entered was reserved for the doctors and had a yellow wooden arm that was raised with a proper ID card before Marshall smashed through it on the way in.

Despite his bizarre driving, the obsessed young man almost made it to the hospital without being noticed by the local police until he ran the wrong way for three blocks on a street divided by a median. A Houston PD blue and white patrol car spotted his antics and tore after him. Marshall's focus was so intense he never noticed his pursuers. The cops pulled into the same doctor's lot only to find an empty, ugly orange OC with the front door open, left crossways in the middle of the driving lane. They spotted a male figure jogging through the parking lot toward the visitor's entrance. The police jumped out of their car, and the chase was on.

The COVID ward was on the fourth floor of the hospital. How to get up there was the question. He bolted past the Emergency Room entrance around the corner to the COVID door, where he had dropped his mom off. As he ran, he slapped on his Cookie Monster mask. He was not surprised as he approached the COVID entrance that there were two orderlies standing there fully decked out in hazmat gear, waiting to receive new patients. With no one to take in at that moment, they were relaxed and chatting. When they saw him coming, both waved and yelled for him to leave the area immediately.

"It's my mother! She's in there and going to be injected with some kind of poison. I need to get to her. Please let me through." he said, gesturing wildly as he spoke.

The men, who were trained to deal with hysterical and irrational people, held their ground. On any normal day, the two brawny orderlies could have easily handled one scrawny teenager, but there were a few factors working against them. First, Marshall was so determined to get to his mom that ten men might not have been able to restrain him. Also, while the hazmat gear was fine for stopping COVID germs, it restricted their mobility to virtual slothfulness. The hoped-to-be CTU wide receiver flew between them and rushed through the glass entrance door. He did so, just ahead of the trailing police officers who burst around the corner. The cops charged after Marshall but were stopped short by when the orderlies. Better to let the hospital's internal security grab him than catch COVID.

Once inside, Marshall faced a small lobby with two elevator doors and another regular metal door. He knew had to go up, so he punched the up button. As he stood there frantically praying the doors would open, he glanced outside and was surprised to see two police officers standing out there, but not coming toward him. He wasn't so lucky with his hazmat friends, who were headed in for him as fast as they could waddle. Just seconds before they reached him, the bell rang and the elevator door slid open.

Thank goodness! Just in time. Uh, no. Facing him just a few feet away inside the elevator were two more uniformed security officers. They were as startled to see Marshall as he was to see them. When they screamed, "Hey! You! Stop, or we'll—", he didn't wait around long enough to let them complete their sentence. He bolted toward the metal door, which thankfully was unlocked, and led to the stairwell. He assaulted the stairs three at a time all the way to the third-floor landing, where he stopped short.

There was a metal barrier and a hefty sign on a stand in the middle of the stairway. In huge bold letters bordered by yellow bio-warning slashes, it read "DANGER AUTHORIZED AND PROPERLY PROTECTED PERSONNEL ONLY BEYOND THIS POINT. COVID VIRUS INFECTION AREA." The hospital had taken every reasonable measure to ensure the isolation of the COVID ward. They locked every access door, and warning signs were posted everywhere. All regular entry points were manned 24/7 by staff who checked IDs, took temperatures, and verified permission to enter the area. They permitted no one other than essential hospital personnel in the ward, and they were especially vigilant in preventing family members from gaining access to their unfortunate loved ones in the hospital. They significantly reinforced and bulked up the security staff. Somehow, Marshall had to penetrate this medical fortress.

Marshall had only his mask for protection but had already been infected. Besides, nothing mattered other than his mom. He had to get to her. He was desperate to reach the fourth floor. There didn't seem to be anywhere to go, and then he heard people coming down the steps below. He had no choice but to throw open the door on the third-floor landing and duck through.

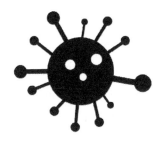

CHAPTER 45

Dr. Clark hung up without another word and tossed the burner phone back into his bag. He took a deep breath. It was showtime again. Sally Morris was his quarry. His vacillation behind him, he was resolute and determined to complete his mission and end this torment. He was done wondering whether to proceed. He headed for the elevator and got off on the COVID ward floor. There were patients scattered about, lying on gurneys in the corridors. A few were leaving; most were coming. There was the usual gaggle of staffers at the nurses' station in the center core of the ward, reviewing charts, preparing meds, and working on hundreds of other sundry tasks.

He automatically sought nurse Carmella but didn't immediately spot her. Could he have gotten lucky? Was she off today? Was she down at the cafeteria? He walked purposefully toward the ICU where Sally Morris was lying. He hoped she was asleep or so labored in her breathing, she wouldn't notice him. He didn't want a repeat of Rodney's doleful eyes. The sweat accumulated on his brow. He kept telling himself what he was about to do was easy. During years as a doctor, he had given thousands of shots. This was just one more. Same old routine. He tried to convince himself, but it didn't work. He knew this one was very different. He was doing his absolute best to stifle his doubts, but they still were there. Do it quickly and get out. He'd be fine if he could steel himself and treat it as a routine and simple procedure.

As he passed into the ICU through the swinging door, he got his answer about Carmella. She was well across the room, totally immersed in an emergency with a patient. That was a touch of good fortune. He knew exactly where she was and was sure she couldn't watch him. It remained only for him to walk up to Sally Morris, locate the injection port on her IV, snap in the vial, ease the medication in, and snap out the vial. Strictly routine, and this whole painful mess would be over.

He approached Sally's gurney, where she was breathing through a ventilator. She was turned away from him. He hoped she was asleep, but she was not. As he stepped closer, she turned her head and looked up at him. A bright smile formed on her lips. Dr. Clark froze. Despite the ravages of the virus, tubes, monitors, and an array of medical equipment, he immediately saw that she was a beautiful woman. He hesitated. Neither spoke. How could he possibly do this to such a gorgeous person? Quickly, he dismissed that thought. He reached into his pocket and pulled out the vial. He reached for the injection port on her IV tube.

***

By this time, the hospital security staff were on full alert in pursuit of an unauthorized individual had breached the building. Teams were roaming the corridors, searching for the intruder. After leaving the third-floor stairwell, he entered a long corridor with doors on each side. As he jogged along, he was about to reach the point where he would be forced to turn left or right. Suddenly, a walkie-talkie transmission squawked from the left. A security team was fast approaching from that direction. If he continued, he would confront them head-on. In the corridor directly to his right was a door that said "Laundry." Marshall didn't hesitate, bolting in just as the two uniformed officers came into view. When they looked to their right, all they saw was an empty corridor where he had been seconds before. They kept on without stopping.

The laundry was a large, open room that was filled with dozens of round commercial grade washers and dryers. There were many folding tables and storage racks. Heaps of soiled linens were scattered around the room, along with neat stacks of clean and folded goods. The noise level from all the equipment was deafening, and the humidity was suffocating. Marshall didn't know what to do next. It didn't look like there was a way out of there to get him up a floor.

At first, he didn't see anyone working until he heard a muffled laugh behind a massive pile of sheets. "Cookie Monster! You've got to be kidding me! Now I've seen everything," a man said as he stepped out from behind the laundry. He was dressed in white hospital scrubs, white pants, a white T-shirt, and a paper hat. He was well under six feet and surely weighed over 200 pounds. The man's face glistened with sweat, and the rolls on his flabby stomach soaked through his T-shirt.

Before Marshall could say anything, the guy spoke. "You must be the temp they promised me. Finally! With this virus, nobody wants to work—especially in a hospital laundry. We're busier than ever and have less help than ever. It sucks."

Marshall hesitated, not knowing what to say. Finally, he blurted "Yeah. That's me." Maybe playing along would buy him some time.

"Good. I'm Sam." He didn't seem interested in Marshall's name. "I'm glad you showed when you did. The COVID ward on four has been screaming at me. They needed their fresh linen an hour ago. I'm here by myself and can't leave. I need you to take it up there to them." He pointed to a large metal cart with bed linen piled high on it. "There is a white coat hanging on a hook over there. You'll also find some gloves and a clear welder's style face mask. Put them on over your cookie mask. You'll be safe and maybe even give them a laugh up there. They need it. When you come back, there's plenty more for you to do. Got it?"

"No problem, Sam. How do I get up there?" *The Covid Ward What luck!*

"Over in the corner, there's our exclusive elevator. It stops on every floor."

Marshall walked over and put on the coat and shield. He couldn't believe his luck. He shoved the heavy linen cart on the elevator and pushed the 'four' button. The old hydraulic beast squeaked and growled, but in seconds, the door opened on four. No one even noticed that he had arrived. He was tempted to leave the laundry and find the ICU, but realized he might need to keep his cover a while longer. The floor was a beehive of activity and organized confusion. He rolled the big cart toward the nurse's central station, but before he got very far, someone pointed to a closet where the fresh linen was kept. He nodded and started pushing it in that direction when he caught sight of a sign denoting the ICU.

At that very instant, the door opened and out walked a man in scrubs. He looked familiar. He couldn't be sure with all the protective gear, but he looked very much like sleazy Dr. Clark. Marshall lost it. His mom was in the ICU. Was he too late? Had he poisoned her? He'd never forgive himself if that happened. Ignoring his cover, he flew down the corridor, bumping and jostling several people on the way. He burst into the ICU and urgently scanned the stations.

He panicked, unable to find her. She had to be there. Where was she? And then he saw the name on station six: "S. Morris" but the station was empty. She was gone! His mom. He was too late. They must have lost her! His worst fears were realized. Life could never be the same. She was everything to him. He collapsed and kneeled next to the bed in his dreadful misery, sobbing uncontrollably.

And then he thought of Dr. Clark, her killer. He'd just seen the lowlife leave. He had to find him. The man had to pay. He couldn't get away. He swallowed hard and got up. By this time, Marshall's antics had caught the attention of everyone. Nurse Carmella stood next to him. She had figured out that he was Sally's son. She tried to console him but was met with blind rage. Marshall elbowed around her and started toward the door. Just as he stepped out of the ICU, however, he was met by three burly security officers. Two grabbed him high and one went low. He tossed and fought, but they were too much. They pinned him on the floor. Suddenly, his world spun and everything went black.

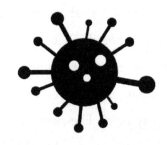

CHAPTER 46

Marshall could hear the murmuring of soft voices but couldn't understand what was being said or who was saying it. Suddenly, his eyes blinked open. Everything around him was white. *Where am I?*

"Marshall? Marshall? Are you awake?"

It sounded like his dear, sweet Mallory. He opened his eyes wider. A blur and gradual focus. There she was. Sitting right next to him. *It was her!*

"Mal, is that you?"

"Yes, Marshall. It's me and my mom, and Paula. We're all here. Just relax."

"It's wonderful to see you all. But where am I?"

"You're in a room at Crystal River Hospital. You've been sleeping for about twelve hours."

"I have? Really? What happ—" It all came rushing back. "Oh no, Mal. My mom. She's gone. Whatever will I do?" Huge tears streamed down his cheeks.

Mallory grabbed his hand and squeezed. "Hang on, Marshall. Hold it for a few seconds." She dug out her cell and pressed a number. "You there? Good. He's awake but still pretty groggy. Here you go." She held her phone up to where Marshall could see it.

"Hi, Marshall. What do you want for breakfast?" A very familiar voice asked.

"Mom! Mom? Is that really you? You're not gone after all. Mom?"

Now all four of them were blubbering.

"Yes, it is really me, son. I'm still in the hospital, but I feel much better. I'm off the ventilator. I might even come home soon. Would you like that?"

"Yes. Yes. But when I couldn't find you in the ICU, I assumed the worst. Where were you?"

"Actually, I had already improved and was due to get off the ventilator and out of the ICU. They were just so busy the staff hadn't moved me. They must have done it just before you came in. I was back in my regular room."

"No kidding. That's so terrific. The nutty doctor, then. Did he do anything to you?"

"No. He came in and walked over to my bed. I smiled at him. He seemed to be brooding over something. He never spoke until he walked out when he said, 'Have a long and wonderful life, Sally,' then disappeared."

"He kind of scared me, but maybe I was wrong about him. I kind of feel bad for him."

"Don't!" came a voice from the doorway. It was COVID ward head nurse Carmella. Everyone looked in her direction.

She smiled. "I'm just making my rounds for my patients that have broken *into* the hospital. Most are trying to get *out*. You are the only one trying to get in. Sorry, we had to sedate you, or you might have torn up our ward and left it in a bigger mess than it already is."

"That's on me, Nurse. My mom is pretty important," Marshall replied.

"Of course. I get it. The separation of families is one of the hardest things about this confounded virus. Let me get back to Dr. Clark for a moment. He was bad news, and you had him pegged right. He had every intention of injecting some foreign substance into your mother. In fact, he actually did it a few days ago, and we lost the patient."

"Rodney Wexford."

"Yes, that poor man fought long and hard. I took losing him personally."

"So, did Clark's drug kill him?"

"Truthfully, we don't know. That is going to be studied by our pathologists."

"I guess I was too late to keep him from my mom. What stopped him from giving it to her?"

"Believe it or not. He had a sudden change of heart at the last second. Instead of giving her the drug, he came to me and spilled the whole thing. His license to practice was in jeopardy, anyway. I guess he felt he had nothing to lose."

"Why did he do it?" Marshall asked.

"Money, of course. Why do crooks do anything? A bunch, I'm sure. He didn't go into that with me, but I'm sure it will come out. Marshall, ladies, I've got to run. I'm happy it all turned out okay. Best of luck and stay healthy. Bye now." She disappeared, but suddenly her head popped back in. "Oh, and Marshall, I almost forgot. Sam in the laundry is plenty pissed at you, but he said you could have your job back."

Only Marshall had a clue what she was talking about, and he grinned broadly.

"So, where is Dr. Clark now?" Marshall asked.

"We think he's in custody. The police are eager to talk to you since you somehow knew he intended to inject your mom," Barbara Jollen said.

"Yes, it was strange. I've been working for Tommy Kinder at Welcome Home Realty for a week. I didn't know Mr. Kinder before I started, but it looked like he had given up on his home selling business. He spent very little time in the office and never told me much of anything. I was just a warm body to answer the phone. Then, one day, Dr. Clark appeared and said he had an appointment with Mr. Kinder. He was cold and unfriendly. He hardly even acknowledged my existence. After his meeting, he rushed right out the door without a word. I was curious about him being a doctor. Maybe he knew something about my mom, but I never got to speak to him."

"So, how did you connect him up with your mom?" Paula asked, jumping ahead.

"A couple of odd things happened. One morning, they delivered a FedEx package for Tommy, who hadn't made it in yet. I thought little about it but noticed the package came from somewhere in New Mexico. I put it on his desk and forgot all about it. The next day, Tommy asked me to take a cloth grocery bag over to the Sam Jacinto monument in the park and give it to Dr. Clark. There was no explanation. On my way, a plastic bag slipped out of the cloth bag. When I put it back in, I noticed it looked like a bottle of medicine. When I met Dr. Clark, he snatched the bag and disappeared without a word."

"Weren't you suspicious?" Mallory asked.

"Darn right I was. I was afraid I'd just played a part in some kind of drug deal. The next day, Tommy was gone. He told me something about going to the Bahamas to look at real estate. I haven't seen or heard from him since. I was so worried about Mom, I thought little about that delivery until I answered a call on the company line, which began, 'Kinder?' Rather than do what I was supposed to do, and state 'Welcome Home Realty,' without thinking, I played along and replied 'yes.' The caller, who was obviously Dr. Clark, then whispered 'Wexford, two days ago. Passed. Sally Morris gets it today.' Then he hung up. He must have been reporting to Kinder and called him on the company line instead of his personal cell phone. I also don't think Clark knew my name or made the connection between mom and me."

"I had just talked to Major Lindsay, who told me about losing Rodney Wexford. I don't know why he picked those two to inject?

Anyway, I went bonkers based upon the medicine I delivered, the secretiveness of Kinder and Clark, and the phone call. I had to get to my mom ASAP before the weird doctor killed her. And here I am. I guess I was too late to stop him. Thank goodness he reconsidered."

CHAPTER 47

Marshall's comment about Clarence Clark's decision not to inject his mom was directly on point. He had come ever so close to injecting her. Right up to the point of reaching for the injection port in her IV line, he had been determined to complete the despicable task. Perhaps it was her lovely smile or the lasting image of Rodney's pitiful eyes, but he just couldn't push that plunger. Sure, the system had done him wrong, but those poor unfortunates writhing with the virus hadn't. He had taken an oath to do everything possible to save them. He faced the stock realization that even with hundreds of thousands of dollars in the bank, he just couldn't live with himself in the future. In the end, his conscience did him in.

He could have taken the cash he had and run, but memories of his actions would never leave him. There was no other viable choice but to admit to his transgressions. He sought Carmella and candidly described his plans to her. As the consummate healthcare professional with over five decades of nursing experience, she listened quietly as

Clarence confessed. She thought she had encountered just about everything in her career, but this situation was unlike anything else she'd ever dealt with. Dr. Clark sat calmly in her office with his head down while she called the senior hospital administrator and security. After showing the head pharmacist where the additional vials of Vennizator were hidden, he was whisked off to the local police station and locked up.

Tommy Kinder arrived back in the Houston area on a late flight. He was concerned that he'd heard nothing from Dr. Clark for several days. Clark was supposed to call him on the burner phone when he had something to report. He was reluctant to place a call himself. He had a terrific trip to the Bahamas and made a sizeable down payment on a gorgeous condo. He was pleased about that and had $750,000 in his offshore account. The agreed deal provided half paid upfront with the balance paid when two injections were done. In fact, if Clark had chickened out, that was fine with him. He'd keep the cash he had and never look back. Either way, Texas was soon to be in his rearview mirror.

Tommy had only the mildest pang of irritation when he arrived at his office the next morning and saw that the kid wasn't there. He seemed to be kind of flighty, anyway. No loss. A few minutes later, however, his blood pressure maxed out when a dozen uniformed police officers barged in with weapons drawn. Though he protested like a stuck pig, they read him his rights, handcuffed him, and hauled him off to jail to join his co-conspirator. Both men hired lawyers, and a long-drawn-out investigation looked likely, although, unlike Kinder, Dr. Clark was more than willing to cooperate with the authorities. It was very unlikely that either of them would get to spend the cash they had already received.

Randy Shiner observed the proceedings with interest. He had some concern that the trail of bread crumbs might lead back to him. He knew, though, that Uncle Sanford had legions of lawyers to fight anything that smacked of involvement of his company or family. Dr. Clark had talked directly to Dr. Nacho Vita about the drug. The cash that had been distributed went directly from Venezuelan sources to the two unfortunates. He wasn't worried. Of course, he would take no calls from Yordan, who'd fled from Caracas, fearing for his life after the plan boomeranged. Instead of gaining credibility, El Presidente was most likely going to look like an even bigger fool to the international community.

Back in Justice, Texas, there was a warm homecoming when Sally Morris walked back into their house after finally whipping the virus. There were some lingering effects of the disease, but in a week, she was almost back to normal. It thrilled Marshall to have her home. In fact, to no one's surprise, his appetite came roaring back. Fortunately, Mom was back to shovel coal into the furnace.

The virus raged on. After seeming to remain steady for a month or two, it suddenly exploded across the nation and world. Finally, precautions such as masks and social distancing were put in place. Also, the government now promised that an effective vaccine would be available by early next year. Marshall still carried the guilt of having infected his mother, although it couldn't be substantiated. Shortly after his mother returned home, she was going through the stack of mail that her son had left untouched while she was gone.

"Hey, Marshall. Look at this," she said, holding up a letter from CTU. He walked over and took it from her. It was from the testing clinic that had been used for the football team before Marshall came home. In part, it read:

"We sincerely apologize, but because of an error in our testing procedures, we previously reported that Marshall Morris was positive for the COVID virus. Upon further review, we have determined that this finding was in error, and Mr. Morris was not infected with the virus based on our exam."

Marshall looked over at his mother. "So, this means I didn't have the virus when I came home?"

"That's what it says. So, you see, after all your worrying, you couldn't have given it to me. I caught it some other way. Don't you feel better now?"

"Yes, I guess so, but just think of all the days I spent as a prisoner in isolation. All for nothing!" Both of them chuckled, and she gave him a big hug.

Made in the USA
Middletown, DE
20 September 2022

10286605R00159